FINDING PEACE

Arlene A. Smith-Scott, JD

FINDING PEACE

2nd Edition

CONTENTS

ALSO BY

"THANK GOD FOR MOM"

"STARTING OVER WITH GOD'S GRACE AND MERCY"

"DEVOTION, STARTING OVER WITH GOD'S GRACE AND MERCY"

"FINDING PEACE"

"DEVOTION, FEAR NOT, FAITH TO MOVE FORWARD"

"WHY WOMEN CAN TEACH AND PREACH THE WORD OF GOD"

"GRANT WRITING: THE UNOFFICIAL RULEBOOK"

DEDICATIONS

How do I begin to thank God for my life and all who has played a part in it, making it beautifully complex and filled with contradictions? Would a simple "thank you" be sufficient? My heart and soul are thankful; and I am filled with gratitude. It is my hope that this book can be used to encourage others as I have been encouraged by the word of God.

My mother, Maxine Smith, has been my inspiration and resource for the continued teaching and reflecting on the word of God. My father, Rupert W. Smith, desired to hear God's word and that desire was shared. My friend and motivator, my Aunt, Mae C. Johns, her wisdom and patience allowed for "possibilities" through the awareness of "what could be?" My uncle, Jerald Johns, who I refer to as "the most loved Uncle." My constant companion, spouse and friend, Kevin E. Brooks, has been a man of his word and consistently present in my life, which has brought stability and peace. God has so lovingly placed each of you in my life. I am blessed to have and to have had your kindness, thoughtfulness and insightfulness.

I am thankful that God sent his only begotten son, Jesus Christ, to die on the cross for me. He is the living sacrifice who provides salvation through faith as well as the holy spirit. His ufficiency has been proven through my trials and tribulations. I have been inspired by the word of God which is shared through this book.

— • —

Stay Connected!

HTTPS://PROD.CONTENT.ATTICUS.IO/IMAGES/DocWribB1toFogJi5p
_CE.PNG

U nlock a wealth of knowledge and exclusive deals! Sign up now to receive free updates and special discounts on services and products related to grant writing, commercial lending, and much more. Don't miss out, join our community today!

Website: www.DocWriteReview.com

Email: Info@DocWriteReview.com

1

THE SEARCH FOR "DRUGS"

How do I ask this doctor for "drugs" without telling her the whole story? The question replays in my mind like a broken record as I sit in this sterile examination room, door closed, trapped with my racing thoughts. I should have rehearsed my lines. Should have practiced in the mirror this morning instead of staring at my hollow-eyed reflection, wondering when I'd become this person, this desperate stranger begging for pharmaceutical peace.

The nurse's chart makes a distinct thump against the door. Muted voices drift through the walls, medical jargon mixing with casual conversation. Someone's on the telephone, their words indecipherable but somehow urgent. Everything feels urgent these days.

The room is painted a dreary institutional green, the kind of color that's supposed to be calming but only succeeds in making everything feel slightly nauseous. A small window offers the room's only salvation, streaming natural light across outdated medical posters. The diabetes advertisement features a blissfully happy couple, their smiles so perfect they seem manufactured. Look how wonderful life can be with the right medication, their faces seem to say. The other poster displays the human nervous system in startling detail, a web of nerves and synapses that looks nothing like the tangled mess inside my head.

Is that what I look like without skin? The weird thoughts that surface these days surprise even me.

I catalogue the room's contents like an inventory: small desk, one chair, a stool, examination table, cabinets lined with glass containers with cotton balls, Q-tips, sterile wipes arranged with medical precision. An old-fashioned blood pressure monitor hangs on the wall alongside other equipment I can't identify. Everything clean, everything in its place, everything under control.

Everything except me.

Standing up, I press my face closer to the small window. The parking lot below looks normal, people coming and going, living their regular lives, sleeping through normal nights.

This is a new doctor for me, which means starting over. Building trust. Explaining without really explaining. I want her to prescribe Xanax for anxiety, though what I really need it for is sleep. Sleep that's been eluding me for weeks now, leaving me suspended in the existence between exhaustion and hypervigilance.

My previous doctor had been different, Dr. Martinez, with his kind eyes and careful questions. He'd prescribed both Xanax and an antidepressant, but only temporarily. "The Xanax is just for two weeks," he'd explained, leaning forward in his chair. "It takes about that long for the antidepressant to kick in. But I need you to understand that Xanax is addictive. A small amount for a short time is all I'm comfortable prescribing."

Point-two-five milligrams. Such a tiny pill for such enormous relief.

The first time I took it, something shifted. The constant chatter in my mind, the endless loop of worry and regret, simply... quieted. My shoulders dropped from where they'd been permanently hunched near my ears. For the first time in months, I could breathe without conscious effort.

Why bother with the antidepressant when Xanax worked so perfectly?

But Dr. Martinez had moved his practice across the country, leaving me here with this new doctor who doesn't know my history, doesn't understand what I've been through. How do I explain that I'm not seeking drugs for recreation, but for survival?

Sitting. Waiting. Checking my phone.

The room still carries the sharp scent of bleach. They must have cleaned it just before placing me here. Should I open the door? Peek out to see if anyone's coming?

Instead, I scroll through emails I've already read, anything to keep my hands busy. My mind refuses to settle, jumping from thought to thought like a ricocheting bullet. Last night was another marathon of insomnia, three hours of sleep interrupted by trips to the bathroom and the relentless replay of memories I'd rather forget.

When had the tide turned? When had I transformed from that fearless girl who could conquer the world on roller skates?

Thursdays were adult nights at Skate Palace, twenty-one and over only. Tuesdays belonged to the teenagers, Sundays to families, but Thursday nights were mine. I'd arrive with my skates already laced, ready to claim the rink like it was my personal kingdom. The music would pulse through the speakers, disco lights spinning overhead, and I'd glide across that polished floor like I was born to fly.

You couldn't tell me nothing back then. Every turn was perfect, every backward skate effortless. I was invincible, wrapped in confidence like armor.

That same fearlessness carried me from Cleveland, Ohio to Washington, DC, though my parents acted shocked when I announced my plans. "It came as such a surprise," my mother would say later, but she was lying. She had to be.

She loved telling the story of our church trip to DC when I was a child. She would say that every time the bus stopped at a landmark or museum, I'd be the last one back, having wandered off to explore every corner, every hidden passage. "You never had any fear," she'd say, pride and worry mixing in her voice. "You always knew exactly where you were going."

What she never mentioned was how I'd fallen in love with the city that day, the monuments reaching toward the sky, the energy humming through the streets, the sense that anything was possible within those boundaries.

Years later, I took a train from Philadelphia (where I'd been visiting my Aunt Dorothy) to DC to meet my half-brothers. William and Thomas, names I'd only recently learned, secrets my family had kept buried until I discovered that wedding photo in our picture album. The groom looked like a younger version of Dad, but the bride definitely wasn't Mom.

"I'm your sister," I'd told William over the phone, my voice steady with certainty. "And I want to meet you."

They picked me up at Union Station. William, Thomas, and Reynold, the adopted brother I hadn't even known existed. They drove me through Georgetown, showed me their DC, welcomed me with open arms. It never occurred to me that our meeting might go badly. Doubt wasn't in my vocabulary back then.

When I announced I was moving to Washington permanently, my parents panicked. I was eighteen, their youngest, their last hope after investing everything in my education at Symphony School for Girls. But college felt like another prison sentence, and I'd just finished basic training at Fort McClellan. I was a 95 Bravo, military police in the Army National Guard. And I was ready for real life.

In desperation, my Dad struck a deal. "If you can find a job by the end of the week, I'll drive you there myself," he said. "I'll visit my mother and the boys for a week. But if you don't have work when I'm ready to leave, you come home with me."

One week. Three job offers. I chose the stockbrokerage firm in Georgetown, only to discover during orientation that you had to be twenty-one. The company liked me enough to offer me a secretary position instead, which lasted exactly one day, turns out, I really couldn't type. My manager took me to an expensive restaurant for lunch and fired me gently, probably the classiest dismissal in corporate history.

But I stayed. Found another job, found my footing, found my future husband on a dance floor when my neighbor abandoned me for his bottle.

I don't think he ever actually proposed. I remember suggesting that if we were still together in a year, we should buy a house. When he agreed, I pushed further: "We should probably get married then."

He agreed to that too.

Just like that, I'd planned my entire future with the same confidence I'd once reserved for roller skating and cross-country moves.

Standing again, I peer out the window, impatience gnawing at my chest. Laughter echoes from the hallway, some shared joke I'm not part of. Here I sit, trying to decode the secret language of prescription requests, wondering how to ask for help without sounding like an addict.

But maybe that's what I am now. Maybe that fearless girl who danced through life is gone, replaced by this anxious woman counting sleepless hours and measuring relief in point-two-five milligram increments.

The door handle turns, and my heart jumps.

Time to perform.

2

"Peace" or a "Piece"

P eace.

The word echoes in my mind like a prayer I've forgotten how to pray. My mother was always hollering about needing peace, usually while creating the exact opposite of it.

I must have been eight or nine when it happened. My sister was still alive then, my brother still lived at home, and the three of us were at each other's throats about something. Probably who got to control the TV remote or whose turn it was to do dishes. We were loud, destructive, the kind of chaotic that makes adults question their life choices.

That's when Mom lost it.

She emerged from the kitchen wielding a can of Crisco, not the liquid oil you see today, but that old-fashioned shortening that came in the blue and white can. Her house shoes slapped against the linoleum as she ran from room to room, praying to the Lord for "peace" while flinging globs of white shortening everywhere.

"I rebuke you, devil!" she shouted, her voice cracking with desperation and something that might have been hysteria. "I rebuke the spirit of discord in this house!"

The three of us slowly stopped our bickering, mesmerized by the spectacle of our usually composed mother turning our home into some kind of evangelical slip-and-slide. She was loud. She was frantic. And despite ourselves, she was hilarious.

We ended up outside on the front porch, united in our bewilderment, watching through the screen door as she continued her spiritual warfare against our childhood chaos. Maybe that was the peace she was seeking, just getting us out of her hair for ten minutes.

Now here I am, decades later, seeking my own version of peace. But what exactly is peace? Is it the absence of worry? The silence of an overthinking mind? Can it be prescribed, bottled, measured in milligrams?

I worry about everything now. Everything.

Will I get COVID-19? Will my friends and family get it? Are my kids safe walking to their cars after work? Will they be treated fairly by their bosses, their colleagues, the world that seems increasingly hostile to anyone who looks like them? Is there enough money in my account to weather this crisis? What catastrophe awaits tomorrow? Should I file that lawsuit against the contractor who destroyed my bathroom? Am I prepared enough to lead Bible study this Sunday? Does Mama have enough groceries? Did I remember to pick up her blood pressure medication?

The questions multiply like cancer cells, spreading through every quiet moment until there's no room left for actual peace.

I can't pinpoint when this unrest began colonizing my mind. Was it when the housing bubble burst, taking my real estate business with it? Was it discovering that people I'd trusted to be fair and equitable were actually condescending and corrupt? Was it watching my beloved father waste away, his strong hands becoming paper-thin in that hospital bed? Or maybe it started with the pandemic, this invisible disease that kills without prejudice, stealing grandmothers and teenagers with equal indifference?

Somewhere along the way, I became estranged from peace. Lost my peace of mind like a set of keys I can't remember putting down.

Would pharmaceutical peace stop this mental hamster wheel? Does tranquility lead to addiction?

My niece Keisha recently made rice krispy treats laced with marijuana. She pressed a small square wrapped in plastic into my palm, her eyes kind but knowing. "Auntie, just break off a little piece before bed. It won't get you high, but it'll help you relax."

That treat has been living in my purse for weeks now. Sometimes, during my 3 AM anxiety spirals, I'll pull it out and stare at it like it holds the secrets of the universe. I've opened the plastic bag to smell its earthy sweetness, even broke off a corner once, but it's still sitting there, untouched, waiting.

My nephew Marcus has a different solution, a small brown bottle of CBD oil and what he calls a "joint," though it looks nothing like the cigarettes from my youth. "Auntie, this is pure CBD," he explained, pulling out his lighter with the casual confidence of someone who grew up in a world where marijuana isn't automatically criminal. "Just a couple puffs. I promise it'll help."

Both offerings are still waiting for me, one in my purse, one on my kitchen counter. So why do I think a prescription drug would be better? Is it because a doctor's involvement somehow legitimizes my need? Makes it medical instead of recreational? You'd think a professionally trained individual would know more about brain chemistry than my well-meaning relatives.

But then again, professionally trained individuals gave us the opioid crisis.

I glance up from my phone, certain I saw movement in my peripheral vision. A shadow in the corner that shouldn't be there. My skin prickles with the sensation of being watched, though logic tells me I'm alone in this sterile room.

Get it together.

Standing, I stretch muscles that have been clenched for hours and crack open the door. The hallway stretches in both directions, all the examination room doors closed, muffled conversations bleeding through thin walls. Down the hall, I catch a glimpse of someone, the back of a head, a left shoulder, someone hunched over a desk with a phone pressed to their ear.

The bathroom door to my right beckons. Might as well take advantage before the doctor finally appears.

Back in the examination room, I check my phone for the time and freeze.

There it is again, that feeling of presence, of being observed by invisible eyes. Are the nurses watching me through hidden cameras? Is the doctor studying my behavior before she even meets me?

Listen to yourself. This is exactly why you need Xanax.

My anxiety level is stratospheric, and even I can recognize it. There was a time when people described me as "calm," "reflective," "thoughtful." Now I'm the woman who suspects surveillance in a doctor's office and talks to rice krispy treats at 3 AM.

Whitney Houston. The thought hits me like a slap.

Didn't she die from Xanax? Or was it the combination of alcohol and Xanax? My fingers fly across my phone screen, googling with the manic energy of someone who suddenly needs to know everything about celebrity overdoses.

February 13, 2012. NBC News reported that Xanax and alcohol may have contributed to her death. TMZ said she took Xanax before big performances. The coroner's report, broken down by ABC News: "A plethora of prescription medication bottles were found in the room... twelve different medications, including anti-anxiety medication Xanax and muscle relaxer Flexeril, prescribed from five different doctors."

Flexeril. Wasn't I prescribed that when I threw out my back last year? How many medications am I already taking? How thin is the line between treatment and self-destruction?

"Why are you here? Your help does not come from man or things made by man."

The voice is clear, distinct, and definitely not coming from my phone.

I jerk my head up, scanning the room with wild eyes. Past the window, the diabetes poster, the neurological diagram, the examination table, the counter, the door. I search for an intercom system, a hidden speaker, anything that could explain the voice that just spoke directly into my soul.

Nothing.

Heart hammering, I stand and yank open the door, peering down the hallway like a woman possessed. The nurse is still on her phone call. The other examination rooms remain closed, their occupants dealing with their own medical mysteries.

I check my phone, no recent calls, no accidentally activated voice messages. Did I actually hear someone speak to me? What did the voice say exactly?

"Why are you here? Your help does not come from man or things made by man."

The words replay with crystal clarity, each syllable etched into my memory with supernatural precision.

I'm losing my mind. That's the only logical explanation. The anxiety has finally broken something fundamental in my brain, and now I'm hearing voices with theological opinions about prescription medication.

My legs carry me down the hallway toward the nurse's station, though I'm not sure what I plan to say. Excuse me, but did you hear a disembodied voice questioning my faith in Western medicine?

The nurse looks up as I approach, covering her phone with practiced efficiency. She appears to be in her early forties, the color of warm caramel, her hair pulled back in a neat bun that suggests competence and no-nonsense professionalism.

"Can I help you?" Her tone is polite but firm, the voice of someone who's dealt with anxious patients all day.

"I was wondering how much longer before the doctor can see me?" My voice sounds surprisingly normal, considering I'm questioning my own sanity.

She glances at her computer screen, then back at me with apologetic eyes. "The doctor had an emergency that's caused some delays. You're third in line to be seen, but I can't give you an exact time."

The phone demands her attention again. I catch fragments of her conversation as she uncovers the receiver: "...waiting for test results for the last half hour... needs the information urgently..."

Test results. Emergency. Urgently.

Someone else's crisis is determining my timeline, their medical drama intersecting with my pharmaceutical quest in ways I'll never understand.

I walk back to my examination room, leaving the door open this time. If I'm going to hear mysterious voices, at least I want witnesses to my breakdown.

The waiting continues, but something has shifted. The voice, real or imagined, has planted a seed of doubt that's growing faster than my anxiety. What am I doing here? Is pharmaceutical peace really peace at all, or just another form of running away?

Outside, storm clouds are gathering. I can see them through the small window, dark and heavy with the promise of rain.

Something's coming. I can feel it building like pressure in the air before lightning strikes.

3

— · —

Peace, Not Suicide

I pace the small confines of the examination room like a caged animal, worn linoleum squeaking beneath my shoes. The internal debate rages: reschedule and flee, or stay and fight for the pharmaceutical peace I came seeking?

On one hand, this delay feels like a sign, maybe I should listen to that mysterious voice and walk away from "things made by man." On the other hand, I'm so desperately tired, so wound tight with anxiety that I might snap if I don't get some relief soon. This new doctor doesn't know my history, my patterns, my careful dance around addiction. She might actually prescribe what I need without the suspicious interrogation I've grown to expect.

I settle back onto the stool, phone in hand, seeking distraction in the endless scroll of information. But instead of escape, I find myself falling down a rabbit hole of statistics that make my chest tighten with recognition.

The articles are damning in their clinical precision: people combine Xanax with alcohol for suicide. The World Health Organization reports approximately 800,000 suicide deaths yearly, one person every forty seconds, a global phenomenon of despair. The National Institute of Mental Health confirms suicide as a leading cause of death in America. The CDC's 2018 report delivers three devastating punches: suicide was the tenth leading cause of death overall, claiming over 48,000 lives; it was the second leading cause of death for ages 10-34; and there were more than twice as many suicides as homicides.

48,000 suicides. 18,830 homicides.

The numbers blur together as I read about rising rates of fear, depression, anxiety, loneliness, substance abuse. The coronavirus has only accelerated our collective descent into mental health crisis. After scrolling through article after article, I feel the familiar weight of depression settling over me like a lead blanket.

That's when the memory surfaces, unwelcome and vivid.

That day. The day I woke up with deadly certainty and whispered to the ceiling, "This will be the day."

I can still feel the weight of Princess curled against my chest, her small body warm and trusting as I held her and cried. She was so little, so full of unconditional love, but even her devotion wasn't enough to anchor me to this world. At least I knew she'd be loved after I was gone. My husband would take care of her, even if he couldn't take care of me.

The morning was gray and soggy, rain having fallen during the night like tears from a weeping sky. I couldn't tell the temperature, but it didn't matter. Nothing mattered except the plan that had crystallized in my mind with terrifying clarity.

Should I shower? Brush my teeth? The rituals of the living seemed pointless now. I pulled on clean underwear, some vestige of dignity, I suppose, but wore yesterday's jeans and shirt. One last walk for Princess, one last feeding, one last hug. She gave me a look I'll never forget, her dark eyes seeming to sense the finality in my movements.

The neighbors clustered near the elevators, their cheerful morning chatter a stark contrast to my inner darkness. "How's your husband doing?" Mrs. Chen asked with genuine concern.

"He's fine," I lied with practiced ease, pushing past them toward the side exit, my smile as artificial as the fluorescent lighting.

In the car, the radio's sudden blast made me jump, my nerves already frayed beyond repair. I fumbled with my phone, searching YouTube for the perfect soundtrack to my final drive, but nothing felt right. The radio would have to do.

Ten miles to the Bay Bridge. Two and a half miles of concrete and steel stretching over the Chesapeake Bay. I'd done the math, researched the timing. Post-rush hour meant lighter traffic, fewer witnesses to my final act.

The familiar landmarks passed like checkpoints on my journey: Route 2, Bay Dale Road, Sandy Point Beach. The tollbooths that should have been there were gone, progress had eliminated even that small ritual. Everything was changing, including me.

Merging onto the bridge, I stayed in the right lane, my heart hammering against my ribs like a caged bird. Fear mixed with determination as I searched for the spot I'd identified during my reconnaissance mission days earlier. Midway across, where the water was deepest, where the fall would be certain.

Tears streamed down my face as I slowed to a crawl, my hazard lights blinking a desperate SOS to the universe. This was it. The jump-off point. The end of everything that hurt.

"Are you sure?" I whispered to my reflection in the rearview mirror. "Really sure?"

My hands shook as I reached for my purse, my keys, my phone. Even in my darkest moment, habit made me gather my belongings, as if I might need them wherever I was going.

That's when the red pickup truck appeared behind me, its horn blaring with increasing aggression. I tried to ignore it, tried to focus on my final preparations, but the driver laid on his horn with the persistence of the truly enraged.

Then he pulled alongside my car, his window already down, his face twisted with road rage. "YOU ASSHOLE!" he screamed, spittle flying from his lips. "GET A LIFE!"

He roared away in a cloud of exhaust and fury, leaving me stunned in my moment of attempted departure. Another car appeared in my rearview mirror, approaching fast, and suddenly survival instinct kicked in. I pressed the accelerator, fleeing the scene of my almost-suicide.

Before I knew it, I was on the other side of the bridge, alive and confused and strangely hungry.

Cracker Barrel seemed like as good a place as any to process what had just happened. As I waited for my French toast, comfort food for the almost-dead, I replayed the encounter with the angry driver.

"Get a life!"

The irony wasn't lost on me. Here I was, trying to end my life, and some stranger was telling me to get one. The absurdity of it hit me all at once, the cosmic joke of carrying my purse and phone to jump off a bridge, as if death required proper identification and emergency contacts.

I laughed and cried simultaneously, my emotions a tangled mess of relief and embarrassment. The waitress approached with concern written across her face.

"You okay, honey?"

"I need to get a life," I told her, and meant it more than she could ever know.

She smiled uncertainly, probably thinking I was having some kind of breakdown. She wasn't wrong.

Sitting in this doctor's office now, I realize how that moment on the bridge changed everything. The angry driver had been my unlikely angel, his crude words the slap I needed to wake up from my suicidal sleepwalk.

But the statistics on my phone screen remind me that not everyone gets their rude awakening. The famous names scroll past like a celebrity obituary: Kate Spade, worth $200 million, hanging herself with a scarf. I'm wearing her shoes right now, comfortable pumps I bought at Nordstrom Rack, designed by a woman who had everything the world said should make her happy.

Anthony Bourdain, traveling the globe, eating with presidents, exploring the undiscovered corners of human experience. Found dead in a French hotel room, his final episode of "Parts Unknown" becoming tragically prophetic.

German billionaire Adolf Merckle, employing 100,000 people, building empires, then stepping in front of a train when the financial crisis threatened his legacy.

Robin Williams, God, Robin Williams. Mork from Ork, the genie in Aladdin, the therapist in Good Will Hunting. Academy Awards, Emmys, Golden Globes, a fortune estimated between $50-100 million. None of it enough to quiet the demons in his brilliant, tortured mind.

Dave Chappelle joked about it in his Netflix special, contrasting wealthy suicides with his friend who lost everything but still showed up to work at Foot Locker in an umpire uniform, seemingly content. But Dave was wrong about one thing, you never really know what's going on in someone else's head. His friend might have been one bad day away from his own bridge.

Money doesn't buy peace. Fame doesn't silence the voices. Success doesn't guarantee satisfaction. The statistics prove it: the rich kill themselves at the same rates as everyone else, sometimes higher. All that wealth and opportunity, yet still they choose the final exit.

A chill runs down my spine as I consider my own proximity to that choice. If not for an angry stranger in a red pickup truck, I might be a statistic myself right now. My name added to those 48,000 annual casualties of despair.

The voice I heard earlier echoes in my memory: "Why are you here? Your help does not come from man or things made by man."

Maybe there's truth in those words. Maybe pharmaceutical peace is just another illusion, another dead end disguised as a solution. Maybe what I'm really seeking can't be found in a prescription bottle.

But then again, maybe that voice was just my anxiety manifesting as auditory hallucination. Maybe I'm overthinking this, letting fear masquerade as wisdom.

Outside the small window, the storm clouds are darker now, pressing against the glass like an omen. Thunder rumbles in the distance, still far away but approaching with inevitable certainty.

Something's coming. I can feel it in my bones, in the electricity of the air, in the way shadows seem to move when I'm not looking directly at them.

The question is: am I ready for whatever it is?

4

The Presence is in the Room

"Why do you speculate on such matters, when Wisdom and Knowledge require understanding of the word of God?"

The voice cuts through my thoughts like a blade through silk, clear, authoritative, unmistakably male but not deep. Not threatening, exactly, but commanding in a way that makes my soul stand at attention.

I bolt upright, my phone clattering to the floor as I leap from the stool. My eyes dart frantically around the examination room: window, posters, exam table, cabinets, chair, stool. Nothing. No one. Just me and the lingering echo of words that shouldn't exist.

Heart hammering against my ribs, I sprint into the hallway, checking my phone for accidental calls, searching for hidden speakers, intercoms, any rational explanation for the impossible. The telephone on the desk stares back at me, innocent and silent.

I know I talk to myself, everyone does, but that was definitely not my voice.

The certainty hits me like a physical blow: I do not need Xanax today.

Not today. Not from this place. Not while something beyond my understanding is trying to communicate with me through the sterile air of a medical office.

I follow the exit signs like a woman possessed, my feet carrying me toward freedom before my mind can overthink the decision. But the receptionist intercepts me at the door, her professional smile tinged with concern.

"Ms. Evans? Did the doctor give you any orders or prescriptions?"

The question stops me cold. "Excuse me?"

"Did the doctor give you any orders for blood work, prescriptions, or a follow-up appointment?" she repeats, consulting her computer screen with the practiced efficiency of someone who's asked this question a thousand times.

"No, I haven't seen the doctor." My voice sounds steadier than I feel. "I was told she was running behind. I'd like to reschedule."

Her expression softens with genuine apology. "She was very behind today. We had a serious emergency in the office, I'm so sorry for the inconvenience. But the worst is over now, and she's catching up. Are you sure you can't wait a little longer? I'd hate for you to leave when she's almost ready to see you."

The pressure is subtle but real, the gentle insistence of someone who's been trained to retain patients, to prevent walk-outs that hurt the bottom line. Under normal circumstances, I might cave to the guilt, might settle back into that green room and wait for pharmaceutical salvation.

But these aren't normal circumstances.

"I have another appointment," I lie smoothly. "I'm afraid I'll be late. Can we reschedule for next week?"

Her fingers dance across the keyboard. "How about next Friday?"

"Perfect."

I'm out the door before she can offer any more gentle resistance, practically running toward the parking lot like a woman fleeing a crime scene.

The heat hits me like a physical wall. I'd forgotten it was a sunny day after sitting in that artificially lit cave for so long. I tilt my face toward the sky, squinting against the brightness, and catch something in my peripheral vision. A movement. A shadow. A presence.

When I turn to look directly, there's nothing there.

But I know. I know with the certainty of prey sensing a predator that someone, or something, is with me.

Should I run to the police station? The thought is almost laughable. Where even is the police station? And what would I tell them? Officer, I'm being stalked by a disembodied voice with theological opinions?

My hip twinges with every step. I should have had that surgery years ago like Aunt Dorothy kept insisting. Can you imagine the scene? Me, limping into the police station, sweating and wild-eyed, explaining that a ghost is following me around dispensing spiritual advice? They'd have me in a psychiatric hold faster than you could say "72-hour evaluation."

My car sits in front of me like a beacon of normalcy, but I can't bring myself to approach it. Not yet. Not while this presence hovers at the edge of my awareness like a song I can almost remember.

Instead, I veer toward the Popeyes restaurant next door, walking quickly but not quite running. The familiar red and orange sign promises the comfort of greasy food and normal human interaction.

But the door won't budge.

"Curbside Service or Uber Eats Only," reads a hastily printed sign taped to the glass. "Due to COVID-19 pandemic, no dining room service."

I stand there like an idiot, watching cars snake through the drive-thru, their occupants eyeing me curiously. I smile back, though they can't see it behind my mask. The expression feels more like a grimace anyway, the kind of smile people wear when they're one step away from a complete mental breakdown.

Should I scream for help? Help me, someone's following me but I can't see them and they keep quoting Scripture!

An employee appears at the door, her face scrunched with concern and suspicion. "Did you place an order? Are you with Uber Eats?"

"No, I'm sorry." I step back from the door, suddenly aware of how I must look. "I thought I could come in to order. My car's over at the doctor's office. I'll go get it and come through the drive-thru."

She nods and disappears back into the safety of her restaurant, leaving me alone with my invisible companion.

As I walk back toward my car, rationality begins to reassert itself. How ridiculous am I, hearing voices and running from shadows? Standing at a chicken restaurant like it's a sanctuary? I begin to laugh at my own absurdity. The kind of shaky laughter that's dangerously close to hysteria.

By the time I reach my car and slide into the familiar embrace of worn leather seats, I'm feeling more grounded. The air conditioning kicks in with a reassuring hum, and I allow myself a moment to breathe.

Maybe I am losing my mind. Maybe the stress of everything. The pandemic, the isolation, watching my husband disappear into medical complications, has finally snapped something fundamental in my brain.

The ignition button responds to my touch with a satisfying purr, and the radio fills the silence with mindless chatter. I'm just starting to relax when my phone rings.

"Hey, baby." My husband's voice flows through the speakers like warm honey, and suddenly I'm crying without knowing why.

"Hi," I manage, pulling out of the parking lot and making a right at the light. "How are you feeling today?"

We talk as I merge onto the highway, and for a few minutes, the world feels normal again. He tells me about physical therapy, about the new roommate who snores, about missing Princess and our quiet house. I don't tell him about the voices or the presence or my aborted quest for pharmaceutical peace.

How can I explain that I'm falling apart while he's fighting just to exist?

He's been my gentle giant for twenty years, all 6'8" of him reduced now to a man in a wheelchair, both legs claimed by diabetes, his kidneys failing, his heart struggling. The disease that runs in his family like a genetic curse. Both his parents died from complications of diabetes, and now it's devouring him piece by piece.

People think diabetes is just about blood sugar, not understanding it's a full-body assault. It attacks blood vessels, kidneys, heart, every organ systematically. It steals circulation from extremities, forces kidneys into failure, weakens hearts until they can barely pump. It's a silent killer that announces itself with amputations and dialysis and strokes.

February 2016. I'll never forget walking into our bedroom to find him face-down on the floor, Princess frantically pawing at him, trying to reach his face. For a terrifying moment, I thought he was dead.

"What are you doing on the floor?" The words tumbled out in panic, ridiculous but human.

When he finally moved, sitting up against the bed, something was wrong with his eyes. They were open but vacant, looking through me rather than at me. His vocabulary had shrunk to three phrases: "What's wrong?" "Are you okay?" "Uh huh."

Not responses. Just repetitions. Like a broken record player stuck on the same three tracks.

The paramedics found his blood pressure at 200-something over something equally terrifying. In the hospital, he became someone I didn't recognize, stripping off his clothes, pulling out IVs, existing in what the doctor called "an altered state." This man who wouldn't go to strip clubs, who wanted privacy in the bathroom after twenty years together, suddenly had no sense of modesty or propriety.

But then came the moment that gave me hope: in the midst of the chaos, with security guards trying to restrain him, he stood up, all 255 pounds and 6'8" of him, walked to the sink, and vomited with perfect precision.

His brain was still working. Still aware. Still him, somewhere underneath the medical catastrophe.

The MRI showed no stroke, no brain bleed. Whatever had happened remained a mystery wrapped in medical jargon and insurance forms. When he finally woke up days later, he was confused and angry: "Why did you leave me in this place? Why am I naked? Did you bring me clothes?"

I was happy and not happy. Happy he was alive and aware, devastated by his confusion and sense of betrayal.

Now he's in rehabilitation, fighting to reclaim whatever independence is still possible. His memory is spotty. He struggles with faces, directions, the geography of our shared past. But he still remembers how to cook, still maintains his wonderful attitude about life. Princess adores him completely, and during these long months apart, she and I have become inseparable companions in worry.

As I drive home to her, I realize something has shifted. The presence I felt outside the doctor's office hasn't followed me into the car. Or maybe it has, but it feels different now. Less threatening. More... protective?

The voice echoes in my memory: "Why do you speculate on such matters, when Wisdom and Knowledge require understanding of the word of God?"

What if it wasn't a symptom of my breakdown, but an answer to my desperation? What if instead of seeking pharmaceutical peace, I need to seek something deeper, older, more permanent?

The storm clouds I noticed earlier are moving closer, darkening the horizon ahead. Lightning flickers in the distance, still far away but approaching with the inexorable patience of nature itself.

Something is definitely coming. The question is whether I'll have the wisdom to recognize it when it arrives.

5

— · —

WHERE IS YOUR FAITH?

H ome at last. The familiar ritual begins automatically in my mind: take Princess out, check the mail, figure out dinner. The elevator announces my floor with its cheerful bing, and I fumble with my keys, expecting to hear the familiar scrabble of tiny paws against hardwood.

Silence.

"Princess?" I call, dropping my purse by the door. By now she should be dancing around my ankles, tail helicopter, spinning with joy. But she doesn't come.

I find her sitting perfectly still in one of the two recliners in the living room, the one closest to the sunroom that catches the afternoon light. She's looking directly at me, her dark eyes bright with recognition, but she doesn't move. Not even a tail wag.

"What's wrong, baby girl?" I approach slowly, concerned. Maybe she's hurt, or sick, or . . .

"Why are you running from peace while saying you are seeking it?"

The voice, that voice, emerges from the recliner with crystal clarity. The same authoritative male tone that spoke to me in the doctor's office, now emanating from my own furniture.

The scream that tears from my throat surprises even me, a sound of pure terror that seems to come from some primal place I didn't know existed. Princess leaps down from the chair and begins barking frantically, not at the invisible speaker, but at me, as if I'm the source of whatever supernatural disturbance has invaded our peaceful home.

My legs buckle. The room tilts sideways like a carnival ride gone wrong. Heat floods my body as my vision starts to tunnel, the same sensation I felt years ago at Kaiser when I fainted in the waiting room. The world is fading to black around the edges, time stretching like taffy.

But I'm falling without landing, suspended in some impossible space between consciousness and something else entirely.

"Where is your faith?"

The question cuts through my panic like a lighthouse beam through fog. Clear. Direct. Impossible to ignore.

Princess has stopped barking and is staring at me with concern, her whole body wiggling with nervous energy. I realize I'm sitting down now, though I don't remember moving. The recliners that were positioned at an angle in the corner, the ones my husband and his sister joked were a waste of money because they wouldn't fit the space properly, are now facing each other in the center of the room.

And I'm no longer alone.

He sits across from me with the casual confidence of someone who belongs here, as if he's been waiting patiently for me to notice him. Princess approaches him without fear, and I watch in stunned silence as he lifts my tiny dog into his lap like they're old friends.

"Where is your faith?" he asks again, his voice gentle but insistent.

I study his face, trying to make sense of what I'm seeing. There's a light surrounding him, not harsh or blinding, but warm and somehow alive. It makes details difficult to discern, as if he exists in a different spectrum of reality than the rest of my living room.

His clothing is the brightest white I've ever seen, not the stark white of hospital sheets or wedding dresses, but something deeper, more complete. Like the color white before it got diluted by human understanding. His features are ethnically ambiguous in a way that suggests he could belong to any culture, or all of them. Middle Eastern, perhaps. Ethiopian. Arabian. Asian. My sociology-loving father would have been fascinated by the puzzle of his ancestry.

He appears ageless, mature but youthful, as if time moves differently around him. There's no jewelry, no ornamentation, nothing to distract from the singular intensity of his presence. This is a being with a mission, though I can't fathom what that mission might be.

"I asked you a question," I finally manage, my voice steadier than I expected. "Who are you? What do you want from me? Why are you in my living room?"

He doesn't answer directly. Instead, he tilts his head slightly, studying me with eyes that seem to see through layers of pretense to something I've forgotten about myself.

"Remember how he told you that one day you would be called to advance his purpose?"

The question hangs in the air like incense. I have no idea what he's talking about.

"I'm sorry, but I don't know what, or who, you're referencing." My voice gains strength as irritation overrides fear. "You're in my home. I deserve answers. Who are you and what do you want?"

His smile is patient, almost paternal. "I am a ministering spirit sent to serve those who seek salvation. I am here to guard his ways."

The words should clarify everything, but instead they deepen the mystery. I think of Chris Tucker in Rush Hour: Do you understand the words that are coming out of my mouth? I hear what he's saying, but comprehension remains just out of reach.

"Where is your faith?" he asks for the third time, and suddenly I hear it, the echo of an old James Cleveland song my grandmother used to play on Sunday afternoons. The lyrics float back to me across decades:

Say you've been sick? Tell me about it.

And you think you can't get well?

Where is your faith? Where is your faith in God?

A conversation between friends, one drowning in despair, the other throwing lifelines of hope.

As the memory settles over me, something shifts in the room. The panic recedes, replaced by an inexplicable warmth. Princess, who had been trembling at my feet, walks calmly to the stranger and allows him to lift her into his lap. She doesn't bark or struggle. She simply settles against him as if she's found exactly where she belongs.

I raise my eyes to meet his gaze fully for the first time.

The light around him makes details difficult to discern, but his presence is utterly peaceful. Non-threatening. I should be terrified, there's a supernatural being sitting in my recliner, holding my dog, asking me theological questions. Instead, I feel safer than I have in months.

"When you were a child," he says, his voice carrying the weight of intimate knowledge, "your faith was limitless. You didn't just believe in the Lord, you knew He had blessed you with a guardian angel. What happened to that child?"

The question pierces something deep inside me. He speaks as if he's known me my entire life, as if he's been watching my journey from fearless little girl to anxious middle-aged woman.

That child. When did I lose her? When did faith become a struggle instead of a certainty?

"What happened to you, old lady?" he asks with a smile that takes the sting out of the words.

I can't help but smile back. "Life happened."

His expression grows serious. "Jesus said to them, 'I am the bread of life; whoever comes to me shall not hunger, and whoever believes in me shall never thirst.' Did you forget John 6:35?"

The directness of the question demands honesty. "No, I didn't forget." I pause, gathering courage for confession. "I guess I've gotten further away from God's word as each day passes. I don't know exactly when or why the shift occurred. As I faced life's problems, I started relying on my own understanding. Through successes and failures, I tried solving everything myself, planning my own strategies, mapping my own routes to happiness."

I take a breath, surprised by my own transparency. "Maybe it was the small everyday choices, the ones that seem insignificant at the time, that gradually shifted my focus away from God and toward myself. But I know I need Him. I know I need Jesus."

He nods as if he's been waiting for exactly this admission. "You must learn not to lean on your own understanding, but on the word of God. The scriptures say, 'Delight yourself in the Lord, and he will give you the desires of your heart. Commit your way to the Lord;

trust in him, and he will act. He will bring forth your righteousness as the light, and your justice as the noonday.'"

He pauses, stroking Princess's fur with gentle fingers. "Do you understand that you cannot find peace because you are paying the penalty for your failure to rely upon the Lord? You are in a self-imposed exile."

The words hit like a physical blow, not because they're harsh, but because they're true.

He laughs softly, a sound like wind chimes in a gentle breeze. "I have been watching you for a long time. There is a contradiction in you. You pray to God for help only after you find yourself in a full-blown crisis. You pray after you worry yourself sick. Then you do not heed the call of the Lord when it comes. You know you make it harder than it has to be, right?"

I'm struck speechless. He's right, completely, devastatingly right. I wait until the crisis suffocates me, then cry out to God like a child who only remembers her parents when she's in trouble. It never occurred to me that I follow this pattern until he names it.

As if reading my thoughts, and maybe he is, he continues: "Do not worry about your life, what you will eat or what you will drink; nor about your body, what you will put on. Is not life more than food and the body more than clothing? O you of little faith."

You of little faith. The phrase settles over me like a diagnosis I've been avoiding.

"Have I lost my faith," I ask quietly, "or am I just afraid to act on it?"

His eyes, warm, ancient, knowing, hold mine steadily. Outside, thunder rumbles closer than before. The storm that's been building all day is finally arriving, and with it, something that will change everything.

"The question," he says, "is not whether you have faith. The question is whether you're ready to use it."

Lightning illuminates the room, and in that brief, brilliant moment, I see him clearly, not just his features, but his purpose. He hasn't come to frighten me or judge me.

He's come to prepare me for what's coming next.

6

— · —

THE VISIT

We sit in comfortable silence, studying each other like chess masters contemplating their next moves. But this isn't a stalemate, it's something deeper. He knows I'm preparing to give him surface answers, responses carefully crafted to contain neither outright lies nor complete truths. Safe answers with strategic omissions, designed to avoid conflict or consequences.

The irony isn't lost on me: I suspect he already knows every answer before I speak. His questions feel rhetorical, probing not for information but for admission. Why do I worry? The uncertainty of each step in this chaotic existence, perhaps. The impossibility of controlling outcomes in a world that seems designed to humble human planning.

A memory surfaces from my recent Bible study preparation, a sermon I'd watched on YouTube by a prominent pastor teaching from Acts. He'd said there were only two questions we should ever ask God: "Who are you, Lord?" and "What do you want me to do?"

This man, this being, sitting across from me with Princess curled contentedly in his lap, had said he was "sent" to me. Surely that implies purpose.

"Yes," he says, reading my thoughts as easily as scanning headlines. "Those are the right questions to ask. Most people assume they know the Lord, yet they fail to understand all that He is and all that He does."

His voice takes on a different quality, not just speaking now, but proclaiming, as if the words are flowing through him rather than from him.

"He is not only the Alpha and the Omega, the first and the last, the beginning and the end. God is spirit, and those who worship Him must worship in spirit and in truth. God is love, and whoever abides in love abides in God, and God abides in him. He is the Rock; His work is perfect, for all His ways are justice. A God of faithfulness and without iniquity, just and upright is He. It is written: 'I AM WHO I AM.'"

He pauses, and I sense the vast weight of eternity behind those words, truths too large for human language to fully contain.

"There is so much more to say, yet I have said enough." Another pause, as if allowing the words to settle into my soul. "The second question: 'What do you want me to do, Lord?' I was asked to come to you. You have been struggling, which has caused you to become both deaf and blind. You have not answered the call, and you don't have much more time."

The last phrase hits me like ice water. "You don't have much more time."

Panic floods my system. Am I dying? Should I be calling people to say goodbye? Getting my affairs in order? How will it happen, heart attack, cancer, accident, COVID? What about all the stuff I've accumulated in storage units? Who wants any of it? Did I make a difference in this life? Why did I even exist?

The questions cascade through my mind like a waterfall of terror until I realize he's watching me with patient understanding.

"He was right," I whisper. "I have been struggling."

Then the other part of his statement penetrates my fear. "You said I haven't answered the call. What call?"

His reply comes with the authority of ancient prophecy: "'For I know the plans I have for you, plans for welfare and not for evil, to give you a future and a hope.'"

He leans forward slightly, his eyes holding mine with uncomfortable intensity. "Who has been calling you, Andrea? Whose voice has been echoing through the wilderness of your daily existence? Whose voice have you heard in your dreams as you sleep, as you eat, as you drive down familiar roads? Whose voice has been calling you?"

The questions pierce through my defensive walls. This is no ordinary man, he's purposeful in a way that transcends human ambition. He's quoting Jeremiah 29:11, a verse I've heard countless times, but now it feels personal, urgent, alive.

My mind races through what I remember about Jeremiah. Called by God to warn the Israelites. Years of telling them to be obedient, warning of judgment and punishment. The Babylonian captivity that followed, seventy years of exile. Then God's message through Jeremiah: build houses and live in them, plant gardens and eat their produce, take wives and have children, multiply, and, most importantly, pray for the welfare of the city where you find yourself, because your welfare depends on its welfare.

And the warning: beware of false prophets who will use the Lord's name but speak lies, for the Lord did not send them.

What is he trying to tell me? Is this a warning about obedience? About false prophets? Or something more personal, that I should accept my circumstances as temporary, make the most of my situation, pray for my community because my fate is tied to theirs?

"All of the above," he says with a laugh that sounds like music. The casual way he reads my thoughts should be terrifying, but instead it's oddly comforting.

"I have been sent so that you will get a better understanding of the forces that are at work, forces that are bigger than you and me. But keep in mind: God's thoughts are not our thoughts, neither are His ways our ways."

I lean forward, desperate for clarity. "You said you were sent so I could understand the forces at work. What exactly does that mean?"

His expression grows serious, almost sorrowful. "You are alive, yet you act as if you have died. You have played with the notion of death. In fact, you have even considered it as an option. Over what, exactly? Because you have been treated unfairly? Because your property was taken from you?"

The words sting because they're true. The bridge. The moment I almost became a statistic.

"Yet food is still plentiful," he continues. "You continue to eat well. You have shelter and you are loved. You have forgotten your many blessings. Do you understand that there are countless people worse off than you?"

I nod, but it's perfunctory. In my heart, I don't really believe it. My problems feel enormous, all-consuming.

"Do you realize how many times you are under attack, but God's mercy and grace have prevented you from being harmed?"

This time I shake my head honestly. "No. I don't know."

The admission hangs in the air between us, heavy with implication. How many unseen battles have been fought on my behalf? How many disasters averted by divine intervention I never recognized?

"He would like you to witness something," the angel says quietly.

"He?" I ask, though I suspect I know the answer.

"Who else would I be talking about?" His smile is gentle but profound. "I have been asked to bring you to Heaven. You are to witness the trial of man."

The words don't make sense. "I'm sorry, I don't understand. Can you say that again? Heaven? Trial of man?"

He doesn't twitch his nose like Samantha from Bewitched or blink his eyes like I Dream of Jeannie. There's no dramatic gesture, no special effects.

One moment we're sitting in my living room with Princess and the afternoon light streaming through the sunroom windows.

The next moment, we're somewhere else entirely.

The transition is so seamless it takes several heartbeats for me to realize what's happened. My recliner is gone. My familiar surroundings have vanished. Even Princess has disappeared, though somehow I'm not worried about her.

I'm standing in a vast space that defies description, not a room, not a landscape, but something that exists beyond the normal categories of earthly architecture. The light here doesn't come from any visible source but seems to emanate from everywhere at once, warm and golden and alive.

And I am definitely not alone.

Figures move in the distance, too far away to make out clearly, but their presence fills the space with a sense of anticipation that makes my skin tingle. Something momentous is about to happen. Something that will change not just my understanding of existence, but existence itself.

The angel stands beside me, no longer the gentle visitor in my living room but revealed in his true nature. a being of such radiant authority that I can barely look at him directly.

"The trial of man is about to begin," he says, his voice now carrying harmonics that seem to resonate in dimensions I can't perceive. "You have been chosen to witness what comes next."

Thunder rolls through the heavenly space, not the earthly thunder I heard building during our conversation, but something infinitely more powerful. The sound of cosmic justice preparing to render its verdict.

I understand now why he asked about my faith.

I'm going to need every bit of it.

7

— • —

ARRIVAL TO HEAVEN

The Ascension

We are flying, though I cannot fathom how such a thing is possible. My chair has vanished from beneath me, yet I remain seated in perfect comfort, suspended in the vast expanse above. This is no ordinary journey; I am experiencing something beyond the physical realm. My spirit has been set free from the confines of flesh and bone.

The sensation is indescribable, light as morning mist, free as wind rushing through canyon walls. Weightlessness envelops me like a gentle embrace, and suddenly I'm transported back to childhood memories of roller-skating. There were moments, brief and magical, when my skates would carry me so swiftly that I felt as though I was soaring above the rink. It had been decades since I'd experienced that pure joy of motion, that split second of defying gravity. But this, this surpasses even those treasured memories.

I move through the heavens with the grace of a prima ballerina caught in her most spectacular grand jeté, suspended at the peak of her leap where time seems to pause. Perhaps this is what astronauts feel in the void of space, this perfect, liberating weightlessness that makes the impossible feel natural.

The Man floats to my left, his serene smile radiating warmth and understanding. As we ascend above the earth, I stretch my fingers forward, watching in wonder as they seem to dissolve into the fabric of the universe itself. The boundary between my physical form and the cosmos blurs until I can no longer distinguish between where I end and eternity begins.

Suddenly, inexplicable joy overwhelms me, and I begin to spiral and dive through the air with childlike abandon. The movement reminds me of Bapsey, my beloved boxer, and those first precious days after I brought her home. She would tear around the backyard in frenzied circles, pure excitement radiating from every bound. That's exactly how I feel now overcome with an explosion of energy and unbridled joy.

The Cosmic View

My vision expands beyond all earthly limitations. As we continue our journey toward the moon, stars, and sun, I turn to gaze back at the world I've left behind. Earth rotates with majestic slowness, a blue marble suspended in the infinite black. I can see every continent, every ocean, river, and sea. Mountain ranges rise like ancient spines across the landscape, and volcanoes pierce the surface like wounds in the planet's flesh.

But then the darker truths reveal themselves. Smoke billows from vast areas of the earth, not the clean smoke of campfires, but the acrid clouds of destruction. My enhanced vision pierces through the atmosphere, and I witness the suffering below: masses of people dying in conflicts and plagues, the sick abandoned without hope, animals crying out in pain and neglect. I see the stark division between the wealthy, protected behind their fortified walls, and the desperate poor who struggle to find even a morsel to feed their starving children.

As we pass beyond Earth's pull, my euphoria begins to ebb like a tide retreating from the shore. I should not have looked back. Some knowledge is too heavy for a heart to carry, even one freed from earthly constraints.

The Heavenly Atmosphere

The temperature shifts as we ascend, cool but not cold, as if the very air has been perfected. I draw in a deep breath, and the atmosphere fills my lungs with something purer than any-thing I've ever experienced. The air is crisp and clean, so pure it makes me feel lightheaded with its perfection. On impulse, I extend my tongue to taste this celestial atmosphere, knowing it must seem foolish but unable to resist. And yes, it tastes sweet and pure, like water from a mountain spring that has never known pollution.

We glide through layers of mist that somehow remain dry, neither damp nor oppressive. I glance toward the Man, but his expression has transformed entirely. Gone is the peaceful ease with which he watched my wonder. Now his face bears the gravity of someone preparing for a conference that will determine the fate of nations, or perhaps something far greater.

This change in his demeanor sends a chill through my spirit. I become alert, sensing that our destination holds more than beauty and wonder.

The Holy City

As we approach our destination, a city materializes in the distance but calling it a city seems inadequate for what I behold. Several magnificent structures rise before us, their domed roofs gleaming with what appears to be pure gold, reflecting light that seems to come from within rather than from any external source. The architecture defies earthly categories, blending ancient grandeur with timeless perfection. Intricate inscriptions and engravings cover every surface, telling stories in languages I cannot read but somehow understand in my spirit.

Streets of gold, not merely gold-paved, but streets that seem to be living gold, wind between buildings of impossible beauty. Open spaces are designed with such perfect proportion that they inspire both awe and peace. The entire city radiates light, not harsh or blinding, but warm and welcoming, as if each building is lit from within by divine fire.

People move through the streets, though, 'people' may not be the right word. Alongside recognizable human forms walk animals I know and creatures I've never imagined, all moving in perfect harmony. There is no hurry, no conflict, no fear. Joy emanates from every interaction, and peace flows like a river through every gathering.

I hover above this miraculous city, trying to absorb every detail, knowing that no earthly words could ever adequately describe what I'm witnessing.

The Great Arena

We continue past the city to what can only be described as a cosmic amphitheater, though even that description falls short. Before I can fully comprehend the transition, I find myself seated, my chair having materialized beneath me once again. The air itself seems to vibrate with anticipation.

Thousands upon thousands of beings are arriving simultaneously, each one unique in ways that stretch the boundaries of imagination. As I observe this gathering multitude, the Man's earlier words echo in my mind: "I was asked to bring you to Heaven so you could witness the trial of man."

The questions burn within me: Why me? What trial? But there is no time for clarification now. Whatever is about to unfold, I am here to witness it.

The Throne Room of Heaven

The arena, if such a mundane word can be applied to this place, defies every expectation and comparison. It has no walls, no ceiling, no roof. Instead, it forms a perfect circle with tiered seating that seems to stretch infinitely upward. We sit suspended above the clouds yet beneath the sun, with stars glittering in the vast distance. Massive pillars rise beyond the limits of sight, supporting nothing and everything simultaneously.

The clouds create an ethereal atmosphere, like being enveloped in gentle fog, yet visibility remains crystal clear. When I look down, I gasp. The earth itself appears to serve as the floor of this cosmic courtroom, its continents and oceans visible far below.

At the center of this impossible arena stands the staging area for what can only be described as the ultimate courtroom. The sight that greets me there drives me to my knees in reverence and awe.

The Throne of the Almighty

One great white throne dominates the center, flanked by twelve smaller thrones on each side, forming a perfect semicircle. But the beings seated upon these thrones are unlike anything I could have imagined. They are not quite human, not quite spirit, something between mist and substance, transparent yet undeniably present. Their forms shift like living fog, making it impossible to distinguish individual features. Only their garments, their crowns, their positions, and the aura surrounding each one allows me to tell them apart.

The great white throne is a masterpiece beyond human comprehension. I am certain no living person has ever beheld such majesty, not unless they too have stood in this very place. A brilliant rainbow of impossible colors arches over the throne, its hues more vivid than any earthly spectrum. The throne itself is adorned with precious stones: jasper and sapphire, agate and emerald, onyx and ruby, chrysolite and beryl, topaz and turquoise, jacinth and amethyst. Each gem seems to contain its own inner fire, contributing to the overwhelming radiance.

The Figure seated upon the great white throne blazes with light that illuminates the entire arena. Behind Him burns a flame, not the wildfire of destruction, but something more like a sacred campfire, steady and warm, giving Him an otherworldly glow that speaks of both power and intimacy.

Instinctively, I bow my head, though I cannot resist raising my eyes to behold this wonder. I turn to the Man beside me and whisper, "Is that God?"

His answer is simple yet profound: "God is everywhere."

The truth hits me like a wave: I am in the presence of the Almighty. Not just looking upon Him but surrounded by His presence. The entire arena pulses with His essence, warm, safe, and inviting, yet terrible in its absolute holiness.

The Sacred Furnishings

Seven golden lampstands, crafted from what appears to be diamonds and gold, stand beside the great white throne, their flames dancing without consuming. Behind the throne sits a table, not of gold or precious stone, but of meticulously carved wood, its surface covered with engravings depicting scenes from ages past. Upon this table rests an ornate silver bowl filled with burning incense, its fragrance filling the entire arena with the scent of prayers ascending to heaven.

Four living creatures surround the throne. I am struggling to process what I'm seeing. Each creature possesses four faces: man, ox, eagle, and lion, representing all of creation. They move on four legs with six wings each: two above their shoulders, two at the middle of their backs, and two above their hindquarters. When they rest, the wings fold to cover their bodies completely.

Most astounding of all, these creatures are covered with eyes. Eyes on their backs, their bodies, their wings. Eyes everywhere, suggesting they see all that transpires in heaven and earth. They move constantly around the great white throne, alert guardians protecting the sacred space.

The Twenty-Four Elders

The smaller thrones, while beautiful beyond earthly standards, pale in comparison to the great white throne. The spirits seated upon them wear garments of purest white, similar to the Man's clothing but each with unique designs and cuts. Each wears a golden crown studded with precious stones, marking their authority and honor.

From their thrones come lightning and thunder, rumbles and vibrations that cause the arena to flash with supernatural colors. The very air trembles with the power of their presence, creating the sensation of gentle earthquakes that remind all present of the awesome forces at work.

The Adversary, the Prosecutor, Satan, himself.

At the central podium stands another figure, a spirit dressed in purple and gold, shimmering with flecks of precious stones from diamonds, sardius, topaz, beryl, onyx and jasper,s that catch and reflect the divine light. His crown is larger and more elaborate than those of the twenty-four elders, yet subordinate to the crown of the one on the Great White Throne. Behind him sits his entourage, arrayed in colors and styles that are truly out of this world. It is not surprising that In Ezekiel 28:12, that it was said that "you were the seal of perfection, full of wisdom and perfect in beauty," when God spoke of Satan.

There is something undeniably impressive about this figure, he stands with perfect posture, taking in all that surrounds him with apparent confidence and determination. His beauty is undeniable, as is the beauty of those who accompany him. Yet despite their magnificence, their presence brings something darker into the arena. The very atmosphere shifts, and I feel the temperature of the space change subtly.

The Coming Storm

Tension fills the cosmic courtroom like a gathering storm. Uncertainty hangs in the air, thick and palpable. The pieces of an enormous puzzle are falling into place in my mind, and I realize with growing dread and anticipation what I am about to witness.

This magnificent being at the podium, beautiful, powerful, determined, is the one bringing charges against humanity. He is the Opposition, the Adversary, the Accuser of mankind. Satan, himself. And I, a simple human being, have been brought here to witness what can only be described as the trial of the century, the trial of all humanity.

The eternal question is about to be answered: Does mankind deserve salvation, or does justice demand condemnation?

As I sit in my seat high above the earth, surrounded by beings of unimaginable power and beauty, I realize that I am about to witness the ultimate courtroom drama, one where the fate of every human soul hangs in the balance.

The trial of man is about to begin.

8

SATAN SEEKS THE JUDGMENT OF MAN

The Call to Order

The resonant chime of celestial bells reverberates throughout the cosmic arena, their harmonious tones cutting through the atmosphere like a divine command. Instantly, the multitude falls silent. Every conversation ceases, every whisper dies away. The focus of countless beings turns toward the magnificent Spirit seated upon the great white throne, the Almighty Himself.

Yet surprisingly, the voice that addresses the assembly does not emanate from that sacred throne. Instead, a herald's voice, clear and authoritative, fills the vast space:

The Herald: "This is a special session, called at the request of the Adversary and granted by the grace of Almighty God. There shall be two sessions today: the morning session will allow the Adversary, Satan, to present his petition before God and His Council. The afternoon session will be the Love March and the demonstration of the Love Principle."

The pauses, and I sense a shift in the atmosphere, something unprecedented is occurring.

The Herald: "We also acknowledge the invited guests who have been permitted to witness these proceedings."

A murmur of understanding ripples through the assembly. Invited guests, like myself, are clearly an unusual addition to these heavenly courts. The silence that follows is pregnant with anticipation and unease.

Satan's Opening Gambit

Movement stirs at the podium as the magnificent looking figure in purple and gold steps forward, his entourage shifting behind him like a living tapestry of otherworldly beauty.

Then, without warning, a voice erupts from the podium, deep, resonant, commanding attention through sheer force of presence.

Satan: "The humans that You have created must be judged NOW! How many times will You allow them to go unpunished? They have failed to follow even ONE of Your commandments, not one! You would think they could manage to love You with all their heart, mind, and soul. After all, You created them! Where is their gratitude to their Creator?"

The words boom across the arena with the force of a cosmic thunderclap. There is something both magnificent and terrible in the Adversary's voice. Beautiful in its power, yet chilling in its accusation.

From the circle of smaller thrones comes a response, gentle yet firm, carrying the weight of infinite compassion:

Azure Voice (Senior Elder): "You sent Your beloved, only begotten Son into their world so that He might dwell among them and know their nature intimately. Through Him, the sins of mankind were forgiven, for He became their Redeemer. Salvation has been offered to all who seek it, by Grace and Mercy alone, not through the perfection of prior commandments or covenants."

Satan's form seems to grow more imposing as he prepares his rebuttal, his jeweled robes catching and reflecting the divine light in patterns that are almost hypnotic.

Satan: "Yes, the world knows You sent Your one and only beloved Son, but that was AFTER mankind proved themselves incapable or unwilling to keep ANY of Your commandments or covenants! Whether made with Abraham, Jacob, Moses, or David, they failed every one. And years later, Your own chosen people slaughtered Your beloved Son and denied His teachings, YOUR teachings!"

His voice rises with what sounds like righteous indignation, but there's something else beneath it, something that makes my spirit recoil.

Satan: "I stand before You today to seek the judgment of mankind due to their failure to comply with even ONE commandment given by Your 'beloved, only Son.' He specifically commanded them while dwelling among them: 'You shall love the Lord your God with all your heart and with all your soul and with all your mind. This is the great and first commandment. And a second is like it: You shall love your neighbor as yourself.'"

He pauses dramatically, letting his words resonate through the arena.

Satan: "They have failed even this most basic requirement. My Lord, I request time to provide extensive evidence of their failures."

The Divine Response

The voice that responds comes from the great white throne itself, not loud, yet it fills every corner of the arena with its presence. It is the voice of absolute authority, yet somehow intimate, as if speaking directly to each individual's heart.

Golden Voice (The Almighty): "How much time do you require for your arguments?"

Satan: "I have prepared ten distinct points demonstrating mankind's inhumanity to their fellow man, each requiring detailed exposition."

Azure Voice (Senior Elder): "I request equal time for rebuttal, my Lord."

Golden Voice (The Almighty): "Both requests are granted. Present your case."

The Nature of Man

The Adversary straightens, his confidence radiating throughout the arena as he begins what is clearly a well-prepared presentation.

Satan: "It is the very nature of man to be corrupt. While some argue that Adam and Eve were merely deceived by the serpent, I contend that it is mankind's fundamental nature to be disobedient to God. From the moment man was formed from the dust of the earth, he has been rebellious, uncontrollable, and destructive. My argument will focus on mankind's systematic inhumanity to their own kind."

A new voice enters the debate, youthful, passionate, perhaps speaking with the enthusiasm of one not yet tempered by eons of observation.

Emerald Voice (Young Elder): "But mankind was created in Our image! What do you mean by 'rebellious, uncontrollable, and destructive'?"

Another voice responds, this one carrying the weight of ancient wisdom:

Sapphire Voice (Ancient Elder): "Mankind is made in Our image, a likeness of Us, but they are not Us. There is a distinction that must be acknowledged."

Emerald Voice (Young Elder): "Wait! Is the Adversary suggesting that WE are rebellious, uncontrollable, and destructive? Why should he be permitted to come before Us with criticism and comparison?"

Divine Clarification

The rainbow above the great white throne suddenly blazes with intensified brilliance, its colors more vivid than any earthly spectrum. The atmosphere in the arena shifts as the Almighty Himself addresses the growing tension.

Golden Voice (The Almighty): "If the heavens and earth were created once, could they not be created again? If light was brought forth from darkness, could that light not be made brighter still? If the waters under the heavens were gathered together to form dry land, could not water and land be reorganized to recreate the earth anew? What is impossible with God?"

A rumble of understanding passes through the assembly, countless voices murmuring in harmonious acknowledgment of divine omnipotence.

Golden Voice (The Almighty): "Remember, Our likeness is not Our portrait, not a mirror image. It is the dominion granted over the fish of the sea, the birds of the air, the cattle, all the earth, and every creature that moves upon it. The image is found in the authority given, not in perfection of nature."

He pauses, and I feel the weight of divine attention shift back to the podium.

Golden Voice (The Almighty): "Continue with your presentation."

An Unexpected Interruption

The Adversary draws himself up, preparing to launch into his systematic destruction of humanity's character.

Satan: "I have ten carefully documented points that will demonstrate mankind's inhumanity to man and prove why they must be judged without further delay."

Suddenly, a voice cuts through the arena like a sword of righteousness. A woman's voice, clear and strong, filled with both wisdom and barely contained indignation.

Pearl Voice (Wise Woman): "With all due respect, I cannot hold my tongue! His audacity! His arrogance! His manipulation knows no bounds!"

The arena falls into absolute silence. The interruption is so unexpected, so bold, that even the four living creatures pause in their eternal patrol around the throne. I strain to see the source of this voice, trying to stand before realizing I'm somehow already on my knees.

Pearl Voice (Wise Woman): "Is he not the very one who has been 'going to and fro in the earth, and walking up and down in it,' influencing those in his path? Why should he be permitted to argue that humans are inhuman when they operate under his own influence and deception?"

The reference is unmistakable. Her words come directly from the book of Job, who described Satan's own admission of his activities on earth. The accusation hangs in the air like a challenge thrown down before the throne of God.

The Divine Response to Challenge

Golden Voice (The Almighty): "Mankind has been given the sacred gift of free will, the ability to choose between right and wrong, light and darkness, good and evil. And it is written that mankind will indeed be judged."

Azure Voice (Senior Elder): "But concerning that day of judgment, no one knows the day or the hour, not even the angels of heaven, nor the Son, but the Father only."

The woman's voice rises again, and I sense she is not finished with her challenge.

Pearl Voice (Wise Woman): "Again, please pardon my boldness, but I must ask: Was it perhaps a weakness to grant mankind the power to choose between good and evil? Did that choice itself set them up for inevitable failure? Should mankind have been given dominion over all earthly things when their morality is, at best, questionable?"

The Moment of Truth

The question hangs in the cosmic air like a thundercloud ready to burst. Has this woman, this Pearl Voice, challenged the wisdom of the Almighty's creative decisions? Or has she asked the question that needed to be asked, the question that strikes at the very heart of the cosmic drama unfolding before us?

The reaction is immediate and overwhelming. The Spirits on their thrones begin to shimmer and shine with increasing intensity. Lightning erupts from the twenty-four smaller thrones, sending colorful streaks across the heavens, brilliant blues, deep purples, soft pinks, pure whites, vibrant greens. The very fabric of the arena seems to pulse with divine energy.

Thunder rolls like the sound of a thousand earthquakes approaching but never quite arriving. The vibrations pass through my very being, and I feel them in ways that earthly senses could never register.

The four living creatures around the great white throne intensify their patrol, their countless eyes scanning in every direction. They move with new urgency, in front of the throne, beside it, behind it, their vigilance now clearly on high alert.

Heavenly Witnesses

For the first time, I notice movement high above the great white throne, near the massive pillars that stretch into the infinite cosmos. Perched on ledges and outcroppings are figures I had somehow missed before, cherubim, but not as I imagined them.

These are not the winged babies of religious art, but mature, powerful beings that appear more like perfected men. They have no wings, contrary to every painting I've ever seen. They watch the proceedings with calm attention, aware of every nuance but seemingly untroubled by the cosmic tension unfolding below.

Above the arena itself, I now see the seraphim in flight, magnificent beings with six wings each. Two wings cover their faces in reverence before the divine presence, two cover their feet in humility, and two enable their graceful flight through the heavenly atmosphere.

The Human Witnesses

The Man who brought me here, my guide and companion, is now on his knees in prayer, his head bowed in reverence and perhaps concern. As I look around, I'm startled to realize that there are many more people near me than I had initially noticed.

To my right sit dozens of individuals, not spirits or angels, but humans like myself. All are on their knees, heads bowed in attitudes of worship and awe. To my left, past the Man, I see even more people in identical postures of reverence.

I realize I should follow their example, and as I attempt to move into a kneeling position, I discover I'm already there! When did this happen? I have no memory of kneeling, yet here I am, and remarkably, I feel no pain whatsoever.

This is particularly astounding given my arthritis, which normally makes kneeling nearly impossible. Just recently, I had fallen while walking Princess and couldn't even get my knees positioned to push myself up from the ground. I had to crawl up a hill and use my hands to push myself upright. Yet here, in this sacred space, I kneel without discomfort, as if my earthly limitations have been temporarily suspended.

Waiting for Divine Response

We all wait. Humans, angels, spirits, creatures, etc., for the response to the Pearl Voice's challenging questions. The woman has questioned the very foundations of God's creative plan: Was free will a mistake? Did the gift of choice doom humanity from the start? Should beings with questionable morality have been given dominion over the earth?

The atmosphere in the arena is electric with a mixture of apprehension, tension, and anticipation. This is no ordinary theological debate, this is a challenge to the fundamental nature of God's relationship with His creation.

My mind races through biblical precedents. I remember Habakkuk questioning God about justice and receiving divine answers. I recall Job's agonized questions about suffering, which ultimately led to a deeper understanding of God's nature. But what about direct challenges to God's wisdom in creation itself?

The book of James comes to mind: "If any of you lacks wisdom, let him ask God, who gives generously to all without reproach, and it will be given him. But let him ask in faith, with no doubting, for the one who doubts is like a wave of the sea that is driven and tossed by the wind."

But were the Pearl Voice's questions asked in faith, or do they constitute the kind of doubt James warns against? The distinction may determine not just the answer, but the very fate of the proceedings, and perhaps of humanity itself.

The Calm Before the Storm

As we kneel in this cosmic courtroom, suspended between heaven and earth, I sense that we are witnessing something unprecedented in the history of creation. Satan's accusations, the Pearl Voice challenges, and the growing tension among the heavenly council suggest that this trial will be unlike anything that has come before.

The very air seems to vibrate with the weight of cosmic decisions yet to be made. Lightning continues to flash from the thrones, thunder rolls like distant battles, and the cherubim and seraphim maintain their eternal watch.

Something momentous is coming. I can feel it in the depths of my spirit, in the very atoms of this divine atmosphere. The trial of mankind is about to begin in earnest, and the outcome will determine the fate of every human soul who has ever drawn breath.

The greatest courtroom drama in the history of existence is unfolding before my eyes, and I am both witness and, in some mysterious way, participant in this cosmic judgment that will echo through eternity.

9

DISAPPOINTMENT AND SATISFACTION

T he Divine Reflection

The cosmic arena holds its breath as the Spirit on the great white throne prepares to address the Pearl Voice's challenging questions. When He speaks, His words seem to transcend time itself, as if He is drawing from the eternal wellspring of divine memory. The Golden Voice carries both infinite sadness and profound love, speaking to everyone yet somehow addressing each heart individually.

Golden Voice (The Almighty): "There was indeed a time when I questioned whether mankind should continue to exist, given their relentless propensity toward evil. The Scriptures record My heart in that dark hour: 'Then the Lord saw that the wickedness of man was great in the earth, and that every intent of the thoughts of his heart was only evil continually. And the Lord was sorry that He had made man on the earth, and He was grieved in His heart.'"

A profound silence settles over the arena. Even the seraphim pause in their eternal flight, and the four living creatures slow their vigilant patrol. The weight of divine grief, the Creator mourning His creation, is almost unbearable to witness.

Golden Voice (The Almighty): "'So the Lord said, "I will destroy man whom I have created from the face of the earth, both man and beast, creeping things and birds of the air, for I am sorry that I have made them."'

Satan's form seems to straighten with satisfaction, his jeweled robes catching the divine light as if reflecting his pleasure at this admission. But the Golden Voice continues, and the tone shifts subtly.

The Great Flood and the Righteous Remnant

Golden Voice (The Almighty): "Mankind's very existence hung in the balance. I was prepared to unmake what I had made, to return the earth to the void from which it came. The judgment was swift and complete: 'And the waters prevailed exceedingly on the earth, and all the high hills under the whole heaven were covered. The waters prevailed fifteen cubits upward, and the mountains were covered. And all flesh died that moved on the earth: birds and cattle and beasts and every creeping thing that creeps on the earth, and every man.'"

The arena trembles slightly, as if the very memory of that cosmic judgment still reverberates through creation.

Golden Voice (The Almighty): "'All in whose nostrils was the breath of the spirit of life, all that was on the dry land, died. So. He destroyed all living things which were on the face of the ground: both man and cattle, creeping things and birds of the air. They were destroyed from the earth.'"

A pause, pregnant with meaning.

Golden Voice (The Almighty): "All... except one. Noah, through his obedience and righteousness, found grace in the eyes of the Lord. He and his family alone survived the judgment that consumed the world."

I feel a stir of hope in my chest. Even in divine judgment, mercy found a way.

The Value of the Righteous

The Golden Voice grows warmer, tinged with something that sounds almost like pride, not in Himself, but in His faithful servant.

Golden Voice (The Almighty): "The value of one righteous man proved greater than the corruption of countless wicked ones. Witnessing Noah's faithful obedience, I entered into a covenant, saying in My heart that I would never again curse the ground for man's sake, though the imagination of man's heart is evil from his youth. Never again would I destroy everything as I had done."

The word "But..." hangs in the air like a storm cloud, and I sense the Adversary leaning forward with renewed interest.

Golden Voice (The Almighty): "But..."

The pause stretches across eternity. The very cosmos seems to wait for the completion of that thought.

The Perfect Paradise Lost

When the Golden Voice resumes, it carries the ache of a parent recalling a child's innocence before the fall.

Golden Voice (The Almighty): "When Adam and Eve were created, they received everything necessary for a life of perfect fulfillment and joy. Apple trees heavy with fruit, pear trees drooping with sweetness, orange groves glowing like sunset, grapes cascading from abundant vines, watermelon patches stretching across fertile ground, every conceivable fruit to delight their senses."

The description paints a picture so vivid I can almost taste the perfect sweetness of that untainted world.

Golden Voice (The Almighty): "Chickens pecking contentedly in the grass, turkeys strutting with pride, gentle lambs, woolly sheep, sure-footed goats, cattle lowing in green pastures, mighty buffalo roaming free, every form of sustenance they could desire. Catfish swimming in crystal streams, perch dancing in dappled sunlight, trout leaping in mountain brooks, sea bass gliding through deeper waters, grouper dwelling in ocean depths, the waters teemed with abundance."

I close my eyes, overwhelmed by the vision of a world without want, without scarcity, without the desperate struggle for survival that marks our current existence.

Golden Voice (The Almighty): "Herbs yielding seeds of every variety, shelter that needed no construction, fresh water flowing eternally from pure springs. They had no need to toil for survival, no requirement to earn their keep through the sweat of their brow. They could have had a hundred children, a thousand descendants, and none would have known want or need."

The beauty of this description makes what comes next all the more tragic.

Golden Voice (The Almighty): "There was only one thing. ONE THING, held back from them: the Tree of the Knowledge of Good and Evil."

The emphasis reverberates through the arena like a cosmic bell tolling.

Golden Voice (The Almighty): "In exchange for all this abundance, all this perfection, only one simple request was made: 'Do not eat from the Tree of the Knowledge of Good and Evil, for in the day that you eat of it you shall surely die.'"

The Image of God

The Golden Voice grows more intimate, more personal, as if sharing the deepest secrets of the divine heart.

Golden Voice (The Almighty): "But the gifts were not merely material. When man and woman were created, they were fashioned in Our very image. The greatest blessing that could be bestowed upon any created being. When their creation was complete, the declaration rang throughout all creation: 'Indeed, it was very good.'"

I feel tears I didn't know I could shed in this place begin to well up in my eyes.

Golden Voice (The Almighty): "Both man and woman were loved with a love beyond human comprehension. The desire of My heart was for a relationship with them, not the relationship of master and slave, not the cold transaction of ruler and subject, but the warm intimacy that exists between a loving father and his beloved children."

The tenderness in that divine voice is almost overwhelming.

Golden Voice (The Almighty): "I desired a relationship built on gratitude, willing obedience born of love, and mutual affection. There was no need for the fear that drives a slave to obey his master, no threat of retaliation or punishment hanging over their heads. In Our home, there are no slaves, only children who choose their response to love."

The Gift and Burden of Choice

The Golden Voice takes on a different quality now, still loving, but tinged with the weight of cosmic responsibility.

Golden Voice (The Almighty): "The relationship I desired required the ability to choose, voluntarily, freely, without coercion. They needed the capacity to decide for themselves how they would live, whether for good or for evil. But with that sacred gift came an equally sacred responsibility: they must be willing to accept the consequences of their decisions."

From somewhere in the arena, I hear what sounds like a sigh. Whether from angel, spirit, or human witness, I cannot tell.

Golden Voice (The Almighty): "It has been suggested that since the outcomes of mankind's actions can be perceived before their physical manifestation, they are being controlled like marionettes on strings. This is a fundamental misunderstanding. Knowing an outcome and controlling an outcome are entirely different things."

The explanation that follows strikes me with its simple profundity.

Golden Voice (The Almighty): "Consider an attentive parent who knows their child intimately. The parent understands their character, their weaknesses, their tendencies. When that child ventures beyond the parent's direct supervision to spend time with peers, is the child physically controlled by the parent? Can that parent prevent the child from drinking too much alcohol or from making the decision to drive while intoxicated? Of course not."

The analogy hits home with startling clarity.

Golden Voice (The Almighty): "The parent does not physically control the child's actions, but if that child is obedient and has internalized the parent's teachings, their behavior will reflect those lessons even in the parent's absence. However, if the child encounters temptation and chooses to be led astray, that choice belongs entirely to the child."

The Necessity of Choice

Golden Voice (The Almighty): "Mankind must possess the genuine ability to make moral decisions. In response to Divine love, they must choose to love and obey, not from compulsion, but from the overflow of a grateful heart. Without the possibility of choosing evil, the choice of good becomes meaningless. Without the option to reject love, the decision to embrace it loses all value."

The logic is inescapable, yet I find myself wrestling with its implications. The very gift that makes love possible also makes betrayal possible.

The Challenge Continues

The atmosphere shifts as the Golden Voice addresses Satan directly, and I sense that the real battle is about to begin.

Golden Voice (The Almighty): "But let us move forward. You spoke of 'mankind's inhumanity to mankind.' Were you prepared to present your examples?"

Satan's form seems to pulse with anticipation, his purple and gold robes shimmering with otherworldly light. His entourage leans forward as one, their beautiful faces marked with expressions of eager expectation.

Satan: "Indeed, my Lord. I have prepared ten comprehensive examples that will demonstrate beyond any shadow of doubt that humanity has failed Your test. They have proven themselves unworthy of the love You have lavished upon them, ungrateful for the gifts You have bestowed, and incapable of the obedience You have every right to expect."

His voice carries the weight of absolute conviction, and I feel a chill run through my spirit.

Satan: "Each example will show not just individual failure, but systematic, cultural, generational patterns of evil that prove mankind's fundamental corruption. They have had thousands of years to demonstrate their worth, and instead they have consistently chosen darkness over light, hatred over love, cruelty over compassion."

The Pearl Voice (the Wise Woman) that challenged so boldly before remains silent now, and I wonder if she is preparing her own response or if the Adversary's confidence has given her pause.

The Weight of Anticipation

As Satan prepares to present his case against humanity, the arena seems to hold its breath. The lightning from the twenty-four thrones flickers more rapidly, creating an almost stroboscopic effect across the cosmic courtroom. The thunder rumbles continuously now, like the sound of an approaching storm that will reshape the very foundations of creation.

The four living creatures around the great white throne have increased their vigilance, their countless eyes scanning not just the arena but seeming to peer into dimensions beyond my comprehension. The cherubim on their distant perches lean forward slightly, their mature faces showing the first signs of concern I've witnessed.

Above us, the seraphim continue their eternal flight, but their movements seem more urgent now, their six wings beating with increased tempo as they call out their eternal song: "Holy, holy, holy is the Lord of hosts; the whole earth is full of His glory!"

I remain on my knees, along with all the other human witnesses, feeling the weight of what is about to unfold. We are about to hear humanity put on trial not by earthly judges, but by cosmic forces beyond our comprehension. Satan believes he has an unshakeable case.

The defenders prepare their rebuttals. And somewhere in the balance hangs the eternal fate of every human soul.

The trial of mankind is about to begin in earnest, and I sense that what we are about to witness will determine not just the judgment of humanity, but the very nature of divine justice itself.

The Calm Before the Storm

In this moment of suspended anticipation, I find my mind racing through the implications of what I've heard. The Almighty's love for humanity is undeniable. The pain in His voice when describing the flood, the tenderness when recalling the original paradise, the careful explanation of why choice was necessary for genuine love.

But Satan's confidence is equally unmistakable. He believes he has evidence that will prove humanity's unworthiness beyond question. And given what I witnessed when looking back at earth during our ascent, the wars, the suffering, the inequality, the cruelty, I fear he may be right.

Yet the Pearl Voice's (the Wise Woman) questions echo in my mind: Was the gift of choice perhaps a setup for failure? Did the granting of free will doom humanity from the start? And if so, is it just to judge them for fulfilling their nature?

These questions hang in the cosmic air as we prepare to hear the prosecution's case against the human race. Whatever comes next will determine whether mercy or justice prevails in the ultimate court of appeals.

The greatest trial in the history of creation is about to unfold, and I am both terrified and honored to be a witness to whatever divine judgment awaits.

10

SATAN'S EVIDENCE

The anticipation in the cosmic arena is palpable. My heart pounds as I realize I am about to witness something unprecedented. Satan's systematic case against humanity! The question I had hoped would be addressed about free will and predestination now seems trivial compared to the gravity of what unfolds before me. Indeed, God's ways are not man's ways, and I am about to discover truths that no earthly theology could have prepared me for.

Satan steps forward from his magnificent entourage, his purple and gold robes catching the divine light like captured Starfire. When he speaks, his voice carries the weight of several lifetimes spent observing human failure.

Satan: "The most prized possession that any man or woman could have is their family. A protective and thoughtful father and husband, a loving and generous mother and wife, obedient and disciplined children. All learning, sharing, and imitating the word of God together."

He pauses, letting the beauty of this vision settle over the assembly before delivering his devastating blow.

Satan: "Yet behold what has become of this sacred institution! The family unit has been devalued, undermined, and torn apart at its very foundation. For entertainment purposes alone, there are television programs whose entire premise revolves around the shameful question, 'Who is the father?' Men deny their own children, abandoning their God-given responsibility, while women have become so promiscuous they cannot identify their children's fathers!"

Lightning flickers across the smaller thrones as his words strike home. I feel the weight of truth in his accusations, and it makes my spirit ache.

Satan: "The family lies in ruins at its core. Let us examine the consequences of this destruction, particularly the plague of fatherlessness that has swept across the nations."

He gestures broadly, and somehow, I can see images forming in the air above us; statistics, charts, and heartbreaking scenes of broken homes across the earth.

Satan: "In one of the richest nations on earth, the United States, one-third of all households are fatherless. ONE-THIRD! The father was ordained by the Almighty to be the head of the household, the protector and guide of his family. He was to be the provider, the teacher of values and morals, walking in the ways of the Lord as commanded in Ephesians 6:4: 'Fathers, do not provoke your children to anger, but bring them up in the discipline and instruction of the Lord.'"

The images above us shift to show empty chairs at dinner tables, children walking alone to school, mothers working multiple jobs while their children raise themselves.

Satan: "The absence of fathers has unleashed an epidemic of evil upon humanity. First. Children without fathers in their homes are exponentially more likely to engage in wicked and evil behavior. They are not exposed to the word of God, therefore they do not know the word of God. They become spiritual orphans in a world that desperately needs righteousness."

The thunder rumbles, and I notice the cherubim above us leaning forward, their perfect faces etched with sorrow at these revelations.

Satan: "Second. These fatherless children fill the prison systems of the world like a plague. They turn to criminal enterprises, gangs, and violence because they have no moral compass, no strong hand to guide them toward righteousness."

Satan: "Third. The economic devastation is staggering. Women, often earning less or working in lower-paying fields, struggle to provide for their children alone. These children are four times more likely to live in poverty, robbed of opportunities that might have led them toward productive lives."

Satan: "Fourth. Education becomes a luxury they cannot afford. Their dropout rates from schools soar higher than those with fathers present. Without education, they cannot break the cycles of poverty and despair that entrap them."

Satan: "Fifth. They turn to drugs and alcohol to numb the pain of their abandonment. But this is compounded by the mental illnesses that plague them. Depression, anxiety, and hopelessness so profound it drives them to seek escape through chemical means."

The arena grows quieter as the full weight of these statistics settle over the assembly. Even the seraphim have slowed their eternal flight, their six wings moving with what seems like mourning.

Satan: "But the greatest tragedy, the one that pierces the very heart of creation is the loss of identity. When a child has no father, they lose the very essence of who they are: their qualities, beliefs, personality, and even their understanding of how they fit within the greater tapestry of humanity."

His voice drops to almost a whisper, yet somehow every being in the arena hears every word.

Satan: "How does a soul answer the question 'Who am I?' when the fundamental pieces of their identity puzzle are missing? If a person feels incomplete, they will chase after false identities. Joining gangs, seeking belonging in destructive relationships, pursuing validation through sin and rebellion."

I think of the genealogies in Scripture, how important family lines were to God's people, and I understand the deeper spiritual meaning of what the Adversary is revealing.

Satan: "The Bible overflows with genealogies! They placed supreme importance on family ancestry. The Scriptures include these family records to show how Jesus Christ was related to King David, to Abraham, to Adam himself. Land inheritance, temple roles, tribal identities, all were determined by familial relationships."

His voice rises with what sounds like genuine anguish.

Satan: "But what happens when you belong to nothing and no one? What role can you fulfill? How does a lost sheep find protection and safety without a shepherd? These children wander through life like spiritual orphans, easy prey for every form of evil that stalks the earth!"

Suddenly, the Pearl Voice cuts through his presentation like a sword of righteous indignation.

Pearl Voice (The Wise Woman): "Again, with all due respect. Are we here to receive a lesson on the consequences of fatherless homes when YOU have been the driving force demolishing the family structure itself?"

The lightning from the smaller thrones intensifies, and I can see the Spirits upon them leaning forward with interest.

Pearl Voice (The Wise Woman): "Are you not the very one who has been 'going to and fro in the earth, and walking up and down in it,' influencing and possessing those in your path? Yet you have the audacity to stand before the throne of the Almighty and argue for the judgment of mankind due to the breakdown of families, when YOU are the destroyer of those families!"

Azure Voice (Elder): "Hypocrite!"

Sapphire Voice (Ancient Elder): "Opposer!"

Emerald Voice (Young Elder): "False Teacher!"

The names are hurled at Satan like spears of truth. Lightning explodes across the arena in brilliant displays of divine anger. Thunder rolls like the sound of approaching armies. The very foundations of the cosmic courtroom seem to shake with righteous indignation.

To my right and left, I hear the human witnesses whispering among themselves, their voices filled with a mixture of fear and recognition. They, like me, are beginning to understand the cosmic nature of the battle being waged over human souls.

But then, in the midst of this divine storm, Satan raises his voice with a question that cuts through the chaos like a blade:

Satan: "If there is no choice available to mankind, then how can there be free will?"

Silence.

The question hangs in the cosmic air like a cosmic thunderbolt waiting to strike. The lightning diminishes. The thunder fades to distant rumbles. Even the whispering among the human witnesses ceases.

No one responds to his question. The silence is deafening, pregnant with implications that stretch to the very foundations of creation itself.

I realize that Satan, the Adversary, has just asked the question that goes to the heart of everything, the relationship between divine sovereignty and human responsibility, the tension between God's omniscience and mankind's moral accountability.

The great white throne seems to glow brighter, the rainbow above it pulsing with colors that have no earthly names. The four living creatures around the throne move with heightened alertness, their countless eyes scanning the assembly as if something momentous is about to unfold.

In this moment of cosmic silence, I understand that we have reached a turning point. Satan's evidence against humanity has been devastating, but his final question has revealed the deeper issue at stake: the very nature of free will itself.

And in the silence that follows, I sense that something unprecedented is about to be revealed, something that will forever change how we understand the relationship between God and humanity, between divine sovereignty and human choice.

The trial of mankind is about to take a turn that none of us, not even the celestial beings, could have anticipated.

11

SLAVERY AND CONCENTRATION CAMPS ARE NOT DEAD

The silence following Satan's piercing question about free will seems to stretch across eternity itself. But then, like a master prosecutor who knows he holds the winning evidence, he straightens his magnificent frame and continues his systematic destruction of humanity's character.

Satan: "Let us proceed to my second point of evidence against mankind's inhumanity to their own kind."

He pauses, his jeweled robes catching the divine light as he shifts position, quickly glancing back at his otherworldly entourage as if drawing strength from their presence.

Satan: "The superiority, entitlement, and arrogance of human beings. Their insatiable desire to enslave other men, women, and children, this evil has not only continued but flourished across the millennia. You would think that after thousands of years, mankind would have matured, would have grown wiser concerning the treatment of their fellow human beings. But they have not. They have become more sophisticated in their cruelty, more systematic in their oppression."

Images begin to form in the air above us again, and I feel my stomach turn as I witness the scope of human suffering he's about to reveal.

Satan: "Slave trade was recorded as early as 3500 BC in Mesopotamia, and it continues to plague the earth today. At this very moment, an estimated 40.3 million souls are trapped in modern-day slavery. One in four are children, innocent lambs led to slaughter. Seventy-one percent are women and girls, treated as commodities to be bought and sold."

The arena grows darker as the weight of these statistics settles over us. Even the seraphim seem to slow their eternal flight, their six wings moving with what appears to be mourning.

Satan: "Behold the faces of modern slavery: child soldiers, their innocence stolen and weapons placed in their small hands. Men and women, boys and girls caught in the web of illegal sex trafficking, their bodies sold like merchandise in the marketplace. Forced laborers, working unto death in conditions that would make the Egyptian taskmasters seem merciful."

He gestures broadly, and the images shift to show the horror he describes.

Satan: "Many think only of the transatlantic slave trade, where ten to twelve million Africans were transported in the bellies of ships like cargo. But that historical evil pales in comparison to what exists today. In the year 2020, merely yesterday in cosmic terms, migrants from West Africa were being sold in open-air slave markets in Libya. Imagine the irony! Men, women, and children fleeing war zones, extreme poverty, and crippling criminality, only to be sold into conditions worse than what they escaped!"

The thunder begins to rumble from the smaller thrones, and I can see the Spirits upon them leaning forward with growing indignation.

Satan: "Modern slaves are forced into every conceivable form of labor: making bricks until their hands bleed, cleaning houses while being treated as less than human, producing clothing in sweatshops that would horrify the ancient world, picking fruit and vegetables under scorching suns with no rest, performing sexual acts that defile the very image of God within them, digging for diamonds and precious gems while living in squalor."

He pauses, letting the full weight of human cruelty sink into our consciousness.

Satan: "They even found slaves working on construction projects for the 2022 Qatar World Cup, a celebration of human achievement built on the backs of the enslaved! And in the United States, supposedly one of the most advanced nations on earth, more than 400,000 modern slaves labor under forced conditions, primarily in for-profit prison systems that make inmates work for pennies while generating over one hundred and fifty billion dollars annually in profit."

The lightning begins to flash across the smaller thrones, and I notice the cherubim above us standing at attention, their perfect faces etched with righteous anger.

Satan: "But here is the most damning evidence of all. People who profess to believe in You, my Lord, in Your Son Jesus Christ, and in the Holy Spirit, have decided to play God themselves! They look upon other human beings as inferior, arguing that the color of skin, the language spoken, the clothes worn, somehow entitles them to enslave their fellow image-bearers."

His voice rises with what sounds like genuine anguish.

Satan: "And they use Your very word to justify their evil! They twist the inspired Scriptures, the Holy Bible itself, as a weapon against their fellow human beings!"

Suddenly, a new voice cuts through the arena, a tenor voice, clear and strong, filled with both authority and heartbreak.

Violet Voice (The Historian): "'Love the Lord your God with all your heart and with all your soul and with all your mind.' And 'Love your neighbor as yourself.' Is this not the greatest commandment given to mankind? How could anyone use the word of God to enslave another human being? The wickedness that surrounds us is beyond comprehension!"

The Violet Voice continues, his tone becoming more urgent.

Violet Voice (The Historian): "They used the inspired word of God, the very breath of the Almighty, to treat their fellow human beings as somehow inferior to themselves! They perverted the sacred Scriptures, twisting them into chains and whips against their own kind!"

A low whisper ripples through the arena, voices too soft to distinguish but carrying the weight of collective sorrow and indignation.

Satan: "I would like to continue, if I may, with even more devastating evidence."

Satan's voice takes on an even more ominous tone as he prepares to reveal the depths of human cruelty.

Satan: "Concentration camps are not relics of the past, they still exist, though the names have been sanitized to 'refugee camps' or 'detention centers.' When people hear 'concentration camp,' they think of the Nazi Holocaust and the Soviet Gulag system, where millions of Jews were systematically murdered. Auschwitz, Treblinka, Belzec, names that should forever stain human history. These death factories built poison-gas chambers that could accommodate 2,000 people at once, with 12,000 souls gassed and incinerated each day."

The images above us shift to show modern horrors that mirror ancient evils.

Satan: "But today, China has constructed approximately 400 camps to detain Muslim minorities and Uighurs. Many are built in industrial areas near factories, turning the imprisoned into forced laborers. A perfect fusion of slavery and concentration camps."

Satan: "India, following China's example, is placing Muslims in large camps, stripping millions of their citizenship and declaring them illegal immigrants in their own home-land. Myanmar has built camps for Rohingya Muslim refugees who fled persecution in Bangladesh, only to find themselves imprisoned again."

Satan: "In Syria, nearly twelve million refugees, half of them children, live in conditions that mock human dignity. The Greek island of Lesbos houses the Moria camp, built for 3,000 refugees but crammed with over 13,000 souls fleeing Afghanistan, Syria, Turkey, and Africa. In Juarez, Mexico, camps hold those escaping Central American violence and poverty, denied entry to the United States."

Satan spreads his arms wide, encompassing the cosmic scope of human suffering.

Satan: "There are so many camps scattered across the globe that eternity itself would not provide enough time to name them all. Humanity has forgotten the lessons of Jesus Christ and the clear commands written in Your word. Leviticus declares: 'If a stranger dwells with you in your land, you shall not mistreat him. The stranger who dwells among you shall be to you as one born among you, and you shall love him as yourself.'"

He continues, his voice building to a crescendo of accusation.

Satan: "Deuteronomy proclaims: 'He administers justice for the fatherless and the widow, and loves the stranger, giving him food and clothing. Therefore, love the stranger.' And Genesis warns: 'You shall not oppress a stranger, for you know the heart of a stranger.'"

Suddenly, the Pearl Voice interrupts with the sharp precision of a sword cutting through deception.

Pearl Voice (The Wise Woman): "Are you not leaving something crucial out of those quotes from God's word?"

Silence falls across the arena like a heavy curtain. Satan's confidence wavers for the first time.

Satan: "What do you mean?"

Pearl Voice (The Wise Woman): "Your quotes are incomplete. Each of those passages ends with the reminder that the Israelites were once foreigners themselves, slaves in Egypt, strangers in a strange land. The question is: do human beings have the capacity to remember their own suffering, to put themselves in the shoes of another?"

Satan: "Apparently not!"

Pearl Voice (The Wise Woman): "Do you mean 'apparently not' because YOUR influence has been so overwhelming that they have forgotten their capacity for compassion?"

Suddenly, movement erupts throughout the arena. I can see figures rising from the smaller thrones, the cherubim standing at full attention, the seraphim increasing their patrol flight, and the four living creatures moving with heightened urgency around the great white throne.

Then, a new voice pierces the cosmic atmosphere, high-pitched, androgynous, carrying an authority I haven't heard before.

Indigo Voice (The Reasoner)"Is he capable of making his case without indicting himself? So far, he has shown remarkable audacity, coming before this holy assembly seeking the judgment of mankind. But each time he argues for human failure, he conveniently omits his own spectacular success at undermining the relationship between God and humanity!"

The words hit me like a cosmic thunderbolt, and suddenly the full scope of what I'm witnessing crashes down upon me with terrifying clarity.

Wait a minute. Is Satan arguing that mankind, us, me, you, our fathers, mothers, sisters and brothers, friends, acquaintances, should be judged NOW and sent to hell? To burn? Forever? Is he arguing that not one of us should be saved? That we should all be treated the same: the murderer, the liar, the thief, the fornicator, all sinners without regard to the word of God and the promise of salvation?

Wait a minute... Wait! Not sometime in the distant future, but NOW?

"OH MY GOD! OH MY GOD!"

The words escape my lips before I can stop them, ringing out across the cosmic arena with the force of a human scream in a cathedral of silence.

The Man beside me is staring at me. The people to his left are watching me with wide eyes. The people to my right are looking at me with expressions of alarm. Did I say that out loud? I didn't mean to say it out loud!

The purpose of this "trial" has just crashed into my consciousness with the force of a divine revelation, and it terrifies me to my very core.

There is absolute silence. No lightning. No thunder. No rumbling or vibrations. The cosmic courtroom has gone dead quiet.

I look desperately at the Man, trying to speak, but no words come. None. I glance toward the center of the arena. The Spirit on the great white throne and the twenty-four smaller thrones seem unaffected by my outburst. The four living creatures continue their eternal patrol. The cherubim maintain their vigilant watch. The seraphim continue their flight patterns.

But the human witnesses, the people to my left and right, they're all looking at me. I must have spoken loudly enough for them to hear but not loud enough to interrupt the divine proceedings.

The Man speaks to me, but he's not speaking with audible words. I'm looking directly at him, his mouth isn't moving, yet I hear him clearly in my mind and heart.

The Man (speaking telepathically): "Calm yourself and do not interrupt these proceedings. You are a guest in their house, here for observation and learning, like those around you. You are an invited guest because you questioned God. You wanted to know 'why' things were the way they were. You wanted to understand what God was thinking when He made you, me, this world, and whether it was worth living in it."

He's smiling at me, not with a big grin, but with kindness and understanding. His words feel tender and loving even though they're an admonishment.

The Man (continuing telepathically): "Do you not remember the words of Habakkuk: 'O LORD, how long shall I cry for help, and you will not hear? Or cry to you "Violence!" and you will not save? Why do you make me see iniquity, and why do you idly look at wrong?' Do you remember that?"

I do remember. The book of Habakkuk. Only three chapters, but it asks the same questions that have tormented my soul. Questions about the inequity and injustice of life. I remember thinking this life was not worth living.

The Man (with a raised eyebrow): "Do you remember that God gave you a spirit, not of fear, but of power and love and self-control? So, act like it."

As his words sink into my spirit, I feel a strange peace settling over me. But the terrifying realization remains: I am witnessing a cosmic trial where the very fate of humanity hangs in the balance. Satan is systematically building a case for our immediate judgment and condemnation.

And something tells me his most devastating evidence is yet to come.

The great white throne pulses with increasing intensity, and I sense that we are approaching a climactic moment in this cosmic drama, a moment that will determine whether mercy or judgment will prevail for the human race.

The trial continues, and eternity itself holds its breath.

12

Environmental Hazards

The cosmic arena still thrums with the aftermath of my outburst, but Satan, seems reinvigorated by the silence that followed. He stands taller, his purple and gold robes shifting like liquid starlight as he prepares to deliver what I sense will be another devastating blow against humanity.

Satan: "I need no one else to make my point. The actions of mankind speak with deafening clarity. Let us proceed to the next issue in my systematic case against them."

He gestures broadly, and images begin forming in the cosmic air above us. Images of a beautiful blue planet, pristine and perfect as it once was.

Satan: "Mankind is destroying their own home. The very earth beneath their feet. Allow me to illuminate this catastrophic failure. For it was written that the waters under the heavens were gathered together into one place, while dry land appeared. The earth was called forth, and the waters were called seas. And God looked upon His creation and declared it GOOD."

The images shift to show the same planet, now scarred by pollution, deforestation, and industrial waste.

Satan: "Yet humanity has found ingenious ways to alter, corrupt, and destroy what the Almighty declared perfect. Two primary forces of destruction ravage the earth: global warming and climate change. Both bearing the fingerprints of human negligence and greed."

I watch as the visual displays above us become more detailed, showing rising temperatures, melting ice caps, and extreme weather patterns.

Satan: "Global warming. The relentless rise in earth's surface temperature caused directly by human activities. They burn fossil fuels with reckless abandon, trapping heat and greenhouse gases in the very atmosphere that sustains their breath. Climate change follows! The systematic alteration of weather patterns across the globe. Do not confuse these twin harbingers of destruction, though they work in deadly harmony."

His voice takes on the cadence of a funeral dirge as he continues.

Satan: "The results of their environmental vandalism: sea levels rising like a slow-motion flood judgment, ocean temperatures climbing toward ecological death, glaciers melting like tears from heaven, polar ice disappearing as if the earth itself is weeping. They have unleashed intense flooding reminiscent of Noah's time, hurricanes that rival divine wrath, heat waves that mock the fires of judgment, and droughts that make the seven years of famine seem merciful."

The images above us shift to show refugee camps and disaster zones.

Satan: "These catastrophes cause death, destruction, and displacement. They are always striking hardest at the most vulnerable, the poor, the powerless. And here is the most damning evidence: what began as unintentional destruction during the industrial revolution has become willful environmental murder. They KNOW what they are doing, yet they continue to destroy their only home."

Lightning flickers across the smaller thrones as his accusations build momentum.

Satan: "But their environmental crimes extend far beyond climate destruction. In 1984, the worst industrial accident in human history occurred in Bhopal, India. Forty-five tons of poisonous methyl isocyanate gas leaked from an insecticide plant, killing thousands instantly and condemning half a million to lifetimes of respiratory and eye problems."

Satan: "In 1989, the Exxon Valdez spilled eleven million gallons of oil across 1,300 miles of pristine coastline, murdering 250,000 seabirds, 2,800 sea otters, 300 harbor seals, 250 bald eagles, 22 killer whales, and billions of salmon—an oceanic holocaust of God's creatures."

The seraphim above us seem to fly with greater urgency, their six wings beating with what appears to be righteous indignation.

Satan: "Pacific Gas & Electric's negligence caused the Camp Fire of 2018, incinerating eighty-five human beings and destroying nineteen thousand buildings. The entire town of Paradise became a literal hell on earth."

Satan: "Between 1961 and 1971, the United States military unleashed rainbow herbicides. Agent Orange, Blue, Purple, and Pink, was released across the jungles of Vietnam. Beyond the massive environmental devastation, four hundred thousand Vietnamese people were killed or maimed, and American soldiers also died from exposure to their own chemical weapons."

The images above us now show dying oceans and barren landscapes.

Satan: "The world's oceans, those same waters the Almighty gathered and called 'good' are dying. In 1992, Newfoundland's cod population collapsed so completely that forty thousand people lost their livelihoods overnight. From Iceland to Chile, marine ecosystems have been devastated by human greed."

Satan: "The Great Barrier Reef, Australia's crown jewel of coral diversity, suffers from massive bleaching events. A slow-motion apocalypse beneath the waves. Louisiana's wetlands, crucial for flood control and water filtration, are being destroyed by human interference, allowing salt water to poison fresh water supplies."

His voice rises to a crescendo of accusations.

Satan: "Lake Victoria, Africa's largest lake, shrinks by 150 feet in some areas while forty million people in Uganda, Kenya, and Tanzania depend on it for survival. Chemical pollution, raw sewage, overfishing, and invasive species choke the life from these sacred waters."

Satan: "The ultimate irony: humanity's destiny is inseparably bound to earth's destiny, yet their leaders deny the obvious truth. Government officials who possess the power to enact life-saving policies instead choose profit over survival. They seem to believe that money is more valuable than having a planet to inhabit."

Suddenly, the Pearl Voice cuts through his presentation like a sword of truth.

Pearl Voice (The Wise Woman): "Pardon my interruption, but you have painted all of humanity with the same brush of condemnation. You group everyone together without distinction, ignoring those individuals who have dedicated their lives to protecting and healing the earth. Are you not aware of the countless environmental advocates working tirelessly to reduce the damage?"

Satan: "My task is to present facts that support my case for judgment, not to make excuses for humanity's failures. As far as I am concerned, it is far too late for distinctions. All humans possess the same propensity for destruction! They should be judged as one unit."

Pearl Voice (The Wise Woman): "There is a crucial difference between having the propensity to act destructively and actually choosing to act destructively. Many individuals have chosen the path of environmental stewardship. Allow me to present evidence of humanity's potential for good."

The atmosphere in the arena shifts as the Pearl Voice begins her counter-testimony.

Pearl Voice (The Wise Woman): "Consider Wangari Maathai, who died in 2011 but was awarded the Nobel Peace Prize in 2004 for founding the Green Belt Movement. Her organization planted thirty million trees, preventing soil erosion while providing employment to thousands in Kenya. She served both the environment and her fellow human beings."

Images begin forming above us showing reforestation efforts and restored landscapes.

Pearl Voice (The Wise Woman): "Gaylord Nelson founded Earth Day and created the Outdoor Recreation Acquisition Program, saving over one million acres of parkland. He helped establish a national trails system, including the Appalachian Trail, and contributed to passing the Clean Air Act, Wilderness Act, and Clean Water Act."

Pearl Voice (The Wise Woman): "David Brower founded Friends of the Earth, the Earth Island Institute, and the League of Conservation Voters. Under his leadership, Sierra Club membership grew from 2,000 to 77,000, and they successfully introduced legislation protecting the environment."

Pearl Voice (The Wise Woman): "Chico Mendes was murdered for his environmental activism calling for land reform and Amazon rainforest preservation. He pioneered the world's first tropical forest conservation initiative led by forest peoples themselves."

Pearl Voice (The Wise Woman): "Aldo Leopold wrote 'A Sand County Almanac,' a passionate plea for wilderness preservation. He is considered the godfather of wilderness conservation and modern ecology."

Pearl Voice (The Wise Woman): "Rachel Carson faced persecution for protecting oceans, rivers, and seas. Her book 'Silent Spring' exposed how pesticides devastated the environment. Despite being scorned, her work led to banning DDT and other harmful chemicals."

Pearl Voice (The Wise Woman): "Vandana Shiva founded Navdanya and fights for biodiversity conservation and farmers' rights. She declares: 'I don't want to live in a world where five giant companies control our health and our food. Food is life, food is health! Growing food ecologically is care for the Earth and regeneration of soil, water, and biodiversity.'"

Pearl Voice (The Wise Woman): "Even a child, Greta Thunberg, spoke truth to power at the 2019 UN Climate Action Summit, demanding accountability with her passionate cry: 'How dare you!' She fearlessly criticized world leaders for their failure to address the climate crisis."

Pearl Voice (The Wise Woman): "Al Gore, the forty-fifth Vice President of the United States, chairs the Alliance for Climate Protection. His books 'Earth in the Balance' and 'An Inconvenient Truth,' along with the accompanying documentary, earned him co-winner status for the 2007 Nobel Peace Prize for 'informing the world of the dangers posed by climate change.'"

The Pearl Voice's testimony seems to fill the arena with a different energy—one of hope battling against despair.

Pearl Voice (The Wise Woman): "Should these individuals and countless others who dedicate their lives to environmental protection suffer the same consequences as those who possess the power to make changes but choose destruction instead?"

Silence falls across the cosmic arena. Even Satan seems to consider the weight of her question. The cherubim above us lean forward with interest, and the seraphim slows their eternal flight as if listening intently.

Then, a familiar voice enters the debate, one I recognize from earlier proceedings.

Sapphire Voice (Ancient Elder): "For it is written: 'Son of man, speak to your people and say to them: If I bring the sword upon a land, and the people of the land take one from among them and make him their watchman, and he sees the sword coming upon the land and blows the trumpet to warn the people, then if anyone who hears the sound of the trumpet does not take warning, and the sword comes and takes him away, his blood shall be upon his own head.'"

Ancient Elder's voice carries the weight of cosmic wisdom.

Sapphire Voice (Ancient Elder): "'He heard the sound of the trumpet but did not take warning; his blood shall be upon himself. But if he had taken warning, he would have saved his life. But if the watchman sees the sword coming and does not blow the trumpet, so that the people are not warned, and the sword comes and takes any one of them, that person is taken away in his iniquity, but his blood I will require at the watchman's hand.'"

Sapphire Voice (Ancient Elder): "The question before us is this: Should those who warn of impending environmental catastrophe be held responsible when those in power hear their warnings yet refuse to act? Who bears the ultimate responsibility, the people, the watchmen, or both?"

Pearl Voice (The Wise Woman): "The watchmen. Those entrusted with the power to enact change bear the primary responsibility. However, all will ultimately pay the price. Earth is humanity's only home, and if it becomes uninhabitable, all will suffer the consequences of environmental destruction."

A triumphant gleam enters Satan's eyes as he seizes upon her words.

Satan: "I believe you have just proven my point perfectly! ALL will pay the price! Environmental stewards and destroyers alike will face the same fate when the earth can no longer sustain life. This is precisely why humanity must be judged NOW, before their environmental crimes make judgment academic!"

The lightning from the smaller thrones intensifies, and thunder rolls across the cosmic arena like approaching drums of war. I sense that we are building toward something momentous, a climactic decision point in this trial of mankind.

The great white throne pulses with increasing intensity, and the rainbow above it seems to bend toward us as if the very presence of the Almighty is drawing closer to this crucial moment.

Something tells me that Satan's most devastating evidence is yet to come, and when it arrives, it will shake the very foundations of heaven and earth.

The fate of humanity hangs in the balance, suspended between divine justice and mercy, between environmental destruction and the slim hope of redemption.

And I am witnessing it all unfold in this cosmic courtroom where eternity itself holds its breath.

13

WEAPONS, THE PLAGUE AND COVID-19

The cosmic arena hums with an electric tension as Satan prepares to unveil what I sense will be his most damning evidence yet. The very air seems to grow heavier, and I notice the four living creatures around the great white throne moving with increased urgency, their countless eyes scanning the assembly as if anticipating something unprecedented.

Satan: "Speaking of environmental destruction, we must now examine mankind's most deliberate and calculated assault upon creation itself. I am talking about the development and deployment of weapons of mass destruction."

He gestures dramatically, and horrifying images begin materializing above us in the cosmic atmosphere.

Satan: "These instruments of apocalypse, forged from nuclear, radiological, chemical, and biological agents. Not only do they slaughter multitudes but systematically poison the very biosphere that sustains all life. They represent humanity's ultimate rebellion against the sanctity of creation."

Suddenly, a new voice cuts through his presentation, clear, authoritative, and unmistakably feminine, yet different from the Pearl Voice we've heard before.

Amber Voice (The Deaconess): "Did you not already address environmental destruction through rainbow herbicides and industrial disasters? It appears you've simply rebranded 'environmental abuse' as 'weapons of mass destruction.' The underlying argument remains unchanged, that mankind is destroying the earth. Please do not repeat identical accusations. Once was sufficient."

The Satan pauses, and for the first time, I see a flicker of something that might be irritation cross his magnificent features.

Satan: "Very well. Allow me to clarify the distinction. This evidence concerns the deliberate engineering of weapons designed for one specific purpose, the systematic extermination of human life on a massive scale. These represent the pinnacle of mankind's inhumanity to their own kind, killing in brutal and perverse manners that mock the very image of God within them."

The images above us shift to show mushroom clouds and devastated cities.

Satan: "On August 6th, 1945, the United States Air Force dropped an atomic bomb on Hiroshima, Japan. Three days later, a second atomic bomb obliterated Nagasaki. The first bomb instantly vaporized approximately 180,000 souls. The second murdered between 50,000 and 100,000 more. But death was merely the beginning of their suffering."

The cosmic display shows the aftermath, shadows burned into stone, people with melted flesh, children crying for parents who had been reduced to ash.

Satan: "Others died slowly and agonizingly from burns and radiation, a living hell that lasted weeks, months, years. Even today, decades later, children born to survivors carry the genetic scars of humanity's nuclear sin: small brain sizes, delayed development, blindness, increased susceptibility to leukemia and cancers. The very DNA of creation bears witness to their crime."

Lightning flickers across the smaller thrones, and I can see the Spirits leaning forward with expressions of profound sorrow and mounting anger.

Satan: "But their appetite for destruction knows no bounds. In October 1961, Russia tested the 'Tsar Bomb' over the Arctic, a fifty-megaton behemoth equivalent to fifty million tons of TNT detonating simultaneously. Thousands of times more powerful than the weapons that destroyed Hiroshima and Nagasaki."

The images show a mushroom cloud that seems to touch the edge of space itself.

Satan: "Detonated 2.5 miles above ground, yet the shockwave stripped nearby islands bare of all life. The flash could be seen 600 miles away. The heat was felt from impossible distances. The mushroom cloud climbed nearly to the edge of space, a satanic tower of Babel reaching toward heaven with the power to destroy worlds."

Satan: "Yet they continue developing delivery systems for maximum carnage: bombs, shells, spray systems, landmines, hand grenades, even using animals as vectors of death. They target food sources, crops, livestock, anything that sustains life becomes a weapon against life."

The display shifts to show more recent horrors.

Satan: "On March 16th, 1988, thousands of Kurdish civilians in Halabja were systematically murdered. Government forces spent two days shelling the city with rockets and napalm, an incendiary that adheres to human skin like hellfire itself. The second day brought mustard gas and nerve agents: sarin, tabun, and VX."

Satan: "Nearly 5,000 people died within minutes, their nervous systems shutting down as they convulsed in agony. Ten thousand more were crippled, injured, or condemned to lifelong suffering, a chemical holocaust that demonstrated humanity's boundless capacity for evil."

The seraphim above us seem to fly with increasing agitation, their six wings beating with what appears to be righteous fury.

Satan: "They've weaponized the very building blocks of life itself: bacterial agents like plague, anthrax, and Q fever; viruses including smallpox, hepatitis, and avian influenza; toxins such as botulism, ricin, and staphylococcus. These biological weapons infiltrate through skin, gastrointestinal tract, and lungs, turning the human body into its own destroyer."

Then his voice takes on an even more ominous tone, and I sense we're approaching something that will shake the very foundations of this cosmic trial.

Satan: "But perhaps the most damning evidence of all is occurring at this very moment. The world currently suffers under a plague. The coronavirus known as COVID-19, whether naturally occurring or engineered as a biological weapon, it has exposed the depths of human selfishness and incompetence."

The images above us shift to show overcrowded hospitals, mass graves, and people dying alone.

Satan: "Consider the United States, a nation that comprises only 4.25% of global population yet accounts for over 24.8% of all COVID-19 cases. As of this moment, they have recorded 22,221,548 cases out of 89,500,000 worldwide. Their death toll stands at 369,000 souls, 19.2% of the global total of 1,920,000 deaths."

Satan: "If COVID-19 were indeed a biological weapon, America would be losing both the battle and the war. Despite their supposed preparedness, their financial superiority over other nations, they proved utterly incapable of protecting their own people. Seven catastrophic failures expose their moral bankruptcy:"

He begins counting on his fingers like a prosecutor delivering final arguments.

Satan: "First, they denied the virus even existed, calling it a hoax while people died. Second, they stood aside watching neighbors, friends, and family torn down by disease. Third, they argued over who was responsible while bodies piled up in morgues. Fourth, they failed to implement nationwide mask mandates. Fifth, they failed to secure adequate vaccines. Sixth, they failed to distribute the vaccines they obtained. Seventh, they played politics with human lives, sacrificing innocent souls on the altar of political convenience."

The thunder from the smaller thrones grows louder, and I can feel the mounting tension throughout the cosmic arena.

Satan: "But here is the most damning evidence of mankind's selfishness. COVID-19 spreads through droplets from infected persons, remains airborne for up to three hours, and transfers through contaminated surfaces. Face masks have been proven effective against transmission. Yet people refuse to wear them!"

His voice rises to a crescendo of accusation.

Satan: "Government officials refuse to mandate mask-wearing. Citizens argue that masks violate their civil rights. Their supposed right to spread disease supersedes the safety of family, coworkers, friends, and neighbors. Their 'freedom' matters more than the lives of doctors, nurses, and healthcare workers dying on the front lines of hospitals, the very hospitals where these maskless individuals may themselves end up fighting for breath!"

The cosmic display shows the ultimate irony he's about to reveal.

Satan: "The President of the United States himself was given the ultimate test. When he contracted COVID-19, along with his youngest son, his wife, his namesake son, close aides, Secret Service agents, business associates, friends, and supporters, while he was rushed to elite medical facilities with experimental treatments unavailable to ordinary citizens."

Satan: "He recovered. His family suffered only mild cases. Most of his inner circle experienced minor symptoms. A few required hospitalization, but most survived. This experience could have transformed a man capable of reflection and empathy, but he failed the test spectacularly."

Satan: "Even after surviving the very plague he had denied, even after being recorded acknowledging the disease's deadly potential, he continued endangering lives through reckless behavior. He learned nothing. Changed nothing. A living example of humanity's incapacity for growth or redemption."

Suddenly, the Sapphire Voice erupts from the circle of smaller thrones with barely contained indignation.

Sapphire Voice (Ancient Elder): "Are human beings truly that selfish? Would they refuse to wear a simple piece of cloth to protect their families, friends, and neighbors? Was it not proven that masks protect both the wearer and those around them?"

Satan: "Yes, it has been scientifically proven that masks protect the wearer. And yes, humans are precisely that selfish. In fact, many believe there's a racist ideology underlying COVID-19 policies or the deliberate lack thereof."

The Pearl Voice cuts through the tension with sharp precision.

Pearl Voice (The Wise Woman): "Explain what you mean by 'racist ideology.'"

The silence that follows is pregnant with anticipation. I sense that the Satan is about to reveal something that will take this cosmic trial into even darker territory, something that will expose the very heart of human evil.

The great white throne pulses with increasing intensity, and the rainbow above it seems to bend closer to the proceedings. The four living creatures move with heightened alertness, and the cherubim above us stands at full attention.

Whatever Satan is about to reveal, I have the overwhelming sense that it will push this trial toward its climactic moment, the point where divine patience meets the ultimate test of whether humanity deserves judgment or mercy.

The cosmic arena holds its breath as we await his response, and I feel that the very fate of our species hangs in the balance of his next words.

14

— • —

THE TOOL OF THE DARK, RACISM

The cosmic arena seems to hold its breath as Satan prepares to answer the Pearl Voice's question about racist ideology. The very atmosphere grows heavier, and I notice the rainbow above the great white throne beginning to pulse with colors that seem almost angry, deep crimsons, and violent purples mixing with the traditional hues of divine promise.

Satan: "Certainly. Racism is prejudice, discrimination, or antagonism directed against someone of a different race, based on the belief that one's own race is superior to all others."

Suddenly, a grumble erupts from across the arena. An interruption from one of the smaller thrones. A new voice emerges, hoarse but commanding, with the strength of a soprano voice that has witnessed too much suffering.

Silver Voice (The Stewardess): "Racism has plagued humanity for millennia. We are well aware of its existence! It has festered since mankind first learned to notice differences between themselves. The tragic irony is that they were ALL made in the image of God, yet some humans have always needed someone to look down upon so they could prop themselves up."

The Silver Voice's tone grows more pointed, cutting through the cosmic air like a blade of truth.

Silver Voice (The Stewardess): "Any differentiating characteristic became sufficient justification for hatred: large nose versus small nose, tall versus short, light skin versus dark skin, different customs, beliefs, geography. You name it, we have witnessed it all throughout history. What we demand to understand is the racial element specifically related to COVID-19 policies."

Then another voice emerges, deeper, richer, carrying the weight of ancient observation.

Bronze Voice (The Deacon): "There are two distinct aspects of racism at play concerning COVID-19. The first relates to the virus's origins in Wuhan, China, an Asian nation with nearly 1.5 billion souls. China has four times the population of the United States, and while America has long considered itself the financial, educational, and scientific hub of the world, tectonic shifts are occurring."

Images begin forming above us in the cosmic display, showing the two superpowers in their eternal struggle for dominance.

Bronze Voice (The Deacon): "China rises as a world leader while America's reputation declines. These nations have clashed repeatedly: the 1950s Korean conflict where China supported the North while America backed the South; the 1954 skirmish over Quemoy and Matsu islands in the Taiwan Strait; the Tibetan uprising that left thousands of Tibetans dead at Chinese hands, drawing American condemnation; the Vietnam War era when China tested nuclear weapons and amassed troops along Vietnam's border."

Bronze Voice (The Deacon): "The underlying factor in many of these conflicts is the poison of racial supremacy. The United States has maintained an imperialistic attitude, treating the Chinese as inferior, as a 'third-world' nation, even threatening nuclear annihilation. Many Anglo-Saxons have long believed themselves superior to the Chinese and all people of color."

The cosmic display shifts to show disturbing scenes of anti-Asian violence and hatred.

Bronze Voice (The Deacon): "With COVID-19's outbreak, people of Asian descent became targets of derogatory language, physical assaults, and systematic intimidation. Government leaders encouraged hate speech by deliberately referring to COVID-19 as the 'Chinese Virus' and 'Wuhan Virus', weaponizing language to fuel racial animosity."

Bronze Voice (The Deacon): "This racism extends beyond America's borders. An Italian governor declared: 'Italians have culturally strong attention to hygiene, washing hands, taking showers, whereas we have all seen the Chinese eating mice alive.' Other nations accused China of planning world domination through viral warfare."

The Bronze Voice pauses, and I can feel the weight of what he's about to reveal next.

Bronze Voice (The Deacon): "The second aspect of racism is even more sinister, the deliberate sacrificing of Black and brown lives. In March 2020, when COVID-19 cases began rising in the United States, the nation entered lockdown for 10-12 weeks. But once reports emerged showing that Black, Hispanic, and Native American populations were 2.5 to 4.5 times more likely to be hospitalized and their mortality rates were 2-3 times higher than whites, the national lockdown was mysteriously lifted."

Lightning begins flickering across the smaller thrones as the horrible truth becomes clear.

Bronze Voice (The Deacon): "Even after experts warned that reopening would have dire consequences, especially for people of color already under siege by COVID-19, the decision stood. Why? Because due to centuries of systemic racism, Black Americans suffer disproportionately from underlying health conditions, high blood pressure, diabetes, obesity. They work in low-wage positions with minimal benefits like health insurance, yet many of these jobs were deemed 'essential' during the pandemic."

Bronze Voice (The Deacon): "This forced Black and brown families onto the front lines of infection while white Americans, with lower risk profiles, benefited from policy decisions that prioritized economic reopening over human lives. The lockdown wasn't lifted for everyone, it was lifted because certain lives were deemed more expendable than others."

The atmosphere in the arena grows darker as he continues.

Bronze Voice (The Deacon): "COVID-19 struck during a presidential election year, amplifying racial tensions between America's two political parties. The Democratic party maintains more diversity, while Republicans increasingly cater to Anglo-Saxon interests. That year, Republicans embraced racism as electoral strategy, believing their best path to victory lay in suppressing Black American votes."

Bronze Voice (The Deacon): "They instituted voter identification laws, reduced polling locations, and spread conspiracy theories, all designed to discourage Black participation in democracy. Even after losing the election, the President and Republican establishment attempted to disqualify votes in states and counties with high Black populations, arguing that white voices somehow possessed superior value to Black votes."

Suddenly, the Bronze Voice's tone becomes even more grave, and I sense we're approaching something that will shake the very foundations of this cosmic trial.

Bronze Voice (The Deacon): "During the COVID-19 pandemic, another epidemic raged simultaneously, the systematic killing of unarmed Black men by police officers whose sworn duty was to protect and serve their communities."

The cosmic display above us shifts to show a scene that makes my soul recoil in horror.

Bronze Voice (The Deacon): "On May 25th, 2020, George Floyd left a convenience store in Minneapolis, Minnesota. A clerk called the police, suspecting the twenty-dollar bill he used was counterfeit. Four officers responded. They restrained him and forced him to the ground."

Bronze Voice (The Deacon): "Derek Chauvin placed his knee on George Floyd's neck and pressed his full body weight down. Even as George Floyd pleaded 'I can't breathe,' Chauvin maintained his deadly position. The other three officers stood by and watched. The crowd screamed that he was dying beneath Chauvin's knee, but still he didn't stop."

The Bronze Voice's next words seem to echo through eternity itself.

Bronze Voice (The Deacon): "For NINE MINUTES AND TWENTY-NINE SEC-ONDS, Derek Chauvin knelt on George Floyd's neck. In broad daylight. In front of witnesses. On camera. Next to fellow officers. Under the guise of 'protection,' 'safety,' and 'policing.' Nine minutes and twenty-nine seconds of deliberate, calculated murder."

Bronze Voice (The Deacon): "NINE MINUTES AND TWENTY-NINE SECONDS!"

Suddenly, the phrase begins echoing throughout the cosmic arena like a drumbeat of divine judgment.

"NINE MINUTES AND TWENTY-NINE SECONDS!"

The chant erupts from everywhere at once. The Spirits on the smaller thrones. The human witnesses to my left and right. Even the Man beside me joins the rhythmic accusation. Lightning explodes across the arena in patterns I've never seen before. Thunder rolls like the footsteps of approaching armies. The very foundations of the cosmic courtroom shake with vibrations that seem to emanate from the heart of creation itself.

"NINE MINUTES AND TWENTY-NINE SECONDS!"

The four living creatures around the great white throne become intensely agitated, moving away from their eternal patrol and approaching the smaller thrones. Their countless eyes begin displaying different images, scenes of racial violence, injustice, and suffering throughout human history. I'm horrified to realize that their eyes appear on every part of their bodies, even on parts that defy description.

"NINE MINUTES AND TWENTY-NINE SECONDS!"

A bass drum begins beating in perfect synchronization with the chant, each strike coming after the word "seconds" like a cosmic heartbeat counting down to judgment.

Satan tries to speak above the cosmic outcry: "Nine minutes and twenty-nine seconds. What type of . . . "

Suddenly, the voice from the great white throne itself cuts through the chaos with absolute authority.

Golden Voice (The Almighty): "Enough. Let there be silence."

Instantly, the arena falls silent. The chanting stops. The lightning ceases. Even the thunder fades to whispers. The cosmic drums fall silent.

Satan: "What type of person kneels on another human being's neck for nine long minutes and twenty-nine seconds? What thoughts and feelings consume someone as they watch life drain from their victim? What does this reveal about a society and its values?"

His voice builds to a crescendo of accusation.

Satan: "What does it say when you can murder someone in broad daylight, on camera, and feel no fear of consequences? How can anyone claim self-defense when your victim lies helpless beneath your knee? This was not the first such murder, nor was it the last. This is not merely racism, this is racism within a system specifically designed to protect those who kill."

Satan: "The victims of police brutality in America form a litany of the dead: Rayshard Brooks, Daniel Prude, Breonna Taylor, Atatiana Jefferson, Aura Rosser, Stephon Clark, Botham Jean, Philando Castile, Alton Sterling, Michelle Cusseaux, Freddie Gray, Janisha Fonville, Eric Garner, Akai Gurley, Gabriella Nevarez, Tamir Rice, Michael Brown, Tanisha Anderson, and the list continues growing daily."

The cosmic display shifts to show scenes from around the globe.

Satan: "But America is not the only nation plagued by this evil. Consider the land called Israel, named after Your servant Jacob. This promised land knows no peace. The Israelites lost their inheritance long ago for being disobedient and stiff-necked, yet those claiming to be distant relatives of the remnant, along with others, have placed their knees on the necks of Palestinians who lived there before their return."

Satan: "Palestinians have been displaced and degraded while the world watches in silence. Racism is a global epidemic: Muslims face persecution in India, Rohingya suffer in Myanmar, Africans experience discrimination in the United Kingdom. Racism infects every corner of Your creation."

Satan spreads his arms wide, encompassing the scope of human evil.

Satan: "What will it take for humanity to mature? Are they even capable of growth? Mankind's inhumanity to their own kind continues in ways that defy comprehension, yet they persist in choosing hatred over love, division over unity, murder over mercy."

The silence that follows is deafening. I can feel the weight of divine attention focusing on this cosmic trial with unprecedented intensity. The rainbow above the great white throne now pulses with colors that seem to reflect both infinite sorrow and mounting anger.

The cherubim above us stand at perfect attention, their faces grave with the knowledge of what they've witnessed. The seraphim flies with increased urgency, their six wings beating with what appears to be preparation for something momentous.

I realize we have reached a crucial turning point in this trial. Satan has systematically built his case against humanity: the breakdown of families, environmental destruction, weapons of mass destruction, pandemic selfishness, and now the ultimate sin, racism that denies the very image of God in which all humans were created.

The great white throne pulses with light so intense it's almost blinding, and I sense that we are approaching the climactic moment of this cosmic trial, the point where divine justice and mercy will collide in ways that will determine the eternal fate of the human race.

Something tells me that the next words spoken in this arena will echo through eternity itself.

15

—•—

CHILD ABUSE, A TOOL OF THE DEVIL

The cosmic arena falls into a silence so profound it seems to absorb sound itself. The electric energy and righteous anger of the previous moments dissipates, replaced by something far more ominous, the terrible calm before a storm that threatens to tear the very fabric of creation apart.

Satan stands motionless at his podium, his purple and gold robes no longer catching the divine light but seeming to absorb it, creating shadows that appear to move with malevolent purpose. When he finally speaks, his voice carries a weight that makes my soul recoil.

Satan: "Before I present my final and most damning evidence against humanity, let us remember what the Almighty Himself declared about the precious souls I am about to discuss."

He opens what appears to be a cosmic scroll, and his voice takes on the cadence of divine scripture as he reads:

Satan: "For it is written in Psalm 127:3-5: 'Behold, children are a heritage from the LORD, the fruit of the womb is a reward. Like arrows in the hand of a warrior, so are the children of one's youth. Happy is the man who has his quiver full of them; they shall not be ashamed, but shall speak with their enemies in the gate.'"

The silence that follows is pregnant with anticipation and dread. Even the seraphim have slowed their eternal flight, hovering as if afraid to move.

Satan: "And from the lips of Jesus Christ Himself, in Mark 10:13-16:"

His voice swells with the authority of divine truth as he continues:

Satan: "'Then they brought little children to Him, that He might touch them; but the disciples rebuked those who brought them. But when Jesus saw it, He was greatly displeased and said to them, "Let the little children come to Me, and do not forbid them; for of such is the kingdom of God. Assuredly, I say to you, whoever does not receive the kingdom of God as a little child will by no means enter it." And He took them up in His arms, laid His hands on them, and blessed them.'"

Satan pauses, letting the beauty and sanctity of these words settle over the assembly like a blessing. Then his voice drops to a whisper that somehow carries to every corner of the cosmic arena.

Satan: "'For of such is the kingdom of God...'"

Suddenly, his voice explodes with the force of cosmic fury:

Satan: "YET CHILDREN ARE IN CAGES!"

The words hit the arena like a physical blow. Lightning doesn't just flicker across the smaller thrones; it erupts in violent cascades of divine anger. The very foundations of the cosmic courtroom seem to shudder under the weight of his accusation.

Satan: "Children, these arrows in the hand of the Almighty, these inheritors of the kingdom of heaven, are seeking shelter, safety, and justice, only to be placed in cages not fit for the lowest animals!"

Images begin forming above us in the cosmic display, and I have to close my eyes against the horror of what I see.

Satan: "The government of the United States, one of the richest nations on earth, ripped children from the arms of parents seeking refuge from violence and poverty. Everyone crossing their borders, even those seeking lawful asylum, was treated like common criminals."

Satan: "They gave these innocent souls blankets resembling aluminum foil. They held them in cages within locked warehouses and converted shopping centers. What happens to a child's soul when treated this way by those who claim to follow the Prince of Peace? They become abandoned, grief-stricken, traumatized beyond repair."

The cosmic display shifts to show even more disturbing scenes, and I feel my stomach turn with revulsion.

Satan: "But if you think government cruelty represents the depths of human depravity, wait until you hear what those who claim to serve the Most High have done to the lambs entrusted to their care."

His voice takes on the tone of a prosecutor delivering a death sentence.

Satan: "In August 2018, a 1,356-page grand jury report from Pennsylvania revealed that 300 priests over a seventy-year period systematically covered up the abuse of over 1,000 children. Can you comprehend the cosmic horror? The church, the supposed sanctuary of God on earth, became a den of predators!"

Satan: "When Bishops and leaders of the Roman Catholic Church were discovered abusing the very children they were ordained to protect, what happened? Those expected to teach the word of God and imitate divine love violated the most sacred trust imaginable."

The cherubim above us begin to weep, perfect beings whose tears fall like liquid starlight, each drop carrying the weight of cosmic sorrow.

Satan: "This was not an isolated incident or modern aberration. There exists a treatise from 1051 AD called 'Liber Gomorrhianus,' documenting child abuse including sodomy within the church hierarchy for nearly a thousand years!"

Satan: "Pope Leo X was accused of vetoing measures that would have restricted the number of boys cardinals could keep for their perverted pleasure. Martin Luther argued that if the Pope had not protected these predators, society would have known how openly and shamelessly the Vatican practiced sodomy against children."

The cosmic display expands to show a global map marked with countless points of abuse.

Satan: "The Commission to Inquire into Child Abuse in Ireland documented six decades of sexual violence in Catholic institutions, beatings, rapes, and systematic humiliation, while church leaders not only knew but actively covered up these crimes."

Satan: "From 1941 to 2005, the general director of the Legion of Christ in Mexico, the highest-ranking priest ever disciplined for sexual abuse, fathered children by three women while sexually abusing countless minors. When nine men filed charges in 1998, the church protected him until 2010, when they finally acknowledged his crimes."

Satan: "In Australia, the support group 'Broken Rites' documented over 100 cases against Catholic priests, discovering that at least 40 victims committed suicide as a direct result of clerical abuse. Forty souls so damaged by those supposed to represent divine love that they chose death over continued existence."

The weeping that begins in the arena is unlike anything I have ever heard. It starts as a whisper, a soft sobbing from the smaller thrones, but grows into something that threatens to tear the very fabric of creation apart.

Satan: "Sexual abuse by priests has been documented in the United States, Canada, Ireland, the United Kingdom, the Philippines, Belgium, France, Germany, Australia, and throughout the world. Many cases span decades, brought forward years after the abuse, when victims finally find the courage to speak."

The weeping grows louder, more intense. I can hear it coming from the human witnesses around me, from the Spirits on their thrones, even from the four living creatures themselves.

Satan: "But institutional abuse is only the beginning. Children comprise up to thirty percent of human trafficking victims, sold into sexual slavery, forced labor, and servitude. Many live in such poverty that they become easy prey for traffickers who exploit them in ways that defy imagination."

Satan: "Their organs are harvested like spare parts. The 'National Human Trafficking Hotline' reports that traffickers specifically target those without legal protection, knowing they can commit these crimes without consequence."

The weeping has become wailing now, a cosmic lamentation that seems to shake the very pillars of heaven.

Satan: "Girls as young as twelve forced into marriage with men who exploit them sexually and as domestic slaves. In Malawi, teenage boys work as farm laborers while girls are sexually exploited in nightclubs. Children mine gold in Venezuelan death traps. Myanmar traffics girls abroad for sexual exploitation."

Satan: "In Nepal, 34% of children between ages 5 and 14 are trapped in child labor. In India, Pakistan, and Afghanistan, over 25,000 bonded child laborers work in brick kilns and construction sites under conditions that would horrify demons."

His voice rises to a crescendo of cosmic accusation:

Satan: "These children suffer 2.78 million work-related deaths and 374 million injuries annually. They are deprived of childhood, potential, and dignity, their physical and mental development forever stunted by human cruelty!"

The wailing in the arena becomes overwhelming. It's the kind of weeping that touches the very core of existence, the mourning for innocence lost, for childhoods destroyed, for souls damaged beyond earthly repair.

I lower my head, unable to witness the cosmic grief surrounding me. The weeping is contagious, spreading through the arena like divine sorrow itself. It grows until it seems the entire cosmos is mourning for these violated children.

Then, as recorded in 1 Corinthians 12:26: "If one member suffers, all the members suffer with it." Here, in this cosmic courtroom, all creation suffers for the children.

Suddenly, I smell something unexpected, the clean, calming scent of lemongrass. Candles begin flickering to life throughout the arena, casting everything in a warm orange glow that somehow soothes the overwhelming grief.

Music begins to play, not from any earthly source, but from somewhere beyond the cosmic pillars. It starts as a single harp, then grows to include violin, piano, and finally becomes a full orchestral arrangement so beautiful it defies description. Each instrument remains distinct yet blends into perfect harmony.

The Man beside me nudges me gently, and I look up to see the source of this divine music. Between the cosmic pillars, above the smaller thrones, a Conductor and orchestra have appeared, celestial beings creating music that seems to heal even as it acknowledges the profound sorrow of what we've witnessed.

The four living creatures, previously agitated, have settled around the great white throne, one on each side, one in front, one behind, their countless eyes now closed as if in prayer or meditation.

I glance up at the cherubim and seraphim, and my heart breaks to see them weeping, perfect beings mourning for the children of earth.

Something draws my attention downward, and I realize we're not sitting on a traditional floor but somehow suspended above the earth itself. Through this cosmic window, I can see oceans, mountains, deserts, cities, people coming and going in their daily lives, unaware that their eternal fate is being decided in the courtroom above.

The view is simultaneously wondrous and heartbreaking. This beautiful planet, this precious creation, is the same world where such unspeakable evil is perpetrated against the most innocent.

As the divine music continues and the cosmic grief slowly transforms into something approaching peace, I realize that what we've just witnessed was more than testimony, it was a cosmic breaking point. Satan has systematically built his case: broken families, environmental destruction, weapons of mass destruction, pandemic selfishness, racism, and now the ultimate violation, the abuse of children, those whom Christ himself declared to be the very essence of His kingdom.

I sense that this is indeed a divinely appointed intermission, a necessary pause before what will surely be the climactic moment of this cosmic trial. The evidence against humanity has been presented in all its devastating totality.

Now comes the time for the defense of mankind, if such a defense can even be mounted after what we've witnessed.

The fate of every human soul hang in the balance, suspended between divine justice and the slim hope of mercy, while the music of heaven itself plays a requiem for innocence lost and a prayer for redemption yet to come.

16

Roll Call

The cosmic weeping slowly fades, replaced by the familiar symphony of divine authority with the lightning crackling across the arena, thunder rolling like approaching armies, rumbling vibrations that make the very foundations of creation tremble. Yet the atmosphere has shifted dramatically. The overwhelming sadness that followed the revelation of child abuse has transformed into something far more complex, not joy, but grim acceptance, as if all present understand we've reached a pivotal moment in this cosmic trial.

The four living creatures rise from their positions around the great white throne and resume their eternal patrol, their countless eyes now scanning the assembly with heightened alertness. The cherubim above us stands at perfect attention on their platforms, while the seraphim increase their vigilant flight patterns throughout the heavenly atmosphere. Every spiritual being in the arena radiates tension, as if preparing for something momentous.

The people around me, both to my right and left, including the Man who brought me here, sit in anticipatory silence. The divine orchestra has vanished, and only the faintest hint of lemongrass lingers in the cosmic air, like the memory of comfort in a time of approaching judgment.

Suddenly, a formal voice rings out across the arena, the same herald we heard at the beginning of these proceedings.

The Herald: "Roll call will now commence. All members of the divine council will acknowledge their presence."

The Herald: "Senior Elder"

Azure Voice (Senior Elder): "Here."

The Herald: "Ancient Elder"

Sapphire Voice (Ancient Elder): "Here

The Herald: "Young Elder."

Emerald Voice (Young Elder): "Here."

The Herald: "The Technician."

Amber Voice (The Technician): "Here."

The Herald: "The Wise Woman)"

Pearl Voice (The Wise Woman): "Here."

The Herald: "The Historian."

Violet Voice (The Historian): "Here."

The roll call continues methodically, the title is called, each voice responding with solemnity as their presence is verified. When the final name is called and acknowledged, an expectant silence settles over the cosmic arena.

Then, the voice from the great white throne itself breaks the silence, a voice that carries the weight of infinite authority yet somehow feels intimate, as if speaking directly to each soul present.

Golden Voice (The Almighty): "Your argument is persuasive."

The words are directed toward Satan, and I feel the cosmic significance of this divine acknowledgment. Satan has indeed built a devastating case against humanity.

Golden Voice (The Almighty): "When given the opportunity to choose between right and wrong, mankind has consistently chosen the path of wickedness. You have made evil appear attractive, irresistible. Thus far, you have systematically outwitted humanity. For it is written in Second Corinthians 2:11: 'So that we would not be outwitted by Satan; for we are not ignorant of his designs.' Yet it appears that even knowledge of your schemes has not been sufficient to protect mankind from your deceptions."

Suddenly, the Pearl Voice cuts through the proceedings with the sharp precision of divine advocacy.

Pearl Voice (The Wise Woman): "Forgive my interruption, but while it is understood that this is a trial of mankind for their wickedness and the evil that has been allowed to overcome them, I must ask: Is humanity the only party that should face judgment here?"

Her voice rises with passionate conviction.

Pearl Voice (The Wise Woman): "From the very beginning, mankind was deliberately led astray! The serpent in the Garden of Eden was not merely crafty, he systematically sowed seeds of doubt regarding the meaning of God's word, then twisted that word for his own malevolent purposes."

The cosmic display above us shifts to show the primordial garden, beautiful beyond earthly description.

Pearl Voice (The Wise Woman): "The serpent questioned Eve while Adam stood beside her: 'What do you believe were God's instructions to you?' When she responded, 'We may eat fruit from the trees in the garden, but God did say, "You must not eat fruit from the tree that is in the middle of the garden, and you must not touch it, or you will die,"' Satan immediately began his campaign of deception."

Pearl Voice (The Wise Woman): "He created doubt through questioning, fostering confusion about God's clear command. This marked the beginning of Satan's systematic interference with the relationship between God and humanity."

Pearl Voice (The Wise Woman): "Then Satan directly contradicted the word of the Almighty, saying, 'You will not certainly die. For God knows that when you eat from it your eyes will be opened, and you will be like God, knowing good and evil.' Two deliberate lies that severed the bond between Creator and creation."

The Amber Voice joins the defense with additional scriptural evidence.

Amber Voice (The Technician): "Allow me to add to my learned colleague's testimony. I would like to read from Ezekiel 28:14-17, which reveals the true nature of the one who has systematically corrupted humanity:"

Her voice takes on the authority of divine scripture:

Amber Voice (The Technician): "'You were an anointed guardian cherub. I placed you; you were on the holy mountain of God; in the midst of the stones of fire you walked. You were blameless in your ways from the day you were created, until unrighteousness was found in you. In the abundance of your trade you were filled with violence in your midst, and you sinned; so I cast you as a profane thing from the mountain of God, and I destroyed you, O guardian cherub, from the midst of the stones of fire. Your heart was proud because of your beauty; you corrupted your wisdom for the sake of your splendor. I cast you to the ground...'"

Pearl Voice (The Wise Woman): "Thank you for that crucial inclusion. Satan, you were 'a murderer from the beginning,' as Christ himself declared in John 8:44. 'You do not stand in the truth, because there is no truth in you. When you lie, you speak out of your own character, for you are a liar and the father of lies.' Humanity has been your subject, possessed and influenced by your deceptions for millennia. Should mankind alone face judgment for crimes committed under your systematic manipulation?"

The silence that follows is pregnant with cosmic significance. Then, the voice from the great white throne begins to speak, and I detect something that sounds almost like... reminiscence? Divine nostalgia for what might have been?

Golden Voice (The Almighty): "Mankind was created to enter into an intimate and loving relationship with their Creator. They were not only made in Our image but were granted dominion over all fish in the sea, birds in the sky, and every living creature on earth. They were designed to be kind, compassionate, sympathetic, wise, generous, curious, etc., reflections of divine character."

The cosmic display shows humanity as they were meant to be, radiant beings walking in perfect fellowship with their Creator.

Golden Voice (The Almighty): "They were given a kingdom under their stewardship, the Garden of Eden. It was My hope that they would grow into themselves, becoming the humans they were meant to be, enjoying personal and intimate relationship with their Creator, free from death and sin. Their glory would have been Our glory. They would have declared Our praise throughout creation."

A pause, heavy with divine sorrow.

Golden Voice (The Almighty): "But that was not to be. They ate from the forbidden tree and entered into covenant after covenant, only to break each one. Humanity has tested their fate from the very beginning. They have sinned and fallen short of the glory of God."

Golden Voice (The Almighty): "Yet the final covenant was made through My beloved Son, Jesus Christ. He died so that humanity might live. He became the living sacrifice, dying on the cross so that those who follow Him might have eternal life and their sins forgiven. Understanding their continued need, I provided the Counselor, the Helper, who indwells those who believe in Christ."

The divine voice grows more solemn, carrying the weight of ultimate authority.

Golden Voice (The Almighty): "Because the Son of God lived and died for humanity, He, Jesus Christ, will decide who will and will not receive the eternal life offered through faith in Him. For it is written in Matthew 25:31-36: 'When the Son of Man comes in His glory, and all the holy angels with Him, then He will sit on the throne of His glory. All the nations will be gathered before Him, and He will separate them one from another, as a shepherd divides his sheep from the goats. And He will set the sheep on His right hand, but the goats on the left. Then the King will say to those on His right hand, "Come, you blessed of My Father, inherit the kingdom prepared for you from the foundation of the world: for I was hungry and you gave Me food; I was thirsty and you gave Me drink; I was a stranger and you took Me in; I was naked and you clothed Me; I was sick and you visited Me; I was in prison and you came to Me."

Now I detect something that might be anger or . . . perhaps profound disappointment, in the divine voice.

Golden Voice (The Almighty): "But whoever makes a practice of sinning is of the devil, for the devil has been sinning from the beginning. The Son of God appeared among humanity to destroy the works of the devil. Jesus Christ has earned the right to choose His flock through His sacrifice."

Golden Voice (The Almighty): "Yet today there comes a request to judge mankind, not on the appointed day and time, but NOW."

The cosmic arena seems to hold its breath as divine judgment is pronounced.

Golden Voice (The Almighty): "The evidence presented is indeed undisputed. Families have been torn apart. Children are abused in unimaginable ways. Racism and every form of prejudice have not improved over the millennia, if anything, humanity has grown worse. Slave trade, concentration camps, refugee camps, human trafficking continue unabated. Weapons of mass destruction and environmental abuse compound mankind's inhumanity."

Golden Voice (The Almighty): "For it is written in Ezekiel 18:20: 'The soul who sins shall die. The son shall not suffer for the iniquity of the father, nor the father suffer for the iniquity of the son. The righteousness of the righteous shall be upon himself, and the wickedness of the wicked shall be upon himself.' Humanity will indeed be judged according to their work."

The pause that follows feels like eternity condensed into a moment.

Golden Voice (The Almighty): "Therefore, there is no need to proceed any further. The request for immediate judgment of all humanity CANNOT be granted! Not today. As you well know, judgment belongs to individuals, not to groups as a whole. The time and place of mankind's judgment have already been appointed. Humanity will indeed face judgment... and YOU know this perfectly well."

Suddenly, movement erupts from behind Satan's podium. Whispers and agitated voices emerge from his magnificent entourage.

Unknown Voices (The Darkness): "That is not fair! He has not been permitted to complete his arguments!"

All attention snaps to the area behind Satan. The four living creatures instantly move to high alert. The cherubim on their platforms peer intently into the entourage, and I notice for the first time that they're holding what appear to be flaming swords in their hands. Several seraphim swoop down to hover over the area where the rebellious voice emerged.

The Spirits on all twenty-four smaller thrones move in perfect unison, and the thunder, lightning, and cosmic vibrations that had been sporadic now form unified waves of divine authority pulsing through the arena.

The Man beside me and others throughout the arena rise to their feet in response to this cosmic emergency. Yet remarkably, the Spirit on the great white throne shows no alarm whatsoever. In fact, the rainbow above His head grows larger and more brilliant, and He radiates additional light that seems to push back whatever darkness threatens to emerge.

Satan, still standing at his podium, slowly raises his right arm with his hand open and fingers spread apart. He turns toward his entourage, and as he does, his purple and gold robes catch the divine light and sparkle with otherworldly beauty. He doesn't speak, but his look conveys volumes including a mixture of command, warning, and perhaps... disappointment in his followers' breach of cosmic protocol.

Golden Voice (The Almighty): "Is there a problem?"

The question is directed at Satan, but it's clear that the answer is already known. This is not a request for information but a divine challenge.

Satan: "No, there is no problem. Just... consequences."

The single word "consequences" hangs in the cosmic air like a threat, a promise, and a warning all combined. I realize that while Satan's request for immediate judgment has been denied, something far more ominous has been set in motion.

The trial may be over, but I sense that the real battle, the one that will determine the ultimate fate of humanity, is just beginning.

The cosmic arena pulses with tension as we all wait to see what these "consequences" might entail, and I have the overwhelming feeling that we are witnessing the prelude to events that will shake the very foundations of heaven and earth.

17

CONSEQUENCES

The word "consequences" hangs in the cosmic air like a death sentence, and suddenly I understand that what we're about to witness will be unlike anything we've seen in this trial. The very atmosphere of the arena shifts, becoming heavier, more ominous, as if creation itself is holding its breath.

Emerald Voice (Young Elder): "Yes, there are consequences."

The voice carries a weight of cosmic inevitability that makes my soul tremble.

Emerald Voice (Young Elder): "All actions have consequences. Consequences that serve as warnings, consequences that offer hope, but consequences, nonetheless. Are human beings now suffering the consequences of their actions? For it is written in Revelation that seven trumpets will sound, and these trumpets will be warnings that the day of judgment draws near."

Suddenly, the cosmic arena transforms in a way that defies description. The earth itself appears before us, not as an image or projection, but as if the planet has been transported into the heavenly courtroom. A massive globe hovers in the center of the arena, every detail visible with startling clarity: oceans that shimmer with divine light, mountains that stretch toward infinity, plains that roll like cosmic carpets, deserts that gleam like scattered jewels.

But something is terribly wrong with this beautiful creation.

Azure Voice (Senior Elder): "With the sound of the first trumpet, a third of the trees will be burned up along with all the green grass."

As he speaks these words from Revelation 8:7, I see smoke, terrible, choking smoke rising from multiple fires across the earth's surface, creating a haze that mars the planet's atmosphere.

Emerald Voice (Young Elder): "Behold the fulfillment of this prophetic warning already unfolding before your eyes. In fourteen of America's fifty states, wildfires have consumed 649,054 acres in a single season. They devour everything in their path; trees, animals, buildings, human beings, an unstoppable wave of destruction."

The cosmic display zooms in to show the devastation in vivid, heartbreaking detail.

Emerald Voice (Young Elder): "Alaska, Arizona, California, Colorado, Florida, Idaho, Montana, Nevada, New Mexico, Oregon, South Dakota, Texas, Utah, Washington, and Wyoming, all burning. Canada has not been spared. In 2018, British Columbia alone saw over 3.3 million acres consumed by flames in a single wildfire season."

The scene shifts to show the Southern Hemisphere.

Emerald Voice (Young Elder): "New South Wales and Victoria in Australia witnessed 1.5 million acres, 2,300 square miles, reduced to ash and char. One hundred thirty-five separate bushfires murdered more than one billion animals, claimed twenty-six human lives, and destroyed nearly 3,000 homes."

But then he reveals something even more terrifying.

Emerald Voice (Young Elder): "Alaska and Siberia now experience record-breaking warmth, causing snow cover to melt and soil to dry at unprecedented rates. This has awakened what scientists call 'Zombie Fires', which are wildfires that burn beneath the surface in the rich organic peat that rings the Arctic Circle."

The cosmic display shows these underground fires like glowing veins of destruction beneath the earth's surface.

Emerald Voice (Young Elder): "Normally, the bitter Arctic winter extinguishes these fires, but the unseasonable warmth allows them to spread unchecked, pumping carbon dioxide into the atmosphere and accelerating global warming in a cycle of destruction that feeds upon itself."

Emerald Voice (Young Elder): "Massive fires have torn through Siberian forests, with the Krasnoyarsk region reaching 100 degrees Fahrenheit, the highest temperature ever recorded north of the Arctic Circle. More than 47 million acres of forests, steppes, and fields have burned in what can only be described as a continental holocaust."

The display shifts to show an area I never expected to see burning.

Emerald Voice (Young Elder): "Even the world's largest tropical wetland, the Pantanal, is on fire. A wetland, something designed by the Creator to be perpetually wet, now burns with unstoppable fury. This biodiversity treasure, home to thousands of aquatic species and terrestrial plants and animals, sees 7,861 square miles, an area larger than New Jersey, consumed by flames."

Emerald Voice (Young Elder): "This wetland provides fresh water for entire populations, but the fires will poison the water quality for generations to come, creating a cascade of environmental destruction that will ripple through creation itself."

The scene expands to show the African continent.

Emerald Voice (Young Elder): "In Africa, Angola and the Democratic Republic of the Congo experience deforestation at rates never before witnessed. Humans deliberately use wildfires to clear land for agriculture, to prepare pastures, to burn crop residue, trading long-term environmental stability for short-term gain."

Emerald Voice (Young Elder): "In 2019 alone, more than 6,290 fires burned in Angola while 3,395 consumed the DRC. By late August 2020, smoke blanketed south-central Africa in a choking pall that stretched nearly 3,000 miles across the continent and over the South Atlantic Ocean."

Emerald Voice (Young Elder): "Even Europe, Spain, Italy, France, and Sweden, suffers above-average temperatures causing wildfires and human casualties. Many buildings lack air conditioning, leaving populations defenseless against the heat."

Then his voice takes on the tone of a cosmic weather report, but one that speaks of planetary death rather than tomorrow's forecast.

Emerald Voice (Young Elder): "These wildfires will only intensify. Global warming accelerates like a runaway cosmic engine. Earth's average surface temperature has risen 2.05 degrees Fahrenheit since the late 19th century, a change that may sound small but represents a planetary fever that threatens all life."

The cosmic display shows ice sheets and glaciers melting in time-lapse sequences that are both beautiful and terrifying.

Emerald Voice (Young Elder): "Greenland and Antarctic ice sheets lose mass at accelerating rates. Glaciers retreat everywhere, in the Alps, Himalayas, Andes, Rockies, Alaska, and Africa. Spring snow cover in the Northern Hemisphere decreases decade by decade, melting faster than any scientific model predicted."

Emerald Voice (Young Elder): "Global sea levels have risen eight inches in the last century, with the rate of increase accelerating. Arctic sea ice, both extent and thickness, declines rapidly. The ocean's surface waters have become 30% more acidic since the Industrial Revolution, creating underwater wastelands where marine life cannot survive."

As I stare at this cosmic display of environmental destruction, questions flood my mind with overwhelming urgency. How long will it take to burn one-third of all trees and grass? Another ten years? Fifty? A hundred? How long do we have? Is this divine warning giving humanity time to repent and change course? What actions should be taken now? Or is it already too late for any action to matter?

The earth before us seems close enough to touch, and the detail is so vivid it's as if we're watching through divine microscopes. I can see individual trees consumed by flames, forests transformed into infernos, foliage disappearing in waves of orange destruction. People flee in terror, some dying in their burning vehicles on highways and freeways as they desperately try to escape the advancing flames.

Animals run in panic, some already on fire, others climbing trees in futile attempts to escape the spreading conflagration, dying in agony as their refuge become funeral pyres. Birds take flight in massive formations, fleeing the smoke and heat. Insects are caught and trapped in the flames; their tiny lives extinguished by the millions.

Buildings burn like giant torches. Homes become crematoriums for families who couldn't escape in time. People's entire lives, their memories, possessions, futures, are destroyed before our eyes in seconds.

The smoke is everywhere, blinding and suffocating, creating an atmospheric shroud that blocks out the sun and turns day into apocalyptic twilight.

And then, rising above the cosmic horror of environmental destruction, I hear something that makes my spirit soar even in the midst of this devastation, voices singing in perfect harmony. Not just one or two voices, but what sounds like a celestial choir filling the arena with words from Psalm 121:

Celestial Chorus: "I will lift up my eyes to the hills, From whence comes my help? My help comes from the LORD, Who made heaven and earth. He will not allow your foot to be moved; He who keeps you will not slumber. Behold, He who keeps Israel Shall neither slumber nor sleep. The LORD is your keeper; The LORD is your shade at your right hand. The sun shall not strike you by day, Nor the moon by night. The LORD shall preserve you from all evil; He shall preserve your soul. The LORD shall preserve your going out and your coming in. From this time forth, and even forevermore."

The psalm rises like incense through the cosmic arena, a declaration of faith in the midst of judgment, hope in the face of consequences, trust in divine protection even as creation itself seems to burn.

Then I hear individual voices raised in fervent prayer. Someone nearby is crying out to God with desperate intensity, pleading for divine intervention:

Unknown Voice: "Deliver mankind, O Lord! Guide and shield them! Provide wisdom and strength to turn from their destructive path!"

To my right, people are praying with voices broken by tears and fear. To my left, more voices join the cosmic petition for mercy. But when I turn to look for the Man who brought me here, my guide and companion throughout this cosmic trial, I realize with a shock that he's no longer beside me.

Where did he go? When did he leave? In the intensity of witnessing earth's environmental destruction, I hadn't noticed his departure. Another voice speaks with heartbreaking vulnerability:

Unknown Voice: "Oh Lord, my Father, hear my cry! I reach out my hand to Thee..."

The prayer is so raw, so desperate, so filled with genuine need that it cuts through all my questions about the missing Man and forces me to confront the reality of what we're witnessing.

I close my eyes, unable to continue watching the environmental devastation unfolding before us. The images are too heartbreaking, too overwhelming. The reality that this destruction represents both divine warning and human consequence is almost more than my spirit can bear.

So I join the cosmic chorus of prayer rising from the arena. In the face of environmental destruction that may represent the beginning of the end, what else can any of us do but pray?

Yet even as I pray, I cannot shake the feeling that this first "consequence" is merely the beginning. If the first trumpet brings the burning of one-third of all trees and grass, what will the remaining six trumpets bring?

The trial of humanity may have ended with divine mercy, but the consequences of human sin are only beginning to unfold. And something tells me that what we've witnessed today is merely the opening movement in a symphony of divine judgment that will reshape the very foundations of creation itself.

18

THE SECOND TRUMPET

The cosmic arena still reverberates with the weight of divine judgment as the Emerald Voice's words about consequences echo through eternity. But now, a new presence commands our attention, that familiar, authoritative voice with the slight accent that has guided us through these apocalyptic revelations.

Copper Voice (The Astrophysicist): "For it is written, the second trumpet sounded. Something like a great mountain burning with fire was thrown into the sea, and a third of the sea became blood. And a third of the living creatures in the sea died, and a third of the ships were destroyed."

As these prophetic words ring out, the earth below us begins to rotate slowly, deliberately, like a cosmic model being presented for examination. The transformation is breathtaking. Suddenly, the oceans, rivers, and seas become crystalline, transparent as the finest glass. It's as if the entire arena has become a massive aquarium, and we can see every living and dead thing within the waters with supernatural clarity.

I lean forward, transfixed by this divine display, but my mind struggles with the central mystery.

Copper Voice (The Astrophysicist): "Observe closely what approaches the earth. Something like a great mountain burning with fire.' But what could this be? The scriptures speak in analogies, parables, and parallels to convey truth. This may not be literal. It may be philosophical. Yet..."

The pause stretches like eternity, heavy with implication.

Copper Voice (The Astrophysicist): "Consider the possibilities. Could this be an asteroid, humanity's own nuclear weapon, a volcanic eruption of unprecedented scale, or some other man-made catastrophe? The word 'something' suggests uncertainty, mystery, but the description 'like a great mountain burning with fire' implies massive scale and devastating power."

Images begin forming in the cosmic display above us, showing celestial bodies hurtling through space with terrifying velocity.

Copper Voice (The Astrophysicist):"It is not beyond possibility that an asteroid could strike earth. In 2013, a meteor the size of a mere bus, weighing an estimated 7,000 tons, exploded on impact with the force of twenty atomic bombs in Chelyabinsk, Siberia. The destruction was catastrophic, yet this was but a pebble compared to what scripture describes."

The images shift to show more recent astronomical events.

Copper Voice (The Astrophysicist):"On November 29, 2020, Asteroid 2000 WO107 swept past Earth at tremendous speed. This space rock measured 1,670 feet in diameter, roughly one-third of a mile of solid destruction. Just two weeks earlier, asteroid 2020 VT4 traveled at 30,014 miles per hour, flying so close over the South Pacific that it passed through Earth's thermosphere, that atmospheric layer 350 to 440 miles above our surface."

The cosmic display shows these near misses with chilling clarity, and I realize how close humanity has come to cosmic judgment through natural means.

Copper Voice (The Astrophysicist):"In August 2020, asteroid 2020 QG came even closer to earth. Two potentially catastrophic encounters in such a brief time span. Coincidence? Or divine warning?"

Suddenly, the tone shifts as the Copper Voice (The Astrophysicist) considers more sinister possibilities.

Copper Voice (The Astrophysicist):"But what if that 'something' is not natural but man-made? Consider this: North Korea conducted a nuclear test on September 3, 2018. Chinese geologists reported that this single test caused an entire mountain range, Mount Mantap, to collapse while triggering a 6.3 magnitude earthquake. If human weapons can literally move mountains, what destruction might they cause if deployed over the oceans?"

Images of missile launches and military exercises flash across the cosmic display.

Copper Voice (The Astrophysicist):"Missiles are fired constantly across Earth's surface. On April 14, 2020, North Korea launched projectiles from both ground installations and fighter aircraft, sending them crashing into the waters off their east coast. On July 28, 2020, Iran's Revolutionary Guard fired underground ballistic missiles at a mock aircraft carrier in the Strait of Hormuz. On November 25, 2020, Yemen's Houthi rebels launched a Quds 2 cruise missile at a Saudi Aramco facility."

Copper Voice (The Astrophysicist):"Could a nuclear missile be the source of this great mountain of fire falling into the sea? The imagery becomes terrifyingly plausible when we consider humanity's capacity for destruction."

The cosmic display shifts focus to the oceans themselves, and what I see makes my heart sink.

Copper Voice (The Astrophysicist):"But examine the second part of this prophetic warning: 'a third of the living creatures in the sea died.' How close are we to this reality? According to the National Academy of Sciences, one-third or more of the 6,300 known species are already threatened with extinction."

The images show dying coral reefs, polluted waters, and massive fish kills.

Copper Voice (The Astrophysicist):"Amphibians, frogs, salamanders, and caecilians, face extinction at unprecedented rates. Habitat destruction, climate change, and diseases like chytridiomycosis accelerate the process faster than previously thought possible. The extinction is not coming, it is here."

A new voice suddenly interrupts, filled with righteous indignation about humanity's treatment of the seas.

Teal Voice (The Limnologists) "Paleontologists worldwide have documented this ocean apocalypse! Each year, fishing trawlers plow an area of seafloor twice the size of the continental United States, obliterating the benthos. Gardens of coral and sponges hosting colorful sea life are reduced to furrowed, lifeless plains. The result? 270,000 sharks are slaughtered every single day!"

The Teal Voice's anger builds as more evidence is presented.

Teal Voice (The Limnologists): "Wikipedia documents mass mortality events that should terrify any thinking person. Between December 28, 2010, and January 3, 2011, 100 tons of dead fish washed ashore on Brazilian coastlines. On January 3, 2011, an estimated two million dead fish were discovered floating in Chesapeake Bay, Maryland. On March 7, 2011, millions of small fish, anchovies, sardines, mackerel, were found dead in King Harbor at Redondo Beach, California."

I remember my own experience with red tide, and the memory makes me shudder.

Copper Voice (The Astrophysicist):"I have witnessed the Red Tide firsthand, that crimson plague that kills fish and sea creatures regularly. During a visit to Mexico, I encountered the Red Algae Bloom. The beach and surrounding area reeked of rotting fish so intensely that even the swimming pools became unusable due to their proximity to the stinking shore."

Copper Voice (The Astrophysicist):"Red algae causes water to turn red, orange, or brown due to the toxins released and the oxygen depletion that follows. Warm ocean surface temperatures, low salinity, and high nutrient content create perfect conditions for this plague. It causes respiratory illness and eye irritation in humans and animals while systematically murdering marine life."

The cosmic display shows the devastating 1996 red tide event.

Copper Voice (The Astrophysicist):"In 1996, a red tide killed nearly ten percent of Florida's manatee population and 162 dolphins in Mexico. These gentle creatures, crafted by divine hands, destroyed by humanity's carelessness."

A pattern of human-caused destruction emerges as the evidence mounts.

Copper Voice (The Astrophysicist):"Excessive fertilizer and sewage runoff creates ongoing pollution that not only causes algae buildup but creates hypoxia and anoxia, low or no oxygen conditions that suffocate marine life. In the Hudson River, thousands of fish died from suffocation. More than 100,000 marine mammals die each year, including whales, dolphins, porpoises, seals, and sea lions. Some consume plastics and other pollutants; others become entangled in humanity's waste."

An even more disturbing revelation follows.

Copper Voice (The Astrophysicist):"Climate change is causing 99% of newborn sea turtles to be female. The link to human-caused climate change is undeniable. The sex of this species is determined by environmental temperature at the time of hatching, not chromosomes. Humanity is literally preventing these creatures from reproducing."

The Pearl Voice that has challenged the Adversary throughout this trial now speaks with deep concern.

Pearl Voice (The Wise Woman): "How much time do we have before we reach one-third of all sea creatures dead? Can this catastrophe be prevented or slowed?"

Copper Voice (The Astrophysicist):"Environmentalists argue that only thirteen percent of the world's oceans maintain intact marine ecosystems. The rest have been plundered and degraded beyond recognition. Rising global ocean temperatures have altered marine life fundamentally, migration patterns, reproduction cycles, everything."

Copper Voice (The Astrophysicist):"Coral reef bleaching and hazardous pathogens have transformed underwater ecosystems into aquatic graveyards. An article in The Guardian expressed astonishment at how little marine wilderness remains. The world's oceans are becoming more acidic and inhospitable to marine life while the global fishing industry overexploits fish populations and kills species unintended for capture, dolphins, sharks, whales, as collateral damage."

Suddenly, the Sapphire Voice speaks with the weight of ancient wisdom.

Sapphire Voice (Ancient Elder): "The signs are undeniable. Whether through natural cosmic events or humanity's systematic destruction of their environment, the second trumpet's warning manifests before our eyes. 'Something like a great mountain burning with fire' may take many forms, but the result remains the same, the death of a third of sea creatures."

The Teal Voice (The Limnologists): "The question remains: Is this judgment or warning? Are these consequences or opportunities for repentance?"

The cosmic arena falls silent as this divine question echoes through eternity. I realize that what we're witnessing is not just prophecy but a choice point for humanity. The second trumpet has sounded, but whether it brings final judgment or final warning depends on how humanity responds to what they can clearly see happening to their world.

The great white throne pulses with increasing intensity, and I sense that the cosmic trial has entered a new phase. No longer are we merely witnessing accusations and defenses, we are seeing the unfolding of divine consequence in real time.

The fate of the oceans, and perhaps all life on earth, hangs in the balance as the second trumpet's warning reverberates through creation itself.

Something massive is coming, whether asteroid, missile, or ecological collapse, and humanity's response will determine whether this is their final warning or their final judgment.

The cosmic arena holds its breath as we await the next movement in this divine symphony of consequence and choice.

19

THE THIRD TRUMPET

The cosmic arena still thrums with the aftermath of the second trumpet's devastating revelation when the familiar voice rises again, carrying the weight of divine prophecy. The earth continues its slow rotation beneath us, but now something has changed, the waters that were once transparent as crystal begin to show signs of distress.

Copper Voice (The Astrophysicist): "For it is written, then the third angel sounded: And a great star fell from heaven, burning like a torch, and it fell on a third of the rivers and on the springs of water. The name of the star is Wormwood. A third of the waters became wormwood, and many men died from the water, because it was made bitter."

The words hang in the cosmic air like a death sentence, and I find myself leaning forward, struggling to comprehend the implications.

Copper Voice (The Astrophysicist): "But what is 'Wormwood'? The name itself carries ominous weight, a woody shrub known for its intensely bitter, aromatic taste. Used as an ingredient in vermouth and absinthe, and sometimes as medicine, but always noted for its overwhelming bitterness that can overpower any other flavor."

Suddenly, another voice joins the discourse, one filled with scholarly precision yet tinged with growing alarm.

Burgundy Voice (The Scholar): "The prophet Jeremiah speaks directly to this mystery in chapter 9, verse 15: 'Therefore, this is what the Lord Almighty, the God of Israel, says: See, I will make this people eat bitter food and drink poisoned water.' The question becomes crucial, is wormwood merely bitter, or does it represent something far more sinister? Poisoned water that brings death?"

As if in response to this question, the rotating earth below us begins to reveal scenes that make my heart sink with recognition and dread.

Copper Voice (The Astrophysicist): "Observe the earth now and witness the fulfillment of ancient prophecy unfolding before our eyes."

The cosmic display shows heartbreaking scenes of desperation across the globe. In some regions, endless lines of people wait patiently for their meager water allowances, their faces etched with the quiet dignity of those who have learned to survive on almost nothing. In other areas, people carry water in buckets and containers balanced precariously on their heads, precious cargo that represents the difference between life and death.

At one location, children gathered around a makeshift well, their faces bright with hope as someone works the primitive pump. When water finally begins to trickle out, clean, precious, life-giving water, they erupt in joyful celebration, their voices rising like a hymn of gratitude.

But the cosmic display also reveals the stark contrasts that define our fallen world.

Copper Voice (The Astrophysicist): "Yet behold the disparities that mock divine justice. While some pray for a single cup of clean water, others languish beside crystal-clear swimming pools and bubbling Jacuzzis, their abundance taken for granted. Still others stand obliviously in their homes, letting precious water run freely from their showers while they talk on telephones or watch television, unaware that their casual waste could sustain entire families for days."

The images shift to show the truly heartbreaking scenes, people and animals dying of thirst, carried to makeshift medical tents where overwhelmed volunteers struggle to ease suffering that water could prevent.

Copper Voice (The Astrophysicist): "Some lie in cots, so wracked with pain from waterborne diseases that they pray for death's mercy. These are the consequences of humanity's poisoned waters, the bitter harvest of environmental destruction and systematic inequality."

A new voice enters the discourse, filled with righteous indignation at the global water crisis.

Satan: "Observe how perfectly this trumpet's warning manifests across your precious creation! People around the world face unprecedented freshwater scarcity. Sources that sustained civilizations for millennia are drying up at catastrophic rates."

Burgundy Voice (The Scholar): "Consider Cape Town, South Africa, in 2018. 'Day Zero,' that's what they called the approaching moment when a city of four million people would be just three months away from complete municipal water failure. The ultimate irony? Cape Town sits surrounded by both the Indian and Atlantic Oceans, endless water in every direction, yet its citizens faced dying of thirst."

The cosmic display focuses on major cities across the earth, revealing a pattern of crisis that spans continents.

Burgundy Voice (The Scholar): "Three major cities in the United States face similar catastrophic water shortages: Los Angeles, Salt Lake City, and Miami. Each crisis has different causes, but identical consequences. Miami's fresh water sources suffer contamination from Atlantic Ocean salt water due to rising sea levels. Los Angeles and Salt Lake City face depletion without adequate backup reserves."

Copper Voice (The Astrophysicist): "The Great Lakes, those massive bodies of water covering both the United States and Canada, have reached their lowest levels in recorded history, losing more than 2.5 million gallons. The Great Salt Lake in Utah, the largest saltwater lake in the Western Hemisphere, measured 3.6 meters below its 1847 level and had shrunk to half its original volume by 2017."

The images become even more disturbing as we witness the systematic destruction of water sources that once seemed inexhaustible.

Burgundy Voice (The Scholar): "The Colorado River, which once flowed majestically from Rocky Mountain National Park through four states and into Mexico, is drying up at unprecedented levels. Scientists estimate that by 2050, it will be completely dry, a river system that sustained millions, reduced to dust and memory."

Copper Voice (The Astrophysicist): "Lake Powell, created by the Glen Canyon Dam along the Colorado River, is down 23.13 feet from just one year ago. Lake Mead, downstream from Powell, has lost 60 percent of its total volume. Owens Lake, once covering 108 square miles, was diverted to supply Los Angeles through an aqueduct system. Now, parts have become dried salt flats that occasionally pool water after rains, but the lake faces complete destruction unless drastic action prevents it."

A somber voice joins the testimony, carrying the weight of global observation.

Sage Voice (The Watcher): "The devastation extends far beyond American borders. The Aral Sea in Central Asia was once the fourth largest body of fresh water in the world. Through systematic diversion of water sources, it has lost an estimated 167 billion gallons and now covers only ten percent of its former surface area."

Sage Voice (The Watcher): "Lake Faguibine in Mali, at 230 square miles, was one of West Africa's largest lakes. Drought caused it to dry up completely, it now covers approximately six percent of its previous area. Lake Chad, which once measured more than 10,000 square miles, has shrunk by 95 percent to just 580 square miles. The devastation is so complete that dust storms block the area, causing dune formation and advancing desertification."

The Pearl Voice that has challenged the Adversary throughout this trial now speaks with deep concern and growing understanding.

Pearl Voice (The Wise Woman): "The pattern becomes undeniable across every continent. The Dead Sea's water levels drop three feet annually. It's no longer one body of water but two distinct, diminished pools. Lake Urmia, once the largest lake in the Middle East, covers less than fifty percent of its original area."

Burgundy Voice (The Scholar): "In China, Lake Poyang, the nation's largest freshwater lake, recently revealed an ancient stone bridge that had been submerged for 400 years when water levels receded to a record low of 28 feet. Lake Chapala in Mexico, once the country's largest lake at 700 square miles, now holds only seven percent of its previous water volume."

Sage Voice (The Watcher): "Lake Poopó in Bolivia, once the nation's second-largest lake and crucial fishing resource for local communities, has essentially vanished. Lake Puzhal in Chennai, India, a rain-fed reservoir serving the nation's sixth largest city, appears to be running dry, along with four other lakes in the same region."

The cosmic display shifts to show the staggering scope of the global crisis.

Teal Voice (The Limnologists): "What humanity fails to comprehend is the mathematical reality of their situation. Only three percent of the world's water is fresh water. Two-thirds of that precious fraction remains frozen in glaciers or otherwise unavailable for human use."

Burgundy Voice (The Scholar): "The consequences are already catastrophic: 2.2 billion people worldwide lack safely managed drinking water services. 4.2 billion people lack safely managed sanitation services. Three billion lack basic handwashing facilities. When people cannot access fresh water, desperation forces them to drink contaminated water, and millions die annually from preventable diseases; diarrhea, cholera, guinea worm disease."

Teal Voice (The Limnologists): "The third trumpet has sounded its warning. 'A third of the waters became wormwood, and many men died from the water, because it was made bitter.' With over 2.2 billion people without safe drinking water, has this prophecy already been fulfilled?"

Satan responds with triumphant satisfaction.

Satan: "Indeed! The star called Wormwood has fallen! But observe how humanity responds to this crisis. Do they repent? Do they change their ways? Do they protect their remaining water sources with sacred care?"

The cosmic display shows scenes of continued waste, pollution, and corporate exploitation of remaining water resources.

Satan: "Instead, they commodify water, turning survival itself into a profit center. Private corporations buy rights to community water sources. Governments sell access to the highest bidders. The wealthy stockpile while the poor perish. They have made the waters bitter not just through environmental destruction, but through the poison of greed and inequality."

Pearl Voice (The Wise Woman): "Yet surely there are those who work to protect and preserve water sources? Environmental activists, scientists, communities organize to protect their watersheds?"

Burgundy Voice (The Scholar): "Some fight valiantly, but they battle against systemic forces far greater than individual efforts. Corporate interests, governmental policies, and consumer habits create momentum toward destruction that overwhelms conservation efforts."

Teal Voice (The Limnologists): "The bitter truth is that Wormwood represents more than physical pollution. It symbolizes the bitterness of a world where abundance and scarcity exist side by side, where technology capable of purifying any water source is available to some while others die of thirst within sight of the ocean."

Sage Voice (The Watcher): "The 'great star' that fell from heaven may be humanity's own moral failure, their inability to share the most basic necessity of life equitably among their own kind."

The atmosphere in the cosmic arena grows heavy with the weight of prophetic fulfillment.

Sapphire Voice (The Ancient Elder): "Three trumpets have now sounded. Each has revealed consequences already manifesting upon the earth. The question remains: Will humanity heed these warnings, or will they persist in the path that leads to their own destruction?"

Teal Voice (The Limnologists): "As the third trumpet's echo fades, we must ask ourselves: If the waters that sustain life itself have become instruments of death, what hope remains for the human race? And what will the fourth trumpet reveal when it sounds across creation?"

The cosmic arena holds its breath as this question hangs in the air like a prophecy waiting to unfold. The earth continues its slow rotation below us, showing scenes of both desperate thirst and wasteful abundance, while the great white throne pulses with light that seems to intensify with each passing moment.

Something greater is coming. I can feel it in the very atoms of this divine atmosphere. The trumpets are sounding in sequence, each revelation more devastating than the last, building toward a climactic moment that will determine the eternal fate of humanity.

The trial of mankind continues, but now it has become something more, a cosmic countdown where each trumpet brings us closer to the ultimate choice between divine mercy and divine justice.

And I sense that when the fourth trumpet sounds, the very foundations of heaven and earth will tremble with the weight of what is revealed.

20

THE FOURTH TRUMPET

The cosmic arena trembles with anticipation as the familiar voice prepares to deliver what I sense will be the most terrifying revelation yet. The earth below us has shifted, either sinking lower or we have been elevated higher, and suddenly I feel as though I'm reclining in a cosmic planetarium where the entire universe spreads out before my eyes like an infinite tapestry of light and darkness.

The Herald: "For it is written, the fourth angel sounded his trumpet, and a third of the sun was struck, a third of the moon, and a third of the stars, so that a third of them turned dark. A third of the day was without light, and also a third of the night."

The words hit me like a cosmic thunderbolt. I lean forward, straining to comprehend the magnitude of what's being revealed.

The Herald: "Look up, witness, and understand what has already begun to unfold across creation. 'A third of the moon, and a third of the stars, so that a third of them turned dark.' The very lights of heaven itself are being extinguished."

A new voice enters the discourse, carrying the authority of scientific observation mixed with growing alarm.

Obsidian Voice (The Astronomer): "I confess, I have read recent articles concerning missing stars, but I dismissed them too casually, a mistake I now deeply regret. There exists a project called 'Vanishing and Appearing Sources during a Century of Observations,' or VASCO, designed to locate objects in space that have appeared or disappeared by comparing historical photographs with recent observations."

The cosmic display above us begins showing star charts and astronomical images that make my blood run cold.

Obsidian Voice (The Astronomer): "Scientists have identified approximately 100 celestial objects that vanished in impossibly short periods. Some rapidly became several thousand times brighter before disappearing entirely, as if screaming a final warning before being snuffed out of existence."

Copper Voice (The Astrophysicist): "On March 16, 1950, astronomers at the US Naval Observatory pointed their telescope toward the constellation Lupus, the Wolf, and captured an image. When scientists examined that same patch of sky decades later, something was missing. Gone. Vanished without explanation."

The implications begin to cascade through my mind like falling dominoes.

Obsidian Voice (The Astronomer): "In 2016, Swedish researchers reported that a star had been lost. One of the distant suns visible in that Naval Observatory image from the previous century could no longer be detected, even with our more advanced and sensitive digital sky surveys."

A new voice joins the testimony, carrying the weight of published scientific authority.

Copper Voice (The Astrophysicist): "The Atlantic published an article titled 'Stars Aren't Supposed to Go Out Like This.' When massive stars disappear, astronomers expect to find supernovae in their place, cosmic explosions that mark stellar death. But in this case, there was no supernova. Nothing. The star simply... ceased to exist."

Copper Voice (The Astrophysicist): "This particular star blazed crystal blue, shining several million times brighter than our sun. Astronomers had studied it for nearly two decades, making its sudden disappearance deeply unsettling. One day they examined the latest observations and realized they could no longer find it anywhere."

The cosmic display shifts to show globular clusters and galaxy formations that appear strangely diminished.

Obsidian Voice (The Astronomer): "In the Astrophysical Journal, researchers published findings titled 'Where Have the Stars Gone?' Globular clusters, massive balls of stars orbiting our galaxy's core like satellites, have revealed that older stars aren't being ejected as previously assumed. They're completely missing."

Obsidian Voice (The Astronomer): "New observations using the Hubble Space Telescope revealed something impossible: massive populations of stars have vanished without trace.

Star clusters around our Milky Way galaxy contain fewer stars than observations suggest they should. Scientists remain completely stumped about their location."

Copper Voice (The Astrophysicist): "On July 5, 2020, astronomers announced that a massive star appears to have mysteriously disappeared from the Kinman Dwarf galaxy in the constellation Aquarius. Previous images captured by NASA's Hubble Space Telescope showed clear 'signatures', unmistakable signs of the star's existence. Now those signatures can no longer be detected."

Suddenly, the Pearl Voice interjects with a question that cuts to the heart of the mystery.

Pearl Voice (The Wise Woman): "If stars, these cosmic furnaces that burn for billions of years, can simply vanish without explanation, what does this reveal about the stability of creation itself?"

Copper Voice (The Astrophysicist): "But consider the second part of the fourth trumpet's warning: 'A third of the day was without light, and also a third of the night.' This speaks not merely of missing stars, but of increasing darkness overwhelming the earth itself."

A new voice emerges, carrying expertise in atmospheric science and environmental observation.

Charcoal Voice (The Environmental Scientist): "There exists documented research titled 'Earth's a Darker Place.' Scientific measurements confirm that the amount of sunlight reaching Earth's surface has declined significantly over the past two centuries, a phenomenon scientists call "global dimming.""

Charcoal Voice (The Environmental Scientist): "Researchers from the University of Oslo calculated that solar energy landing annually on every square meter of land and water has dropped by an average of 2.4 watts. Earth is literally getting darker, not because of changes to the sun, but due to various types of air pollution blocking solar radiation."

The cosmic display shows disturbing images of pollution, smog, and atmospheric interference that blanket the earth like a shroud.

Indigo Voice (The Reasoner): "On February 18, 2014, the Associated Press published research titled 'Study: Arctic Getting Darker, Making Earth Warmer.' The article revealed that the Arctic has lost its bright, white reflectivity due to massive ice melting, creating more dark, open water that absorbs rather than reflects solar heat."

Charcoal Voice (The Environmental Scientist): "The Proceedings of the National Academy of Sciences documented that with darker, open water during summer months, less of the sun's heat reflects back into space. The entire Earth absorbs more heat than expected. The Arctic grew eight percent darker between 1979 and 2011 alone."

Copper Voice (The Astrophysicist: "Here lies the cruel irony. The same pollution that blocks sunlight from entering our atmosphere also prevents heat from escaping. Humanity has created a prison of their own making, trapped between darkness and overheating."

Charcoal Voice (The Environmental Scientist): "But the darkness extends beyond atmospheric pollution. Consider 'light pollution' excessive, misdirected, or obtrusive artificial light that has consequences beyond mere inconvenience. It washes out starlight in the night sky, interferes with astronomical research, disrupts ecosystems, wastes energy, and causes adverse health effects."

The next revelation strikes me with a particular force, a conviction, really!

Charcoal Voice (The Environmental Scientist): "One-third of humanity, and eighty percent of North Americans, can no longer see the Milky Way galaxy. The very cosmic home that should inspire wonder and worship has been rendered invisible by human interference."

Satan suddenly erupts with triumphant satisfaction.

Satan: "Behold the perfection of their self-destruction! They have fulfilled the fourth trumpet's prophecy through their own actions. Stars disappear from their skies not merely through cosmic judgment, but through their systematic poisoning of the very atmosphere that should reveal heaven's glory!"

Obsidian Voice (The Astronomer): "The question becomes inescapable: Can thirty percent of the stars truly disappear? Can one-third of the day become dark? Has the judgment of humanity already begun?"

Pearl Voice (The Wise Woman): "Or perhaps more unsettling: Can the consequences of mankind's behavior inadvertently cause the same events as divine judgment prophesied in Revelation?"

Suddenly, the Golden Voice speaks from the great white throne, and the cosmic arena falls into absolute silence.

Sapphire Voice (The Ancient Elder): "The fourth trumpet has sounded its warning. The lights of heaven grow dim, and darkness encroaches upon the earth. Yet humanity continues in their destructive path, blind to the signs surrounding them."

Copper Voice (The Astrophysicist): "I find myself reflecting on this fourth trumpet's terrible message. When the very stars themselves begin to vanish, when the light of day diminishes, when the night sky becomes an empty void, what hope remains for a species that has turned creation itself into an instrument of their own judgment?"

Burgundy Voice (The Scholar): "Perhaps the most terrifying aspect is the speed of fulfillment. These prophecies, written nearly two millennia ago, manifest before our eyes with increasing acceleration. The trumpets sound not as distant warnings, but as present realities."

Charcoal Voice (The Environmental Scientist): "Humanity possesses the knowledge to reverse these trends, to restore the clarity of their skies, to protect the remaining stars from vanishing behind veils of pollution. Yet they persist in behaviors that deepen the darkness."

Satan: "They have made their choice! Light or darkness, heaven or hell, salvation or damnation, and they choose darkness every time! They prefer the artificial lights of their cities to the eternal lights of heaven!"

The cosmic display now shows the earth as it truly appears from our elevated position, a planet increasingly shrouded in darkness, its natural lights dimming, its artificial lights creating false illumination that blinds its inhabitants to the glory of creation above.

Emerald Voice (Young Elder): "Four trumpets have now sounded. Each revelation builds upon the last: the destruction of vegetation, the death of sea creatures, the poisoning of fresh water, and now the extinguishing of heaven's lights. The pattern accelerates toward an inevitable conclusion."

Sage Voice (The Watcher): "The question that haunts this cosmic courtroom: Will humanity recognize these signs and repent while light remains? Or will they continue their march into darkness until the final trumpet sounds, and all hope of redemption is lost?"

The atmosphere in the cosmic arena grows heavier with each passing moment. I can feel the weight of approaching judgment, the sense that we are racing toward a climactic moment that will determine the eternal fate of every human soul.

Pearl Voice (The Wise Woman): "When the lights of heaven itself begin to fail, when the darkness grows so deep that humanity can no longer see the stars that once proclaimed My glory, what excuse will they offer for their continued rebellion?"

The great white throne pulses with light so intense it nearly blinds me, yet somehow, I understand that this light may be the only illumination left in a cosmos where the fourth trumpet has sounded its warning.

The trial of mankind continues, but now it has become a race against encroaching darkness, both literal and spiritual. The cosmic countdown accelerates, and I sense that when the fifth trumpet sounds, we will witness something that will shake the very foundations of heaven and earth.

Something far greater than missing stars and dimming light is coming. I can feel it in the very fabric of reality itself, approaching like a cosmic storm that will test whether any light can survive the darkness humanity has chosen for itself.

21

WOE! WOE! WOE! THE EAGLE FLIES

The cosmic arena trembles with the weight of four trumpets' warnings when suddenly, Satan's voice erupts with mocking triumph. His purple and gold robes seem to pulse with malevolent energy as he quotes scripture with sardonic precision.

Satan: "As I watched, I heard an eagle that was flying in midair call out in a loud voice: 'Woe! Woe! Woe to the inhabitants of the earth, because of the trumpet blasts about to be sounded by the other three angels!'"

The words hang in the cosmic air like a death sentence, and I feel a chill that penetrates to my very soul. Three more trumpets remain, and if the first four have revealed such devastating truths, what horrors await?

But then, cutting through Satan's mockery like a sword of divine authority, comes a voice I recognize yet have never heard speak with such commanding power.

Golden Voice (The Almighty): "That is enough. This is not the day nor the time of judgment. Let the four trumpets serve as warnings of what is yet to come..."

The arena falls into absolute silence. Even the four living creatures pause their eternal patrol around the great white throne. The seraphim hover motionless in their flight, and the cherubim stand at perfect attention. This is no ordinary voice. He is the Judge, the Alpha and the Omega.

Golden Voice (The Almighty): "But you, who have stood in opposition to the relationship that humanity has with their Creator, should not have come before this heavenly assembly demanding 'judgment of mankind.' Not from this sacred court."

The Almighty's attention turns fully toward Satan, and the very atmosphere seems to crackle with divine authority.

Golden Voice (The Almighty): "You knew perfectly well that the Father judges each person as an individual. You know that He has entrusted all judgment to his Son, so that all may honor the Son just as they honor the Father. Your intent was to come between the Father and His Son... just as you have systematically come between fathers and their children throughout human history."

Lightning begins to flicker across the smaller thrones, and I can see the Spirits leaning forward with intense interest.

Golden Voice (The Almighty): "Satan! You, who pretend innocence while standing before us, seeking to assume a role you were never called to fulfill. Under the pretense of offering humanity 'choice' between right and wrong, you disguise yourself as an angel of light. But you are the Lord of Darkness, seeking to destroy all things that we have made. While you use your cunning, beauty, and the ability to distract, create chaos and sow division."

Satan straightens, his magnificent form radiating defiance even in the face of divine rebuke.

Satan: "I would never attempt to interfere with the relationship the Son has with the Father! As you are well aware, I have come before the Lord seeking permission for actions I have taken on earth. When the sons of God presented themselves before the Lord, I was present among them."

Golden Voice (The Almighty): "We are aware of your presence, and we understand your true purpose. You would interfere with all manner of divine relationships. In fact, you employ the same ancient strategies to achieve the results you desire."

The Almighty's voice grows more pointed, more accusatory.

Golden Voice (The Almighty): "You specifically requested that humanity be judged NOW, but you deliberately failed to acknowledge your role in their demise. You made a request knowing it could not be granted, my word is sacred, and it has been declared that my son, alone, will choose who is his and who is not at the appointed hour that I have set."

Golden Voice (The Almighty): "Second, you question the covenant between the Son and the Father by using the fact that humanity has followed you, been thoroughly captivated by your deceptions, while simultaneously arguing for their condemnation due to their 'inhumanity.' The audacity of such manipulation!"

A pause stretches across eternity, heavy with divine sorrow and righteous anger.

Golden Voice (The Almighty): "My heart remains in a sorrowful state, knowing that my children are so quick to follow you, you who come to them in sheep's clothing but inwardly are nothing more than a ravenous wolf. You, who are of this fallen world, have blinded the minds of those who do not believe, preventing them from seeing the glorious light of the Gospel. They cannot understand the message of love, mercy, kindness, forgiveness, salvation, etc. Yet, they were made in our likeness!"

Satan seizes upon this statement with the cunning of a master debater.

Satan: "Is it my fault that your creation refuses to believe the word of the . . . Creator? Have they not been disobedient from the very beginning? For example, I merely asked Eve two simple questions and let us not forget that Adam stood right beside her throughout the entire conversation. Adam watched Eve eat fruit of the forbidden tree and when she passed it to him, he ate of it, too."

His voice takes on a tone of mock innocence.

Satan: "The first question was whether they were certain that God had commanded them not to eat from the tree in the middle of the garden. A simple yes or no confirmation of what they had been told. The second question was whether they were sure God meant they would literally die, or whether 'death' might mean something entirely different. Again, merely seeking confirmation of their understanding."

Satan: "The fruit was simply offered for them to accept or refuse. Where is the deception in asking for clarification?"

The Almighty's response carries the weight of omniscient authority and barely contained divine anger.

Golden Voice (The Almighty): "Satan, You were perfect in your ways from the day you were created, Till iniquity was found in you. "By the abundance of your trading, You became filled with violence within, And you sinned; Therefore I cast you as a profane thing, Out of the mountain of God! You have remained the same, filled with arrogance and conceit. Your 'questions' raised doubt in the minds of Adam and Eve, and in all who have followed you since. But as it is written: 'He who doubts is condemned if he eats, because he does not eat from faith; for whatever is not from faith is sin."

Satan presses his philosophical attack with relentless precision.

Satan: "With all due respect, the Lord's relationship with humanity requires genuine choice. If they are not given real options, are they nothing more than slaves or subjects, compelled to bow down and praise the Lord without joy or personal benefit? Doesn't freedom of choice allow humans to be free agents, making their own decisions and accepting the consequences?"

The question hangs in the cosmic air like a challenge to the very foundations of divine justice. Then he responds with a counter-question that cuts to the heart of the matter.

Golden Voice (The Almighty): "Is gratitude the same as servitude? That is the fundamental flaw in your argument."

He pauses, and then His voice takes on the cadence of sacred scripture as He recites Psalm 8:3-9:

Golden Voice (The Almighty): "As it is written by my servant, "When I consider Your heavens, the work of Your fingers, The moon and the stars, which You have ordained, What is man that You are mindful of him, And the son of man that You visit him? For You have made him a little lower than the angels, And You have crowned him with glory and honor. You have made him to have dominion over the works of Your hands; You have put all things under his feet, All sheep and oxen. Even the beasts of the field, the birds of the air, And the fish of the sea, That pass through the paths of the seas. O LORD, our Lord, How excellent is Your name in all the earth!"

The cosmic arena falls into reverent silence as these words of divine praise echo through eternity. Even Satan's entourage seems momentarily subdued by the power of scripture spoken with divine authority.

Golden Voice (The Almighty): "Love and Gratitude. From the very beginning, our desire was to have a loving and intimate relationship. Humanity, Adam and Eve was placed in the Garden of Eden and provided shelter, food, and companionship. They were granted dominion over all animals, fish in the sea, and every creature on earth. Does this describe a master-slave relationship? Of course not. Only you could misconstrue the relationship that We desire with our children. When faced with choices between righteousness and evil, light and darkness, good and bad, it was Our hope that humanity would choose correctly. However, when faced with your false statements and deceptive narratives, the choice becomes infinitely more difficult."

Satan launches his most sophisticated theological attack yet.

Satan: "Again, with all due respect, doesn't the Lord know all things? Why didn't He foresee the outcome of providing choice to humanity? Did He not say to Solomon: 'Know the God of your father and serve Him with a whole heart and with a willing mind, for the LORD searches all hearts and understands every plan and thought. If you seek Him, He will be found by you, but if you forsake Him, He will cast you off forever'?"

The implications of this question strike the cosmic arena like a thunderbolt. If God is omniscient, did He create humanity knowing they would fall? The philosophical complexity threatens to tear at the very foundations of divine justice and mercy.

The response comes with the authority of one who has wrestled with the deepest mysteries of divine will and human freedom.

Golden Voice (The Almighty): "You ask and do not receive, because you ask with wrong motives, seeking to turn divine truth like a blade in the souls of humanity."

Golden Voice (The Almighty): "You, who have no right to question God! We know that for those who love God, all things work together for good, for those who are called according to His purpose. What you need to understand is that you, too, will face judgment, you and all who follow you."

The Almighty's voice grows more ominous, carrying the weight of final judgment.

Golden Voice (The Almighty): "The cowardly, the unbelieving, the vile, the murderers, the sexually immoral, those who practice magic arts, the idolaters, and all liars, they will be consigned to the fiery lake of burning sulfur. This is the second death."

The cosmic arena trembles as these words of ultimate judgment echo through creation.

The Golden Voice (The Almighty): "ENOUGH."

The single word detonated across the arena like a cosmic thunderclap, silencing every voice, stilling every wing, freezing every heartbeat in creation itself. The very atoms of heaven seemed to hold their breath.

When the Almighty spoke again, His voice carried the weight of galaxies, the authority that had spoken light into existence, the power that held every star in its course:

"Deceiver. Accuser. Fallen one. You dare stand in Our presence and demand judgment upon those We created in Our own image? You, who corrupted the very paradise We entrusted to your care? You, whose pride cast you from these halls like lightning falling from heaven?"

The golden radiance intensified until it became nearly unbearable, and I felt the tremendous power of divine wrath barely contained within infinite love.

"LET THIS SERVE AS YOUR FINAL WARNING. You exist only by Our sufferance. You move only within the boundaries We have set. You can do nothing, NOTHING, that We have not permitted for Our own purposes. Your petition to judge all of humanity is DENIED. Not delayed. Not postponed. DENIED."

The word 'DENIED' crashed through the arena like a cosmic gavel, final and absolute.

"SO ORDERED! THESE PROCEEDINGS ARE HEREBY CLOSED."

Thunder rolled through dimensions I couldn't name, and lightning split the air with the sound of justice itself.

"YOU AND YOUR ENTOURAGE MUST LEAVE OUR HEAVENLY REALM. NOW."

In that split second, no, in less than a heartbeat, in the space between one breath and the next, reality itself seemed to crack.

Satan and his dark assembly didn't fade away. They didn't dissolve or retreat with dignity. They were ejected, ripped from heaven's presence like infection being purged from a wound, like darkness fleeing before the dawn, like lies crumbling before absolute truth.

One moment they were there, a stain upon perfection.

The next moment, they were gone, not just from the arena, but from heaven itself, cast back into the shadows where they belonged.

The silence that followed wasn't empty, it was full. Full of victory. Full of justice. Full of the kind of peace that comes only when good has triumphed over evil, when truth has vanquished lies, when Love has proven once again that it is the only force in the universe that truly matters.

And in that silence, I heard something that made my soul soar:

The sound of heaven itself exhaling in relief.

Suddenly, movement catches my attention high above the cosmic arena. An eagle, magnificent beyond earthly description, soars through the heavenly atmosphere. Its voice rings out across creation with supernatural power:

The Eagle: "Woe! Woe! Woe to the inhabitants of the earth, because of the trumpet blasts about to be sounded by the other three angels!"

The three-fold cry of "woe" reverberates through the arena like cosmic thunder. I realize we have witnessed not just a theological debate, but a cosmic confrontation between the Almighty and Satan. A battle for the soul of man will determine the outcome of the remaining trumpet judgments.

Pearl Voice (The Wise Woman): "If the first four trumpets have revealed such devastating consequences, and now the eagle proclaims three woes for the final three trumpets, what unimaginable horrors await the earth?"

Azure Voice (The Senior Elder): "The time of warnings draws to a close. Humanity has heard the first four trumpets. They have seen the evidence of their choices manifesting in real time. The final three trumpets will not be mere consequences of human action; they will be direct divine intervention."

The great white throne begins to pulse with light so intense it threatens to overwhelm my senses. The rainbow above it expands and brightens, its colors taking on hues that have no earthly names.

Sapphire Voice (The Ancient Elder): "The eagle has spoken. The three woes are declared. Let humanity choose wisely in whatever time remains, for the final trumpets will sound when mercy gives way to justice, and warnings transform into judgment."

The cosmic arena holds its breath as the implications sink in. We have witnessed the Almighty God, himself defend humanity against Satan's accusations, but we have also heard divine judgment pronounced upon those who persist in following darkness rather than light.

Something far greater than anything we have yet witnessed is approaching. The eagle's three-fold cry of "woe" echoes through my very soul, and I understand that when the fifth trumpet sounds, we will enter a realm of divine judgment unlike anything human history has ever recorded.

The trial of mankind has reached its climactic moment, and the cosmic countdown to ultimate judgment has begun in earnest.

22

MANNA

The confrontation between the Almighty God and Satan still reverberates through my soul. I am digesting the various statements made and conclusions drawn. The questions asked and the statements made; man is inhumane to man. I am relieved that Satan and his entourage is no longer present. They are a dark force. Suddenly, the familiar Herald's voice cuts through the tension.

The Herald: "An intermission has been declared. Further proceedings will continue later today. Invited guests are free to remain, though their assigned guides must stay nearby. Remember these words: 'The wise seek knowledge with all their heart, and those who truly understand listen carefully to learn.'"

As these words echo through the arena, I witness something that defies comprehension. Everything, absolutely everything on the stage, begins to vanish before my eyes. The magnificent thrones dissolve like morning mist. The four living creatures with their countless eyes simply fade from existence. The seraphim and cherubim disappear from their eternal posts. The candles, incense holders, even the grand table with the four corners of divine light—all gone. In moments, the heavenly tribunal that held the trial of humanity itself has vanished into nothingness."

Everything except the earth, still rotating slowly in the center of the arena, surrounded by eternal stars and the sun. These remain, suspended in space like a reminder of what we've witnessed and what is yet to come.

As I stood up from where I had been kneeling, I realized for the first time the absolutely staggering size of this arena. When I look to my right, I see people, thousands upon thousands of people stretching as far as my eyes can perceive.

As I turn toward the rear, my breath catches in my throat. Rows upon rows of seats extend upward; balcony upon balcony, each one hanging over the next, stretching up into the heavens themselves. They are too numerous to count, creating a vertical city of witnesses that disappears into infinity.

Now I can see the cherubim clearly, perched on the various balconies, watching everyone and everything with their ancient, wise eyes. They are not the winged babies of religious art, but exactly as described in earlier chapters, short, round, mature beings with faces like old men, dressed in pristine white robes. Their eyes hold the wisdom of ages, and I understand they are the eternal guardians of this sacred space.

Above us, the seraphim continue their flight patterns, their six wings beating in perfect rhythm as they maintain their watch over the proceedings.

Looking to my left reveals the same breathtaking scene, people everywhere, seated in rows and balconies that circle the entire arena like a cosmic amphitheater. The arena itself gleams white and gray, with blue chairs providing the only splash of color. The steps and floor appear to be part of the sky itself, lit by small guiding lights that help navigate the celestial architecture.

The entire structure blends seamlessly with the clouds, sky, and stars, making it nearly impossible to determine where the arena ends and heaven begins. I wonder how many people this . . . place can hold, surely millions, perhaps billions of souls gathered as witnesses to the trial of humanity.

The diversity of the assembly amazes me. Some people are dressed in various shades of white, similar to the Man who brought me here. I remember shopping with a friend for her wedding dress and being astounded by the variety of whites available, diamond white, ivory, olive, champagne. Here, the designs differ, but the similar colors create a sense of unity that blends beautifully with the heavenly atmosphere.

Others, like me, wear earthly clothing, suits, dresses, jeans, shorts, African apparel, Indian garments, traditional Japanese outfits. Every culture and nation appear to be represented in this cosmic gathering.

The people themselves reflect the full spectrum of human diversity. Some are nearly albino in their paleness, others so richly dark they remind me of the stunning Senegalese model Khoudia Diop. I see faces that could be from any nation on earth, India, China,

Russia, the Netherlands, Ghana, Mexico, Peru, Brazil, Australia, Thailand, Vietnam, etc. Every tribe, tongue, and nation seem to have representatives in this heavenly assembly.

As people begin moving toward the aisles, I'm struck by the perfect order. Unlike earthly venues where crowds push and shove to be first, here everyone moves with patient courtesy. There's no rushing, no anxiety, just peaceful, organized movement toward the ends of the rows where people seem to simply… disappear.

A moment of panic grips me as I realize the Man is no longer beside me. Where did he go? How will I find my way?

A gentle tap on my shoulder draws my attention. I turn to see a woman with a radiant, joyful face pointing across the crowd. Following her gesture, I spot the Man using hand signals to direct me toward the end of the row.

As I walk toward where he's indicating, I watch in fascination as people ahead of me reach the end of their rows and vanish as if stepping through an invisible doorway. No one seems concerned or surprised, this is apparently normal in this heavenly realm.

When I reach the end of my row, I look to the Man for confirmation. He nods encouragingly. Taking a deep breath, I step forward into what appears to be empty space…

And suddenly, I find myself in the most magnificent dining hall I've ever imagined.

"HUGE" doesn't begin to describe this place. It's a cafeteria that could encompass entire city blocks, filled with more people than I've ever seen in one space. Yet despite the vast crowds, there's an overwhelming sense of peace and joy that permeates the atmosphere.

Soft music plays in the background, not overwhelming, but present enough to add to the sense of celebration. The lighting is warm and bright, and the aroma… oh, the aroma takes me back to Christmas Eve as a child, when my mother would spend all day preparing our holiday feast. The scent of baking cakes and pies, simmering greens, ham studded with pineapple and cloves; all the smells that represent love, family, and celebration rolled into one heavenly fragrance.

This place reminds me of my happiest moments, but magnified and perfected beyond earthly experience.

The man who had been gesturing toward the door came up to me with a bright smile. He gave me a friendly hug and said, 'Hello, I'm Benjamin. Are you Andrea?"

He almost catches me off guard. I had become so absorbed in taking in this incredible space that I nearly didn't realize he was speaking to me until he embraced me.

"Yes, I am Andrea. How are you?" I respond.

Benjamin: "Blessed and highly favored!"

The joy and certainty in his voice convince me immediately that he speaks truth. He does indeed look blessed, tall, dark, handsome, with an expression of gentle curiosity and unmistakable divine favor.

Benjamin: "Would you join our group for lunch? We've been looking forward to meeting you."

"I would love it. Tell me, who is "we" and have you really been looking forward to meeting me?" I ask with a smile, both curious and honored.

He smiles and gently takes my arm, guiding me toward a table where nine or ten people are already seated. Their faces light up when they see me approaching.

Prisha: "Hey, Andrea! It's so nice to meet you!"

Diego: "Please sit down and join us!"

The warmth of their welcome makes me feel as though I belong here, as if I've found my heavenly family.

"What are you eating?" I ask, settling into a chair that seems to have been waiting specifically for me.

Benjamin: "Manna."

Prisha: "The bread of heaven!"

"Please don't tell me we're going to eat manna for forty years!" I joke, and their laughter tells me they appreciate the biblical humor.

Diego: "No, we're not in the wilderness anymore!"

Hanna: "Have you ever tasted it before?"

"No, never," I admit truthfully.

A plate appears before me containing what looks like a small, white nougat. The anticipation of the group is palpable as I pick up the plate and examine this legendary food. The aroma of nuts and honey fills my nostrils, rich, sweet, and somehow familiar yet unlike anything I've have seen before.

Under their encouraging gazes, I break off a piece and place it in my mouth. The flavor explodes across my taste buds, a chewy, white, nougat-like confection spiced with cardamom and mixed with the finest nuts imaginable.

Hanna: "It's good, right?"

"Yes, it really is," I respond, taking another bite. The taste is simultaneously exotic and comforting, like coming home to a place I've never been.

Benjamin: "This is different from what the Israelites ate in the wilderness. This is mixed with the finest nuts and honey made by God Himself. In the wilderness, the Israelites couldn't prepare it this way. It was described as being like coriander seed, white, with a taste 'like wafers made with honey.'"

Prisha: "Or they would grind it like grain and make cakes with it, beating it in mortars first."

Will: "Don't forget that in Numbers, the flavor was described as 'fresh oil.' Remember how it tasted like fresh oil when prepared differently?"

Hanna: "The beauty is that manna always provided exactly what each person needed. It satisfied every hunger, fulfilled every nutritional requirement. It was God's perfect provision."

As I continue eating, I notice something remarkable happening. With each bite, I feel more than just physical satisfaction. There's a sense of spiritual nourishment, as if this food is feeding my soul as well as my body.

Benjamin: "You feel it, don't you? The way it satisfies more than just hunger?"

I nod, unable to fully express what I'm experiencing.

Prisha: "That's because this isn't just food, it's communion. It's God's way of reminding us that He provides for every need, not just physical but spiritual and emotional as well."

Diego: "In the wilderness, the Israelites often complained about the manna, wanting the foods they remembered from Egypt. They took for granted the miracle of daily provision."

Will: "But here, we understand what a gift it truly is. Every bite is a reminder of God's faithfulness, His perfect provision, His intimate knowledge of our needs."

As we eat and converse, I become aware that this intermission is more than just a break in the proceedings. It's a time of fellowship, of spiritual nourishment, of preparation for what's to come.

Prisha: "The trial isn't over, you know. This is the calm before the storm. The final three trumpets, the three woes, they're still coming."

The reminder sends a slight chill through me despite the warmth of the fellowship.

Benjamin: "But this is why we're here, sharing this meal. To remind us that no matter what judgments may come, no matter how dark the final revelations may be, God's provision remains constant. His mercy endures forever."

Hanna: "The manna reminds us that even in the wilderness, even in times of judgment and trial, God provides what His people need to survive and thrive."

As I finish the last of the manna on my plate, I feel a profound sense of peace and preparedness. Whatever awaits us when the cosmic courtroom reconvenes, whatever the final three trumpets may reveal, I am reminded that we serve a God who provides for His people even in the midst of judgment.

Prisha: "Are you ready for what's coming next?"

I look around the table at these newfound friends, these fellow witnesses to the trial of humanity, and I realize that somehow, inexplicably, I am ready.

"Yes," I say, surprised by the confidence in my own voice. "I think I am."

The manna has done more than satisfy my physical hunger. It has prepared my spirit for whatever spiritual revelations await when the final trumpets sound and the three woes are unleashed upon the earth.

The intermission continues, but I can sense that something greater approaches, something that will test the very foundations of heaven and earth when the trial of mankind reaches its ultimate conclusion.

23

— • —

THE GUIDES

The warmth and fellowship around the table makes me feel completely at ease for the first time since this journey began. I find myself freely talking and laughing with my tablemates, my anxiety melting away in the face of their genuine acceptance. But curiosity begins to stir within me, who are these people, and how did we all come to be here together?

"I'd love to know more about all of you," I say, settling back in my chair. "Your names, where you come from, how you ended up here."

The introductions that follow reveal something extraordinary. As each person speaks, I realize there are eleven of us at this table, and we fall into two distinct categories that will change everything I thought I knew about spiritual reality.

"I'm Hanna," says a radiant woman with eyes that seem to hold starlight. "I'm a Guide."

"Prisha," announces another with a voice like wind chimes. "Also a Guide."

Benjamin nods. "You already know me, Benjamin, Guide as well."

"Diego," says a man whose very presence radiates authority. "Guide."

"Will," adds another whose alertness suggests he's constantly watching, constantly aware. "Guide."

Then the others introduce themselves with a different designation:

"Ishita," says a young woman whose curiosity mirrors my own. "Invited guest."

"Ho Sung," announces a man with gentle wisdom in his eyes. "Invited guest."

"Ling," adds a woman whose quiet strength is immediately apparent. "Invited guest."

"Simba," says a man whose name fits his bold demeanor. "Invited guest."

"Oliver," concludes a scholarly-looking individual. "Invited guest, like yourself, Andrea."

I am an invited guest too. And suddenly I understand, the Man who brought me here, my mysterious guide whose name I still don't know, belongs to this same category of Guides. Benjamin explains that my Guide asked him to look after me during this intermission.

As our conversation deepens, I begin to understand something that defies earthly comprehension. When Benjamin had said he was "blessed and highly favored," he wasn't using a casual greeting or expressing personal well-being. The Guides possess actual powers and abilities that ordinary humans don't have, supernatural gifts that help them work in both the physical and spiritual realms.

"Tell us about your work," I find myself asking. "What do Guides actually do?"

Hanna speaks first, her voice carrying an otherworldly authority. "I'm a messenger. I appear in person to deliver messages from God directly to those who need to hear them. Think of it as spiritual FedEx, heavenly delivery service with a perfect track record."

Diego's expression grows more serious. "Once a judgment has been issued by the divine court, I oversee its execution, whatever form it may take. More often than not, people have no idea what they're truly asking for when they petition God for their desires. My role is to ensure divine justice is carried out precisely as ordained."

Will's alertness becomes even more apparent as he speaks. "I work in security, patrolling the earth and tracking down those who don't belong in certain spiritual territories. Protecting the boundaries of the Kingdom and monitoring all who come and go is my absolute duty. No unauthorized spiritual activity goes unnoticed."

Prisha's face lights up with genuine joy. "My greatest privilege is to guard the Truth itself, that's my assignment. As it is written: 'You shall know the truth, and the truth shall make you free.' I protect that truth from distortion, deception, and destruction."

Benjamin's voice carries a warmth that immediately comforts. "I help prepare the defense for those who will face spiritual challenges. Always being prepared to make a defense to anyone who asks for a reason for the hope that is within us. No soul faces trial alone if I can help it."

Each of their explanations feels both complete and mysteriously incomplete, as if they're revealing truth while maintaining necessary boundaries. I sense each has a crucial role in God's cosmic order, different but equally important.

"Do you know why we're here?" I ask, gesturing to include all the invited guests. "How did we become chosen for this... this cosmic trial?"

Hanna's response shakes me to my core: "Of course we know! We have been assigned to each of you. We know you completely. We knew you in your mother's womb, knew you as children, watched you grow into adults. And we will always know you... unless..."

The word hangs in the air like a sword suspended over our heads.

"Unless what?" Ho Sung asks quietly.

Hanna's entire demeanor shifts, as if she's about to reveal something that will change everything. "Unless you fail to acknowledge our Lord. Unless you refuse to accept that Jesus Christ was the Living Sacrifice, offered to save humanity from the consequences of sin. Unless you reject the Holy Spirit's presence within you."

Oliver breaks the reflective silence with a question that makes me both smile and nod in recognition: "What do you mean you've been 'assigned' to us? Are we like George Bailey in 'It's a Wonderful Life'? Are you our guardian angels?"

The silence stretches uncomfortably until Benjamin responds with gentle humor: "I think you've oversimplified it, but... yes."

Ling leans forward with another crucial question: "Does everyone have a guardian angel?"

Hanna's answer reveals the breathtaking scope of divine care: "At conception, not birth, but conception, assignments are made. Some people are born with awareness of a spiritual presence. Others never recognize it. But everyone can choose to draw closer to or further from their guardian, depending on how they live their lives and what they value and cherish."

My heart pounds as I ask the question that's been burning within me: "Why were we invited guests chosen to be here today? And where exactly are we? Does heaven really have a cafeteria serving manna?"

Prisha's response stops my world: "First, you have asked for help from our Lord. Your prayers were heard. He commanded his angels concerning you, to guard you in all your ways. He told us to lift you up in our hands, so that you would not strike your foot against a stone."

The words hit me like divine lightning. My prayers were heard. HEARD. Not ignored, not dismissed, not lost in cosmic noise. HEARD.

I sit staring at Prisha, my mouth hanging open, my mind reeling. Which prayers? How many times have I cried out to God in desperation, in doubt, in desperate need? And He heard them all?

As if reading my thoughts, Prisha continues: "And whatever you ask in prayer will be given, if you have faith of a mustard seed and it aligns with God's will." Her voice grows more pointed. "I see you've lost your faith, but you must have had it at some point. You, who are blessed and highly favored, act as if you were a lost sheep with no shepherd, scattered over mountains and hills and in rivers, ready to be killed by lions. But you have a Shepherd, and like us, you have a job, an especially important job."

I cannot speak. I cannot think clearly. My mind keeps cycling through the same revelation: "He heard my prayers! He heard my prayers! HE HEARD MY PRAYERS!"

Which prayers specifically? I must admit I don't pray as often as I should. I recently started kneeling for prayer on Thursday mornings before facilitating Bible study, beginning with the Lord's Prayer and ending with requests for direction and wisdom so I won't distort God's word. But between those bookends, I speak to God. I honestly thanking Him for blessings, making specific requests, confessing my sins, sharing things I might not tell anyone else.

I remember my inadequacy at public prayer. Once, I was asked to give a closing prayer during Bible study, I awkwardly asked everyone to recite the Lord's Prayer with me instead. My mother later tried to encourage me, sharing how she learned to pray publicly using A.C.T.S. Adoration, Confession, Thanksgiving, and Surrender. I never developed that gift like my cousin, who was ordained as an intercessory minister and could pray long, powerful prayers.

But I talk to God like He's sitting right beside me. In my car. While cooking. When worry consumes me. Before earpieces became common, I probably looked like I was talking to myself. Now I can walk through a mall having spiritual conversations without anyone thinking twice.

"He heard my prayers!" The joy explodes within me. GOD HEARD MY PRAYERS!

But the joy is tempered by uncertainty, which prayers did He hear? This past year has been so difficult. I've asked God for help with everything imaginable.

Yes, I asked for God's help! Days when I didn't think I'd survive. Days when I didn't want to survive. Moving from one crisis to another, barely holding on. Death. Disease. Destruction. All the D's. And COVID-19, the C, that turned every day into the same nightmare.

Yes, I cried out for God's help! I felt like screaming, "God, can't You see the ugliness of this world?" Like the Prophet Habakkuk: "How long, LORD, must I call for help, but you do not listen? Or cry out to you, 'Violence!' but you do not save? Why do you make me look at injustice? Why do you tolerate wrongdoing?"

This was my year of mourning, of devastating loss in more ways than I can count.

But God thought enough of me to command His angels to help... ME! Prisha stated it so matter-of-factly, so routinely, as if divine intervention was perfectly normal. But it doesn't diminish how monumentally important this revelation is to me.

Actually, this confirmation doesn't surprise me as much as it moves me. As a child, I told my parents I had a guardian angel. As I grew older, I stopped feeling that presence, stopped believing in angels. I can't pinpoint when faith gave way to doubt, but it happened gradually, insidiously.

There's an old saying: "Just because you don't believe it doesn't make it any less real."

All this time I've been afraid, anxious, unable to sleep, needing faith to believe. Now I discover God not only heard my prayers but responded by commanding His angels to intervene in my life.

But Prisha mentioned an "especially important job." What job could I possibly do? What skills do I have that could make any difference in God's heavenly order? Why would I be given an important assignment? Does God know I'm a failure at so many things?

I still can't speak. My mouth remains open, my mind spinning with questions and revelations that threaten to overwhelm my ability to process them.

"The trial isn't finished," Prisha reminds us gently. "The three woes are still coming. Whatever jobs we've been given, whatever purposes brought us here, they're connected to what's about to unfold when the trial reconvenes."

I can hear the herald's voice beginning to echo through the dining hall, still faint but growing stronger. The intermission is drawing to a close.

Benjamin reaches across the table and gently touches my hand. "Andrea, are you ready to discover what your 'especially important job' might be? Because I think we're about to find out."

The warmth and peace of this fellowship has prepared me for something I couldn't have imagined when this journey began. Whatever revelation awaits, whatever role I'm meant to play in the final movements of humanity's trial, I'm no longer facing it alone.

I have my Guide. I have guardian angels. I have fellow witnesses.

And most incredibly of all, I have a God. My God, who heard my prayers.

The question now is what can I do, what difference can I make when the three trumpets sound, what task will be required, how will the knowledge of the trial of man impact the ultimate conclusion?

24

---•---

TABLE MATES – ISHITA

As I take a moment to think about all that has happened, I glance over this magnificent dining hall that appears to stretch out before me. It is vast enough to encompass entire city blocks, filled with more souls than I've ever seen in one place. Yet despite the overwhelming crowds, there is an undeniable sense of peace and joy that permeates the atmosphere. I didn't realize, until now, that there is soft music playing in the background. I can hear harps, horns, and vocals. The music is beautiful. As I listen, I reflect on what has happened and the souls before me, sitting at the   table.

The herald's words still echo in my mind: "The wise seek knowledge with all their heart, and those who truly understand listen carefully to learn." As I look around at my tablemates, I sense we've been brought together for a purpose beyond mere fellowship.

The manna we've shared has nourished more than our bodies; it has prepared our spirits for what's to come. But there's something else happening here, something deeper than physical sustenance. I notice Benjamin exchanging a meaningful look with Prisha, as if they were talking to one another.

"An intermission from witnessing humanity's trial should be a time of rest," Prisha says gently, her voice carrying an otherworldly authority. "But I believe we should share something more substantial. Sometimes the heaviest burdens become lighter when spoken aloud, and the most difficult truths reveal the greatest strength."

She looks around our table with eyes that seem to sparkle like the stars. Speaking to the invited guest, she said, "Please. Would you share details about your lives that were particularly difficult? Not to dwell in past pain, but to understand how you survived, how you overcame, how you found your way to this sacred gathering." The request hangs in the air like both a challenge and an invitation.

One by one, the Invited Guests begin to speak. Each voice threading together a tapestry of human resilience that will serve as testimony not just to each individual journey, but to the indestructible nature of hope itself.

ISHITA: The Girl Who Learned to Breathe Again

The village dust clung to everything, walls, windows, the folds of Ishita's green and gold salwar kameez as she walked the familiar path home. At seventeen, she moved with the unconscious grace of youth, her thick hair swaying against her shoulders, catching glints of the dying sun. Her brown eyes held depths that seemed older than her years, though she couldn't have known then how much deeper that sadness would grow.

The British accent that flavored her Hindi, a remnant of her English-medium schooling, would later sound strange in London. But on that evening near New Delhi, it was simply part of who she was: a village girl with dreams that stretched beyond the narrow lanes of her world.

The Darkness

The old truck squatted by the roadside like a rusted predator. She had passed it countless times before, never imagining it would become the stage for her nightmare. The grab came without warning, rough hands, the metallic taste of fear flooding her mouth as she was dragged into the shadows.

Five men. The number would burn itself into her memory, along with their faces, their voices, the smell of tobacco and cheap alcohol that clung to their clothes. They beat her until resistance became impossible, until her body was nothing more than broken angles against the truck's corroded floor. One after another, they stole pieces of her soul.

When it was over, they left her there, discarded like refuse among the debris of the truck bed. Blood matted her hair. Her green kameez, torn and stained, barely covered her bruised skin. The white sandals she had worn so proudly that morning lay scattered, one missing entirely.

In the suffocating darkness, she forced herself to move. Each step home was agony, but she walked, stumbled, crawled when necessary, driven by an instinct deeper than pain.

The Silence

Her mother's scream echoed through their small house when Ishita collapsed at the threshold. But after that first raw sound of grief, a different kind of violence began: the violence of silence.

Her father paced their courtyard like a caged animal, his shame radiating outward in waves. "What did you do?" The question hung in the air like smoke. "Did you encourage them? Did you dress improperly? Walk where you shouldn't have walked?"

Each word was another wound. Her mother wept as she bathed Ishita's broken body, her tears mixing with the water that ran pink down the drain. But even her mother's tenderness carried the weight of unspoken fears: Who will marry her now? What family would want damaged goods?

The police station remained unvisited. The family's reputation mattered more than justice, more than truth, certainly more than Ishita's healing. The community's potential whispers terrified her parents more than their daughter's actual screams had.

The Descent

Days blurred into weeks. Ishita's physical wounds began to close, the cuts scabbed over, the bruises faded from purple to yellow to nothing. But her spirit retreated deeper into darkness with each passing hour.

She stopped eating. Stopped speaking. When her uncles and male cousins visited, she would flee to the farthest corner of the house, her heart hammering against her ribs until they left. The men she had once laughed with, once trusted, now seemed like threats lurking in familiar faces.

Sleep brought no relief, only the truck, the hands, the weight of bodies she couldn't fight off. She would wake screaming, her sheets soaked with sweat and terror.

Her parents watched their daughter disappear before their eyes, but they remained paralyzed by their own shame and fear. The village carried on around them, oblivious to the ghost that Ishita had become.

The Exile

London arrived not as salvation but as another form of abandonment. Her parents spoke of opportunities, of a fresh start, but Ishita understood the truth: she was being removed like a stain they couldn't wash clean.

The flight stretched endless hours over dark oceans. She pressed her face to the window and wondered if the girl who had walked that village path still existed somewhere below the clouds, or if she had died in that truck and everything since was just an echo.

The Light

Her Aunt Priya stood in Heathrow's arrivals hall like a beacon. Where Ishita's parents had seen only shame, Priya saw a survivor. Where they had whispered of damaged goods, she spoke of healing.

"You are not what happened to you," Priya said on that first night, holding Ishita as she sobbed. "You are what you choose to become from this moment forward."

The Christianity that Priya had embraced offered concepts foreign to Ishita's Hindu upbringing: grace without earning, forgiveness without penance, worth that couldn't be stolen or diminished. But more importantly, Priya introduced her to the women's survivor group—a circle of faces that had seen the same darkness.

The Awakening

The first time Ishita spoke her story aloud in that London community center, surrounded by women who nodded with recognition rather than judgment, something shifted. The words that had festered like infected wounds in her silence finally found air and light.

"I was raped," she said, and the ceiling didn't collapse. The earth didn't split open. She was still breathing, still whole in ways that mattered more than her attackers could ever understand.

Other voices joined hers, women from different countries, different circumstances, but united by the peculiar strength that comes from surviving the unsurvivable. They had rebuilt their lives not despite what happened to them, but because they refused to let those moments define their worth.

The Return

Ishita's healing wasn't linear or complete, trauma rarely allows for such neat conclusions. But she learned to carry her scars without shame, to speak her truth without apology. The girl who had walked that village path was gone, it was true. But the woman who emerged from that London circle was something new: tested, scarred, but undeniably alive.

Her British accent, once a curiosity in her Indian village, now carried stories of survival across oceans. Her brown eyes still held sadness, but it was tempered now with something harder to describe: the particular wisdom that comes from having walked through hell and chosen to keep walking.

The darkness hadn't disappeared, it never would entirely. But Ishita had learned that even in the deepest night, dawn was possible. And sometimes, that possibility was enough to light the way forward.

25

TABLE MATES - HO SUNG

Ho Sung's gentle smile belied the steel in his spine. At 5'5" and 145 pounds, he appeared fragile in his simple black blazer that hung loose on his small frame. But the red shirt underneath seemed to pulse with an inner fire, and his eyes held the quiet strength of someone who had stared into the abyss of human cruelty and somehow crawled back toward light. His hands, scarred and discolored from years of brutal labor, traced invisible patterns on the table as he gathered the courage to speak.

"I was born in hell," he said simply, his voice soft but unwavering. "Hoeryong concentration camp in North Korea. Some people are born into poverty. I was born into a system designed to slowly murder the human soul, one breath at a time."

His gaze remained downcast, almost submissive, as the weight of memory settled over him. "My parents were teachers before they became ghosts. My father taught mathematics in Pyongyang. He believed education could change the world. My mother taught literature, filling children's minds with stories of heroes and hope. They were intellectuals, which made them dangerous in a regime that demanded only blind obedience."

The dining hall seemed to lean in as Ho Sung's voice grew darker. "They were arrested when my mother was eight months pregnant with me. Their crime? My father had questioned a governmental policy in a faculty meeting. Just questioned it, not openly defied, not protested, just asked if there might be a better way. That was enough to brand our entire family as 'unreliable elements,' traitors to the state."

He paused, his scarred hands clenching and unclenching. "They were supposed to be executed. But someone in the administration had a crueler idea. Why kill them quickly when you could destroy them slowly? So they were sent to Hoeryong, to the farming sector called Naksaeng-ri, Sawul-ri, where they would work until they died, and their children would be born into the same living nightmare."

The brutality of the camp unfolded through his words like a map of human suffering. Families crammed into barracks that were little more than concrete tombs, sleeping bodies pressed against strangers, no privacy, no dignity, no escape from the stench of unwashed humanity and human waste. The outhouses were holes in the ground that reeked of death itself, and in winter, prisoners risked frostbite just to relieve themselves.

"My sister, too, was born in that place," Ho Sung continued, his voice barely above a whisper. "I was five when she arrived in this world, already wasting away from malnutrition. I have no memory of her alive and healthy, only the sound of her cough, wet and rattling, that echoed through our barrack at night. She died when I was seven, her body so small they buried her in a rice sack."

His mother's story was a slow-motion tragedy of sacrifice and starvation. "She gave me everything," he said, tears beginning to trace down his cheeks. "Every grain of corn meal, every scrap of potato peel she could scavenge. She told me stories about the books she used to teach, about princes and dragons and happy endings, even as her body consumed itself to keep me alive. I watched her grow thinner and thinner, her eyes growing larger in her hollow face, until one autumn morning she simply didn't wake up. She died with her hand on my head, as if blessing me one last time."

His father's death was more violent, more sudden. "A tractor overturned in the fields. My father was underneath it, when it happened. His leg crushed to a pulp. In the outside world, it would have been a serious injury requiring surgery. In the camp, it was a death sentence. They left him in the dirt, no medical care, no pain relief, just waiting for an infection to finish what the accident had started. I sat with him for three days, watching gangrene turn his leg black, listening to him deliriously recite mathematical equations as fever consumed his mind."

By the time Ho Sung was fifteen, death had become as familiar as the daily rations. "Friends would simply disappear, beaten to death for stealing food, worked to death in the fields, or executed for attempting escape. Death wasn't just present in the camp; it was the camp's primary product. Hope was a luxury none of us could afford."

Then came the whisper that changed everything. Two prisoners had actually escaped and survived. "It was like hearing that someone had flown to the moon," Ho Sung said, his voice taking on an almost mystical quality. "Impossible, but somehow true. That night, lying on my straw mat, listening to the rats scurrying in the walls, I made a decision that would either kill me or set me free."

The planning was meticulous, born of desperation and years of observation. He studied the guards' routines with the precision of a military strategist, memorized the height of every blade of grass along the fence line. He secretly ate vegetables from the fields to build what little strength his malnourished body could manage.

"The day I chose was overcast, gray clouds hiding the sun like a funeral shroud. I positioned myself at the very front of the work line, as far from the guards as possible. As we bent down to work the soil, I began to lower myself gradually, inch by inch, until I was flat against the earth like a corpse."

What followed was a masterpiece of desperate courage. "I became something less than human, a shadow, a worm, a ghost crawling through the dirt. Right arm forward, right knee bent, push with the toes. Left arm forward, left knee bent, push. Over and over, inch by inch, certain that any second I would hear the crack of a rifle and feel my life explode out of my body."

The fence loomed before him like the gates of another world. "I found a section where the bottom wire had pulled loose from its anchor. I tested it with a blade of grass, no electricity. My heart was beating so loud I was certain the guards would hear it. I turned perpendicular to the fence, made myself as narrow as possible, and pulled the wire toward me while pushing my body underneath with my feet. The metal scraped against my spine, tearing through my shirt and skin, but I didn't dare make a sound."

Once beyond the fence, true terror began. "I was in no-man's land now. If they found me, there would be no trial, no questions, just a bullet in the back of the head. I crawled through vegetation that seemed to stretch on forever, thorns tearing at my skin, my body screaming from exhaustion, but I couldn't stop. I wouldn't stop."

When he finally stood and ran, it was with the desperation of a man fleeing the very gates of hell. "I ran until I tasted blood in my mouth, until my legs gave out beneath me, until I heard something that sounded like salvation, the rushing water of the Tumen River."

The river presented its own impossible choice. "I stood on the bank and wept like a child. The water was dark and cold, moving fast enough to drown a strong swimmer, and I had never learned to swim. But behind me was certain death and ahead was at least the possibility of life."

The log that appeared seemed like divine intervention. "It was trapped in the shallows, thick enough to support my weight if I was careful. I stripped off my shirt, it was all I had to offer as gratitude to whatever god had delivered this miracle. I climbed onto that log like it was Noah's ark, balancing on my stomach with my hands and feet trailing in the water, using them like paddles to guide my makeshift raft."

Night fell as he drifted downstream, cold and exhausted, certain he would die on that log. "But I held on. I held on because my mother had died to keep me alive, because my father had whispered mathematical formulas to the end believing that knowledge mattered, because my sister deserved to be remembered by someone who escaped the place that killed her."

Dawn brought salvation in the form of a Chinese fisherman. "He pulled me from the water like I was a drowned cat, his eyes wide with recognition. He knew immediately what I was, another ghost fleeing the nightmare across the river. He had heard the stories, seen other refugees, but I was perhaps the youngest he had encountered."

What followed was Ho Sung's first experience of unconditional human kindness. The fisherman gave him food and water, communicating through gestures and expressions of compassion that transcended language. "I wept as I ate," Ho Sung remembered, "not from hunger but from the shock of being treated as human."

When they reached the Chinese shore in Jilin province, the fisherman's protection became even more profound. "He gave me his own shirt, made me carry his fishing equipment so we would look like a father and son returning from a day on the water. His wife and children welcomed me into their home without question, understanding immediately that they were harboring a soul in desperate need of sanctuary."

The bath that followed became Ho Sung's spiritual rebirth. "I never knew what it meant to be clean. The fisherman's wife prepared the water, laid out clean clothes, then left me alone with her husband. He could have simply pointed to the tub and walked away, but instead he stayed. He stayed and helped me learn how to bath like a human."

Ho Sung's voice broke as he described the tenderness that followed. "I climbed into that tub and curled into a ball, my knees to my chest, arms wrapped around myself like I was trying to hold my broken soul together. The fisherman sat beside me on an old wooden box and began to pour warm water over my head and back, over and over, like a baptism."

The intimacy was profound but pure. One human being ministering to another's desperate need for dignity. "He washed my hair with soap that smelled like flowers, worked the matted filth from my scalp with gentle fingers. I looked up at him through the water streaming down my face, and I saw something I had forgotten existed, genuine care for another person."

The fisherman showed Ho Sung how to wash himself, how to clean behind his ears, how to scrub away years of accumulated grime and degradation. "When he cleaned my back, moving the soapy cloth in gentle circles, I understood for the first time what love looked like in action. Not romantic love, not the love of family, this was something else, something holy. It was the love of one human being for another, simply because we share the same frail humanity."

When Ho Sung stood to wash the rest of his body, the fisherman's eyes remained kind, never judging the skeletal frame, the protruding ribs, the scars and bruises that mapped his suffering. "He looked at the dirty water, it was black with the filth of my captivity, and I thought he would be disgusted. Instead, he simply helped me step out and wrapped me in clean clothes that felt like clouds against my skin."

The haircut and shave that followed completed his transformation. "When he was finished, I looked in a cracked mirror on the wall and saw a different person. Not the starving prisoner who had crawled under a fence, but a young man with potential, with a future, with worth."

For several days, the fisherman's family sheltered him. "They taught me to clean fish, to make myself useful despite the language barrier. The fisherman's wife would smile at me while I worked, sometimes touching my shoulder gently to show approval. Their children would peek around corners to watch me, curious but not afraid. I was learning to be part of a family again."

The journey to Jilin City on the back of a motorcycle marked his final passage to freedom. "The organization that met me there specialized in helping people like me, ghosts from across the river who had somehow found their way back to the land of the living. They had medical care, counselors, programs to help us build new lives."

Ho Sung looked around the table, his gentle smile returning. "When they finally took me to that organization, I understood something profound: freedom isn't just about escaping physical bars. It's about remembering that you have value, that your life matters, that you deserve to dream of tomorrow. But more than that, it's about learning that there are people in this world who will risk everything to show love to a stranger, simply because love is the most powerful force in the universe."

His voice grew stronger as he concluded. "That fisherman and his family didn't just save my body from the river. They saved my soul from despair. They showed me that even in a world capable of unspeakable cruelty, there are still people who choose kindness. And that choice, that simple, revolutionary choice to treat another human being with dignity, that's what makes freedom possible."

26

Table Mates - Ling

Ling adjusts the delicate gold pha chung hang blouse, its purple accents catching the afternoon light streaming through the conference room windows. At forty-seven, she carries herself with quiet dignity, her traditional chut Thai a deliberate choice, a reclamation of her heritage on her own terms. The intricate embroidery along the hem of her ruean ton skirt tells stories of resilience, each golden thread a testament to survival.

Her curly black hair, now pinned in an elegant bun, frames a face that time has softened but never broken. Behind large, studious glasses, her mismatched eyes, one brown, one green, hold depths that few dare to explore. Those who look closely might notice the thin scar running from beneath her right ear to her chin, a reminder of a past she's learned to carry rather than hide from.

Today, she speaks to a room full of advocates, lawmakers, and survivors. But her story begins far from these polished halls, in a place where childhood ended before it truly began.

The Sound of Childhood

The village south of Bangkok existed in a world apart, where the line between innocence and sexual encounters blurred like watercolors in the rain. For Ling, home was a collection of rooms behind thin walls, where laughter mixed with sounds, she didn't yet understand.

"Nong Ling, come help me with the washing," called Mae Siriporn, one of the many women who mothered the children who belonged to no one and everyone. The brothel's children were raised collectively, like a flock of sparrows who nested wherever they found warmth.

Ling's earliest memories were painted in primary colors: the red dust of the court-yard where she played with broken toys, the yellow fabric of Mae Niran's favorite dress, the blue of the sky she glimpsed between laundry lines heavy with drying sheets. The women who cared for her spoke in hushed tones about her mother, a ghost who had given life and then departed, leaving only questions and a child with eyes like precious stones.

At night, the building came alive with different sounds. Ling and the other children learned to sleep through the symphony of adult business: footsteps on creaking floorboards, muffled voices negotiating in multiple languages, the occasional cry that could have been pleasure or pain, they were too young to know the difference.

"Why do the women work at night, Mae?" six-year-old Ling once asked.

Mae Siriporn's hands paused in her mending. "They do what they must to survive, lúk. We all do what we must."

The Weight of Understanding

Childhood has a way of ending not with a single blow, but with the slow accumula-tion of truth. For Ling, understanding came in fragments, overheard conversations, glimpses through doorways, the gradual realization that her world was not the same as the one beyond the brothel's walls.

At eleven, Mae Kanya pulled her aside with hands that smelled of jasmine soap and desperation. "You're growing up, Ling. Soon you'll need to earn your place here."

The words settled in her stomach like stones. Earn her place? This was the only home she'd ever known, the only family she'd ever had. Where else would she go?

Her new role began simply enough, carrying water from the well, her small hands learning to balance heavy buckets without spilling. She washed endless piles of towels and sheets, scrubbed floors on her hands and knees, and learned to move through the brothel like a shadow, invisible when the men came calling.

The women began to look at her differently, their gazes mixing affection with something that felt like mourning. Mae Siriporn would stroke her unusual curly hair and whisper prayers in Thai that Ling didn't recognize. Mae Niran taught her to braid flowers into chains, as if beauty could be a shield against the inevitable.

"Your eyes are like jewels," Mae Kanya told her one evening as they folded laundry together. "Brown earth and green forest. You have your mother's gift for catching attention."

Ling didn't understand why this made Mae Kanya cry.

The Moment Innocence Shattered

The night Ling first witnessed what the women's "work" truly meant, the world tilted on its axis and never quite righted itself again.

She had been carrying clean towels to room seven when the door stood ajar. Through the gap, she saw Mae Siriporn, kind Mae Siriporn who braided her hair and told her stories, pinned beneath a man whose face was red with exertion and anger. His hands gripped her roughly, one holding her in place while the other yanked her hair so hard that Ling could see the pain etched in every line of Mae Siriporn's face.

The sounds Mae Siriporn made were not sounds of pleasure, despite what the man seemed to believe. They were the sounds of someone enduring, of someone who had learned to perform survival. Her eyes, when they met Ling's through the crack in the door, held a message that would haunt the girl forever: This is what becomes of us. This is what waits for you.

The towels fell from Ling's hands like snow. The man never paused, never acknowledged her presence. Mae Siriporn's slight gesture, a barely perceptible wave of her hand, sent Ling fleeing to her corner of the yard, where she sat shaking until dawn.

That night, the sounds of the brothel changed. What had once been background noise became a symphony of pain she could no longer unhear.

The Price of Beauty

By thirteen, Ling had grown tall and striking, her unusual features marking her as something special in the brothel's economy of flesh. The men began to notice her, their eyes following her movements with a hunger that made her skin crawl.

"She's ready," she heard Mae Kanya whisper to the mama-san one evening. "Look how they watch her. We could ask for a premium."

Ready. The word echoed in Ling's mind like a death sentence.

The first man who bought her was American, his wedding ring catching the lamplight as he reached for her with hands that shook with excitement and shame. He spoke to her in English she didn't understand, his voice gentle even as his actions were not.

"You're beautiful," he whispered, as if the words could transform transaction into romance. "So beautiful."

Beautiful. The word became a curse.

Night after night, they came. Businessmen from Bangkok who spoke of their wives while they hurt her. Tourists with cameras and fantasies about exotic girls. Local men who brought their sons to "become men" at her expense. Each promised her things, love, escape, a better life, but they only left her with bruises and the bitter taste of lies.

Twenty men some nights. Sometimes more. Ling learned to separate her mind from her body, to drift somewhere high above the ceiling where their hands couldn't reach her. She became an expert at reading faces, predicting violence, calculating survival.

The other women taught her their secrets: how to make the pain bearable, how to avoid the worst injuries, how to hide money in places the mama-san wouldn't think to look. But mostly, they taught her to endure.

"This is not your fault," Mae Siriporn would whisper as she tended Ling's wounds. "This is not who you are."

But at thirteen, Ling couldn't tell the difference anymore.

Rescue and Rebirth

The raid came on a Tuesday that had started like any other. Ling was scrubbing blood from a sheet when she heard the commotion, shouting in Thai and English, the sound of doors being kicked in, the mama-san screaming orders that no one was following.

She pressed herself against the wall as uniformed officers and aid workers flooded through the brothel. A woman with kind eyes and a translator's badge knelt beside her, speaking in gentle Thai.

"You're safe now. No one will hurt you anymore."

Safe. Another word that had lost all meaning.

Ling was carried from the only home she'd ever known wrapped in a thin sheet, her body shaking not from cold but from the terrifying prospect of an unknown world. As the van pulled away from the brothel, she watched through the rear window as her childhood disappeared forever.

Questions Without Answers

The shelter in Bangkok was clean and quiet, too quiet for someone who had learned to sleep through chaos. Ling found herself lying awake at night, listening for sounds that never came, waiting for violence that didn't arrive.

The questions began almost immediately. Social workers, police officers, aid workers, they all wanted to know the same things, asked in different ways, as if repetition could unlock secrets Ling didn't know she possessed.

"How many girls were there?"

"Who ran the operation?"

"Can you identify the clients?"

"Why didn't you try to leave?"

The last question stung the most. Why didn't she leave? Where would a child go? How do you escape from the only world you've ever known? How do you run from a place that, despite everything, contained the only mothers you'd ever had?

Ling's answers came in fragments, pieces of a puzzle she was still trying to understand herself. The investigators grew frustrated with her silence, her inability to provide the clear narrative they needed for their reports.

But some stories don't fit into neat categories. Some truths resist the tidy boxes that justice systems require.

Learning to Live

Recovery was not a destination but a daily choice. At the shelter, Ling met other survivors, women and girls who carried similar scars, who understood the language of trauma without words.

She learned to read properly, her hunger for knowledge surprising everyone, including herself. Books became doorways to other worlds, other possibilities. She devoured stories of women who had survived, who had built lives from the ashes of their childhoods.

Slowly, tentatively, Ling began to speak about her experiences, not to investigators seeking evidence, but to counselors helping her reclaim her voice. Each conversation was an act of rebellion against those who had tried to reduce her to silence and shame.

"You are not what happened to you," her counselor, Khun Pranee, would remind her. "You are what you choose to become."

Epilogue: The Woman Who Speaks

Years later, standing before rooms full of advocates and lawmakers, Ling wears her traditional Thai dress like armor. Each speaking engagement is an act of defiance, a refusal to let her story end in the brothel where it began.

She speaks for Mae Siriporn, who taught her that kindness could survive even in the darkest places. She speaks for the other children who didn't make it out, whose voices were silenced before they could learn to use them. She speaks for the thirteen-year-old girl who thought beauty was a curse, who couldn't imagine a future beyond pain.

The scar on her face, a parting gift from a client's ring, no longer feels like a mark of shame. It's become a reminder of survival, proof that wounds can heal even when they leave permanent traces.

"My name is Ling," she begins each speech, her voice steady despite the tremor in her hands. "I am a survivor. I am here to tell you that behind every statistic about human trafficking is a person who deserves dignity, justice, and the chance to reclaim their story."

In the audience, she sees faces that mirror her past, advocates who care, officials who listen, and occasionally, other survivors finding their courage to speak. Her mismatched eyes, brown earth and green forest, hold all the women she's been: the child who played in red dust, the girl who carried water buckets, the teenager who learned to survive, and the woman who chose to transform her pain into purpose.

This is Ling's story. It is not just hers, it belongs to every person who has been bought and sold, to every child forced to grow up too fast, to every survivor who finds the strength to speak truth to power.

And it is far from over.

27

TABLE MATES - SIMBA

He begins his story at his rebirth. In the sprawling refugee camp outside Juba, Simba cuts an imposing figure despite his youth. At twenty-two, he stands nearly seven feet tall, his frame lean but strong, carrying himself with the quiet dignity of someone who has seen too much too early. His skin is the deep ebony of his Dinka ancestors, and when he smiles, which he does more often now, it transforms his angular face completely. The cream and burgundy jalabiya he wears flows around his tall frame like royal robes, the burgundy turban adding to his regal bearing.

Children flock to him as he moves through the camp, their small hands reaching for his long fingers, their voices calling "Ustaz Simba! Teacher Simba!" He has become their anchor in a world that has forgotten how to be gentle with the young.

But there are nights when Simba wakes gasping, his heart hammering against his ribs like a caged bird desperate for freedom. In those moments, he is not the patient teacher or the gentle giant. He is nine years old again, standing in the ashes of his village, learning that childhood ends not with birthdays but with the sound of gunfire.

When the Sky Caught Fire

The morning that changed everything began like any other in their small Dinka village along the White Nile. Simba's mother, Nyandeng, was grinding sorghum for the day's bread, her voice joining the other women in a traditional work song that had been passed down through generations. His father, Deng, sat with the elders discussing the rains and the cattle, their voices a comforting murmur in the early morning air.

Simba was practicing his letters in the dirt with a stick, preparing for another day at the small school the missionaries had built. He loved the way the English alphabet curved and straight-lined across the ground, loved the way his teacher, Sister Mary, would nod approvingly when he read aloud.

The first sound was like thunder, but the sky was clear. Then came the screaming.

The Arab militias descended on their village like locusts, their horses kicking up clouds of dust that mixed with the smoke beginning to rise from burning huts. Simba watched, frozen, as men with rifles and machetes swept through his world like a deadly storm.

"Run, mon!" his mother screamed, using the Dinka word for child as she pushed him toward the tall grass at the village's edge. "Run and don't look back!"

But Simba couldn't help but look back. He saw his father try to shield his mother with his own body. He saw the muzzle flash. He saw them both fall.

The sound that tore from his throat was not quite human; it was the cry of something breaking apart from the inside. But he ran, crashing through the grass, thorns tearing at his skin, his breath coming in desperate gasps as the world he knew disappeared in flames behind him

The Desert of Lost Children

The "salvation camp" was hell disguised as mercy. Located deep in the Sahara, it was meant to "rehabilitate" war orphans, to break them down and build them back up as tools of war. The concrete buildings baked under the merciless sun, and the nights brought cold that cut through their thin clothes like knives.

Simba learned new words here: hunger, thirst, obedience, punishment. He learned that a nine-year-old's ribs could show through his skin, that hope could be rationed like water, that dreams could be beaten out of you with methodical precision.

The commanders spoke of glory, of revenge, of righteous war. But Simba only remembered the weight of the rifle they put in his hands, heavier than any textbook, heavier than the responsibility of childhood. His fingers, once used to trace letters in the dirt, learned to strip and clean weapons with the mechanical precision of the traumatized.

At night, pressed against other skeletal children in dormitories that smelled of fear and unwashed bodies, Simba would close his eyes and try to remember his mother's work song. But increasingly, all he could hear was the sound of gunfire, the crack of boot on bone, the whispered prayers of children who no longer believed anyone was listening.

Brothers in Arms

When the SPLA recruited him at twelve, Simba thought he was being saved. The Christian soldiers spoke of liberation, of fighting for their people, of avenging the dead. They gave him a uniform that hung on his growing frame, boots that were too big, and a purpose that felt like redemption.

But war, Simba learned, was war, regardless of which side claimed righteousness. He was paired with Kwame and Juma, boys like himself, orphaned and recruited, trying to find family in the brotherhood of survival

Kwame was fourteen, built like a boxer with quick hands and quicker laughter that never quite masked the haunted look in his eyes. He came from a village near the Ethiopian border, spoke three languages, and could strip a rifle blindfolded. At night, he would whisper stories about his little sister who used to braid flowers into his hair.

Juma was eleven, small for his age but fierce. His parents had been teachers before the war, and he still carried a battered English primer in his pocket, the only thing he'd saved from his burning home. He could read better than most of the adult soldiers and had memorized entire passages of poetry that he would recite during the long, terrifying nights.

They became a unit, these three, not by choice but by necessity, bound together by shared trauma and the desperate need for something resembling family. In a world where children were weapons, they managed to remain human by protecting humanity in each other.

Martyrdom

The mission briefing came on a Tuesday that felt like any other day of war. Commander Garang spread a hand-drawn map across the wooden table, his finger tracing routes and marking targets with the casual precision of someone ordering dinner.

"Government checkpoint here," he said, tapping a spot where two dirt roads intersected. "Nine soldiers, three vehicles. They're choking off our supply line to the eastern villages."

Simba stared at the map, trying to read his fate in the roughly sketched lines. Beside him, he could feel Kwame's leg bouncing with nervous energy, could hear Juma's breathing quicken.

"Suicide mission," Garang continued, and the words fell into the silence like stones into still water. "We need that checkpoint eliminated. Completely."

The plan was brutally simple. Kwame and Juma would approach the checkpoint together, carrying the homemade vest packed with fertilizer, nails, and enough explosive force to shred everything within a thirty-foot radius. Simba would position himself in the grass with his rifle, tasked with eliminating any survivors who might try to flee or call for reinforcements.

"All three of you might die," Garang said with the matter-of-fact tone of someone discussing the weather. "Probably will. But this is bigger than any of us."

That night, they sat in their shared tent while Simba carefully mixed the chemicals that would end his friends' lives. His hands shook as he worked, and Kwame watched every movement with the intensity of someone memorizing his own death.

"I keep thinking about my mother's ugali," Kwame whispered. "How she used to make it with extra honey when I was sick."

Juma pulled out his battered primer and began reading aloud: "The boy stood on the burning deck, whence all but he had fled..." His voice cracked on the words, but he continued, the familiar rhythm of poetry a shield against the horror of what tomorrow would bring.

Simba said nothing. He focused on the precise measurements, the careful timing, the technical aspects that kept him from thinking about what he was building. This vest would tear his brother apart molecule by molecule. These chemicals would erase fourteen years of Kwame's laughter, his dreams, his stories about the sister who braided flowers.

Walk of Death

They left the forest outpost at midnight, moving through the darkness like ghosts. Kwame wore the vest under his shirt, its weight making him move differently, more carefully, as if he were carrying his own gravestone. Juma had volunteered to go with him, to face the end together rather than alone.

The miles passed in silence broken only by their footsteps and the sound of their breathing. Simba carried his rifle and the weight of knowing he would survive this night while his brothers would not. The injustice of it burned in his throat like acid.

"Remember when we caught that fish in the river?" Juma said suddenly, his voice barely above a whisper. "And we cooked it over the fire and pretended we were just boys going camping?"

"You burned it," Kwame replied, and Simba could hear the smile in his voice. "Worst fish I ever ate."

"Best meal of my life," Simba said, and meant it.

They walked on, these three children dressed as soldiers, carrying death and memory in equal measure. Above them, the stars wheeled in their ancient patterns, indifferent to the small tragedy unfolding below.

As they approached the checkpoint, Simba felt time begin to slow and stretch. Every step carried them closer to the moment when his world would split apart, before and after, the time when he had brothers and the endless time when he would carry their ghosts.

The Long Wait

Simba crawled into position in the tall grass, his rifle trained on the checkpoint two hundred meters away. From here, he could see the guards, young men not much older than himself, smoking cigarettes and talking quietly in Arabic. In the three vehicles, he could make out the silhouettes of sleeping soldiers.

The night was perfectly clear, the air still and heavy with the promise of violence. Simba's finger rested on the trigger, and he tried not to think about the fact that he was about to become a killer in service of his friends' deaths.

Kwame and Juma approached from the east, moving with the careful precision they had practiced a hundred times. Even from this distance, Simba could see the tension in their young bodies, the way they held themselves like men walking to their own execution.

Because that's exactly what they were doing.

At fifty meters from the checkpoint, they stopped. Simba watched through his rifle scope as his brothers turned to look at each other one last time. Even at this distance, he could see Kwame's hands shaking as he reached for the detonator hidden in the vest.

Juma said something, too quiet for Simba to hear, but he could guess. A prayer, maybe. Or a joke. Juma always made jokes when he was scared.

Thirty meters.

Twenty.

Simba's heart hammered against his ribs so hard he was afraid the guards would hear it. His hands were slick with sweat despite the cool night air. Every muscle in his body was coiled tight, ready to fire, ready to kill, ready to witness the obliteration of everything he loved.

Ten meters.

This was it. This was the moment when childhood ended not with birthdays but with the sound of his best friends being torn apart by explosives they had built together. Simba closed his eyes for just a second, trying to memorize Kwame's laugh, Juma's voice reciting poetry, the way they looked when they thought no one was watching and they could still be boys.

He opened his eyes and waited for the world to end.

When Silence Become a Scream

Nothing happened.

Simba watched through his scope as Kwame and Juma reached the checkpoint, as the guards looked up in surprise, as his brothers raised their hands in what looked like surrender. No explosion. No flash of light. No moment of terrible brightness that would have marked the end of everything.

The guards were shouting now, rifles raised, surrounding his friends. Simba could see Kwame fumbling with something under his shirt, the detonator that wasn't working, the death that wouldn't come when summoned.

For a moment that lasted forever, Simba's finger tightened on the trigger. He could kill the guards, save his friends, change the ending of this story. But there were too many of them, and his shots would only ensure that all three of them died instead of just two.

He watched, paralyzed by impossible choices, as the guards dragged Kwame and Juma away from the checkpoint. He watched as they were forced to their knees. He watched as rifles were aimed at the backs of their heads.

The shots, when they came, were sharp and final, two cracks that split the night and Simba's world in half. He bit down on his own fist to keep from screaming, tasted blood, and felt something fundamental break apart inside his chest.

His brothers were dead. Not in the glorious explosion they had planned, not taking enemies with them, but executed like animals by the side of a dirt road while Simba lay helpless in the grass.

The guards dumped their bodies in a ditch and went back to their cigarettes and quiet conversations, as if nothing had happened. As if Kwame's dreams of seeing the world and Juma's love of poetry meant nothing. As if fifteen-year-old Simba hadn't just lost the only family he had left.

The Mathematics of Survival

Simba lay in the grass until dawn, paralyzed by grief and the terrible knowledge that he was still alive while his brothers were not. When the sun finally rose, painting the sky in colors that seemed obscene in their beauty, he began to crawl backwards through the grass, away from the checkpoint, away from the ditch where his friends lay, away from everything that had defined his world.

He walked for days, moving like a ghost through a landscape that no longer made sense. Every step carried him further from the life he had known, but no matter how far he walked, he couldn't escape the sound of those two shots, the sight of his brothers falling, the weight of being the one who survived.

The SPLA would call him a deserter if they found him. The government soldiers would kill him on sight. He was caught between armies, between loyalties, between the boy he had been and the man he was supposed to become.

When he finally collapsed near a cluster of white tents marked with UNICEF logos, Simba was more ghost than boy. The aid workers who found him spoke of trauma and healing, of education and hope. But all Simba could think about was the mathematics of survival: two shots, two deaths, one boy left behind to carry the weight of what love costs in wartime.

Learning to Live

The refugee camp became Simba's monastery, a place where he slowly learned to live with the dead. The nightmares came regularly, dreams where he saved his friends, where the detonator worked, where he made different choices. He would wake, reaching for weapons that weren't there, his body preparing for battles that existed only in memory.

Sarah, the aid worker who befriended him, understood the trauma in ways that surprised him. She had seen too many child soldiers, too many broken young men trying to re-assemble themselves from fragments.

"Survivor's guilt," she called it, as if naming it could somehow make it smaller. "It's not rational, but it's real."

"I should have saved them," Simba whispered one night after a particularly bad dream. "I had a rifle. I could have done something."

"And then all three of you would be dead," Sarah replied gently. "Your friends didn't die so you could join them. They died so you could live for all of them."

28

TABLE MATES - OLIVER

The first thing you notice about Oliver is his eyes, weathered blue. At sixty, his face tells stories he'd rather forget. Long brownish hair streaked with gray which he pulls back into a ponytail, revealing flesh tunnels in his ears and tattoos snaking up his neck like old regrets. He speaks with the slow drawl of Mobile, Alabama, though Brooklyn has been home for forty years now. When people ask about his past, he offers them coffee instead of answers.

The Foundation Cracks

Oliver's father, Jerome, had worked the fryer at Kentucky Fried Chicken for eight months when desperation finally got the better of him. He knew the closing routine by heart, the manager counts the register alone after sending the last employee home. Easy money, he told himself. Simple plan.

He arrived minutes before closing time, ski mask pulled down, .38 Special trembling in his palm. But the moment he stepped through the employee entrance, his plan began unraveling. His distinctive limp, thump-drag, thump-drag, echoed across the empty restaurant like a signature he couldn't hide.

"Don't turn around," Jerome said, trying to disguise his voice as he approached the register where his manager, Mr. Patterson, was counting the day's earnings.

Patterson's shoulders tensed. His head tilted, listening. Then came the words that shattered everything:

"Jerome? Jerome, is that you?"

The mask meant nothing. Patterson had heard that unmistakable gait a hundred times before, the limp from Jerome's childhood accident that made his right leg two inches shorter than his left.

"Don't!" Jerome's voice cracked as Patterson began to turn. "Don't turn around!"

But Patterson was already facing him, lined face showing not fear but weary disappointment. "Son, what are you doing?"

The pity in Patterson's voice triggered something primal in Jerome's panic-flooded brain. This wasn't how it was supposed to go. The manager wasn't supposed to know him, wasn't supposed to look at him with those disappointed eyes.

"I need the money," Jerome said, hating how desperate he sounded.

Patterson nodded slowly, raised his hands. "Okay, Jerome. Let me get it for you. No need for anyone to get hurt."

But when Patterson's hand moved toward something beneath the register, the silent alarm, Jerome saw betrayal everywhere.

"You pressed the alarm!" Jerome screamed. "You called the cops on me!"

"Jerome, I didn't"

"SHUT UP!"

The gun swung wild.

BANG.

The first shot caught Patterson in the chest, spinning him backward against the counter. Dark blood spread across his white uniform shirt.

"Oh God," Jerome whispered. "I didn't"

BANG.

The second shot seemed to fire itself. Patterson crumpled to the floor, breathing shallow and labored.

"Jerome," Patterson whispered, blood bubbling at the corner of his mouth. "Call... call an ambulance."

But Jerome was already running, his broken gait carrying him toward the exit as fast as his damaged leg would allow. The gun clattered to the floor behind him.

Patterson died six hours later.

Three days after that, Jerome turned himself in to police. Second-degree murder. Twenty-five to life.

His infant son Oliver was six months old when the gavel fell.

His mother, Diane, was already lost to heroin by then. She worked the streets for a pimp named Rico, trading pieces of her soul for fixes that never lasted long enough. The night she left Oliver with her father, she kissed his forehead and whispered, "Mama's gonna get clean, baby. Gonna come back for you real soon."

But addiction writes its own promises, and they're all lies.

They found her body in an abandoned house on Dauphin Street, needle still hanging from her arm.

The Last Safe Harbor

Oliver's grandfather, Samuel, was a dock worker with hands like leather and a heart soft as Sunday morning. For eight and a half years, Samuel was Oliver's entire world. They had rituals: Saturday morning pancakes, Sunday football, bedtime stories about sailors and sea monsters.

"Remember, boy," Samuel would say, adjusting Oliver's grip on the baseball, "it ain't about the strength in your arm. It's about the spin. The spin changes everything."

On a cold November evening, with the Saints trailing by fourteen, Samuel clutched his chest and pitched forward in his recliner. The massive heart attack took him before the paramedics could navigate Mobile's evening traffic.

Oliver found him during halftime, still warm, eyes fixed on a television screen full of men playing a game that suddenly meant nothing at all.

The System

What followed was a masterclass in institutional failure. Relatives passed Oliver around like a burden they couldn't afford to carry. Finally, the State of Alabama opened its arms and swallowed him whole.

Seven years. Eight foster homes. Each placement started with forced smiles and ended with packed garbage bags and social workers with tired eyes who had seen it all before.

At sixteen, Oliver had had enough. When his latest foster family was asleep, he climbed out the bedroom window with nothing but the clothes on his back and twenty-seven dollars stolen from a cookie jar. Three friends from school were driving to New York City, chasing dreams of making it big.

"You coming or not?" they asked.

Oliver looked back at the house, another temporary stop in a life full of temporary everything, and climbed into the backseat.

The Wolves

New York City in the late 1970s was a beautiful disaster. Oliver landed in Brooklyn with empty pockets and a stomach that had forgotten what full felt like. The Wolves found him first. A crew that called themselves family in the way that broken people understand family, bound not by blood but by necessity.

"You got nothing to lose," Wolf told Oliver on that first night. "That makes you dangerous. Dangerous is good in this business."

For three years, Oliver learned the streets like scripture. He moved product, ran numbers, and collected debts with the cold efficiency of someone who had nothing left to protect. The Wolves specialized in crack cocaine, manufacturing it in a converted basement laboratory.

Oliver had sworn never to touch it. His mother's face, peaceful in death but destroyed by life, haunted his dreams. But swearing and surviving are different creatures entirely.

Breaking Point

The drive-by happened on a Tuesday. Oliver was working his corner when he noticed the black Chevy Monte Carlo with distinctive silver and gold rims rolling slow down the street. Something about its movement, predatory, deliberate, made his stomach clench.

The window slid down. Sunlight caught the assault rifle's barrel, and time crystallized into slow-motion horror. Oliver dove for the nearest doorway as bullets chewed through brick and mortar.

When the shooting stopped, the silence was worse than the gunfire.

Shaun lay crumpled against a fire hydrant, his young face peaceful despite the dark pool spreading beneath his head. Big Rick was conscious but screaming, clutching his side while blood seeped between his fingers.

The aftermath was swift and merciless. Wolf docked Oliver's pay for the lost product. Business dried up overnight as customers found safer corners. The profitable corners already had crews, and Oliver was now a crew of one.

That's when the rock started whispering his name.

The First Taste

The pipe felt lighter than he'd expected. Just once, he told himself. Just enough to feel strong again, to find the courage to reclaim what was his.

The flame kissed the crack, and smoke filled his lungs like a promise.

The rush was everything they'd said and more, electric confidence flooding his veins, washing away every doubt and fear. Armed with two pistols and chemically enhanced courage, Oliver walked onto Fulton Street like a gunslinger in a modern western.

He pressed the barrel of his .38 against the nearest dealer's ear. "You got five seconds to pack up and find somewhere else to play, or I start making permanent decisions."

They scattered like roaches when the lights come on.

But as the meth wore off, reality came flooding back. He'd just made enemies of an entire crew. He was alone, and the euphoria was fading like sugar in rain.

He needed another hit. Just one more became two more became his entire stash.

The Descent

Addiction is patient. It doesn't announce itself with fanfare. It simply moves in like fog, so gradually that you don't notice the world disappearing until you're lost in gray nothing.

Oliver's world contracted to a simple equation: acquire money, acquire drugs, repeat until unconsciousness. Everything else, pride, morality, self-preservation; became negotiable commodities.

He graduated from petty theft to armed robbery. From robbery to assault. The woman on the 4 train never saw him coming, professional-looking, absorbed in a phone conversation. Her leather purse sat beside her like a wrapped present. One hundred and forty-one dollars and thirteen cents, converted to crystal within the hour.

Months blurred into each other like watercolors in rain. Oliver's body became a stranger, weight melting off his frame, skin picking scabs his fingers couldn't leave alone. He stole, robbed, assaulted people, even prostituted himself. When he robbed people, he would hit or shoot his victims too. Getting the money was no longer enough.

The Reckoning

The beatings were almost a relief when they came. Four men from the crew whose corner he'd stolen found him stumbling out of a meth house, vision blurred by three days of continuous use. They worked him over with methodical efficiency.

Oliver's last coherent thought before the darkness took him was gratitude, finally, the voices in his head had gone quiet.

Three months later, he woke up in Brooklyn Methodist Hospital, handcuffed to a bed that smelled of disinfectant and broken dreams. A detective with kind eyes and a tired face sat beside his bed, reading charges from a manila folder.

Eight counts of armed robbery. Five counts of aggravated assault. One count of second-degree murder.

"You remember any of this, son?" the detective asked.

Oliver stared at the ceiling tiles and tried to recall faces, voices, moments that might explain how he'd become someone capable of taking a human life. But there was only static where his memories should have been.

"The victim was Maria Santos. Sixty-two years old, grandmother of four. You shot her in the chest for thirty-seven dollars and a MetroCard."

Oliver closed his eyes and tried to summon some feeling, remorse, anger, anything that might prove he was still human underneath the chemical wreckage. But there was only emptiness, vast and echoing as a cathedral at midnight.

Thirty Years

The trial was a formality. Security cameras don't lie, and Oliver's fingerprints told a story that no closing argument could rewrite. Thirty years. He was twenty-two years old.

As they led him away in shackles, Oliver caught sight of Maria Santos's family in the gallery. Her daughter, maybe thirty, with Maria's same dark eyes, watched him with an expression that wasn't quite hatred but something deeper and more complicated.

Rikers Island was everything Oliver had expected and worse. But it was in this concrete hell that Oliver encountered something he hadn't felt in years: hope.

The Wednesday evening Bible study met in a room that had once been a supply closet, led by a soft-spoken man named Brother James. Oliver attended initially for the same reason everyone did, it was an hour out of his cell.

But something about Brother James's voice, weathered by compassion rather than bitterness, began working on Oliver's soul like water on stone.

"Y'all think God can't reach you in here," Brother James said. "Think you've done too much, gone too far. But that ain't how grace works. Grace ain't about deserving. Grace is about receiving what you can't earn."

The Long Road

Prison routine became Oliver's salvation. He earned his GED, then a bachelor's degree through correspondence. He learned to meditate, to process his trauma in group therapy sessions where grown men cried like children.

He wrote letters to Maria Santos's daughter, hundreds of them over the years, but never sent a single one. What could he possibly say that would matter?

Brother James kept coming to Rikers every Wednesday for twelve years, until his heart gave out. At the funeral, his widow read a letter he'd written: "Every soul is worth saving. Every person carries a spark of the divine, no matter how deeply buried. Never give up on anyone, because God never gives up on anyone."

Oliver wept for the first time in twenty years.

The Test

At forty-seven, Oliver had become a mentor to younger inmates. His biggest test came when a nineteen-year-old named Devon arrived with the same desperate hunger in his eyes that Oliver recognized from his own mirror decades earlier.

"This place gonna eat you alive," Devon announced with chemical bravado. "But I ain't going out like these other chumps."

Oliver saw himself at twenty-two in Devon's swagger. He could walk away, let the kid learn through violence what words couldn't teach. Instead, he approached Devon after dinner.

"Can I talk to you for a minute, young brother?"

They talked for three hours that first night. Oliver told Devon about crystal meth and drive-by shootings, about Maria Santos and her granddaughters, about the way addiction could make you a stranger to yourself.

It took six months, but eventually Devon started attending Bible study, then GED classes, then group therapy.

"You saved my life," Devon told Oliver the night before Oliver's parole hearing.

Oliver shook his head. "I didn't save nothing, young brother. Just shared what was shared with me."

Going Home

The parole board was composed of three people who looked like they'd rather be any-where else. Oliver sat across from them in his best prison clothes, trying to project the rehabilitation they needed to see.

"You've had an exemplary record," the chairwoman said. "However, you took a human life. Maria Santos's family has written to express their opposition to your release."

"I understand," Oliver said quietly. "I carry what I did to Mrs. Santos every day. I can't bring her back, can't undo the pain. All I can do is try to live in a way that honors her memory."

Six weeks later, the letter arrived: Parole granted.

Brooklyn, Redux

The Brooklyn that greeted Oliver in October 2009 was both familiar and foreign. Gen-trification had transformed the neighborhoods where he'd once dealt drugs. His halfway house was in Bed-Stuy, six blocks from where he'd once worked corners for the Wolves.

He found work at a community kitchen, serving meals to people whose stories echoed his own. At night, he attended NA meetings, sharing hard-won wisdom with people trying to stay clean one day at a time.

"Recovery ain't about becoming someone new," he told his sponsees. "It's about remem-bering who you were before the drugs made you forget."

The Letter

Three years after his release, an envelope arrived with no return address. Inside was a single sheet of paper and a photograph.

Mr. Williams,

My name is Carmen Santos. My mother was Maria Santos. You killed her on February 14th, 1987.

My daughter Elena, the one my mother was saving for her quinceañera, graduated from law school last month. She became a lawyer because she wanted to understand why the system failed my mother.

I don't know if you deserve forgiveness. But my mother believed in redemption, worked with addicts and ex-convicts, believed everyone deserved a second chance.

The photograph is from Elena's graduation. My mother should have been there to see it.

I need you to know that Maria Santos was more than the victim in your case file. She was a woman who laughed at telenovelas, who made the best arroz con pollo in our neighborhood, who worked two jobs so her granddaughter could have the party of her dreams.

Elena had her quinceañera anyway. The whole community came together. She looked beautiful, and we played my mother's favorite songs, and everyone cried because she should have been there.

Maybe I just need to know that her life mattered.

Carmen Santos

Oliver read the letter three times before he could see the photograph clearly through his tears. Elena Santos in cap and gown, surrounded by family, radiant with accomplishment. She had her grandmother's eyes, the same dark eyes that had haunted Oliver's dreams for twenty-six years.

Full Circle

Five years later, Oliver opened his own program for ex-addicts transitioning out of prison. He called it Second Chances, though he privately thought of it as paying a debt that could never be fully settled.

On the anniversary of Maria's death, Oliver visited her grave in Cypress Hills Cemetery. He brought yellow roses, Carmen had mentioned they were her mother's favorites.

"I know sorry don't bring you back," he said to the headstone. "But I want you to know I remember you. I try to live in a way that honors what you stood for."

Last month, Elena Santos, now Judge Elena Santos, spoke at a criminal justice reform conference where Oliver was also presenting. She referenced his program in her remarks, calling it an example of how the system could focus on restoration rather than simply punishment.

"Some crimes can't be undone," she said. "Some losses can't be restored. But that doesn't mean we stop trying to heal what can be healed."

Oliver sat in the back row and wept quietly, understanding finally that forgiveness wasn't something he could earn. It was something that happened in the space between people, in the slow work of building something better from the pieces of what had been destroyed.

The Work Continues

Oliver is seventy now, his hair completely gray, his face mapped with lines that tell stories of hard choices and harder consequences. He still runs Second Chances, though he's training younger people to take over.

He never married, never had children. The family he built consisted of the broken people who found their way to his basement meetings, the ex-addicts who became counselors, the former inmates who discovered they could choose differently.

He still carries Carmen's letter in his wallet, next to a photograph of Brother James and a list of the seven people his program has lost to overdoses over the years. The names serve as reminders that recovery is fragile, that second chances don't come with guarantees.

29

INTERCESSORY PRAYER

T he silence at our table stretched like a tight rope, humming with expectation. Ten pairs of eyes watched me with the gentle patience of people who had already bared their souls and now waited for mine. Ishita's story of violence and betrayal. Ling's tale of abandonment and resilience. Ho Sung's journey through deprivation and loss. Simba's fight against war and oppression. Oliver's descent into addiction and his clawing path back to redemption.

Each story had carved something deeper into my chest, a growing shame that burned hotter than the injustice I'd suffered. Here I sat, surrounded by survivors of unimaginable trauma, and I had nearly thrown away the very gift they had fought so desperately to preserve.

My life.

"We're not comparing pain here," Prisha said softly, reading the conflict written across my face. Her voice carried the weight of someone who had learned to guard truth like a sacred flame. "This is about sharing what shaped us into who we are today."

Ling leaned forward and said, "This is a judgment-free zone, Andrea. We've all carried burdens that felt too heavy to bear."

Oliver nodded, understanding flickering in his blue eyes that had seen the bottom of human experience. "Sometimes the stories we're most ashamed to tell are the ones that need telling most."

Hanna's voice cut through my hesitation like a warm blade. "The Lord already knows your story, child. He chose you and loved you anyway. Let that be your comfort."

But it was Prisha's next question that shattered my carefully constructed walls.

"What was the effect of mental illness on your family, Andrea? And how did it affect you?"

The words hit me like ice water, and I found myself staring at her with complete attention. This woman who claimed her greatest joy was guarding truth had just reached into the most protected chamber of my heart.

Will's follow-up question drove the blade deeper: "Would you say it was mental illness... or influence from the opposition?"

The opposition. Even here, in this place of supposed safety, that phrase made my skin crawl. Because I knew what he was really asking. I knew because I'd asked myself the same question a thousand times in the darkest hours of night, when sleep became my enemy and memories my torturers.

The flood came then, memories I had buried so deep I'd almost convinced myself they were dreams. My sister's face, beautiful and terrible in its madness. The sound of glass breaking at 3 AM. The way my parents' marriage had crumbled under the weight of something they couldn't name or fight or cure.

I opened my mouth to speak, to finally give voice to the thing that had shaped every decision I'd made since childhood, when footsteps approached our table.

"The Man" materialized beside us like he'd been summoned by my desperation. The guides' faces lit up with genuine pleasure as they turned their attention to him, and I nearly wept with relief at the reprieve.

But the other invited guest, Ishita, Ling, Ho Sung, Simba, Oliver, they didn't know him. They offered polite smiles to this stranger who commanded such obvious reverence from our spiritual guides.

"How did it go?" Will asked, and something in his tone suggested this wasn't casual conversation.

"It went well," the Man replied, his voice carrying undertones I couldn't quite identify.

Hanna's next words made my breath catch: "Levi, how long did it take you to pray for her? I'm scheduled to pray for Ling in the afternoon session."

Levi.

The name hit me like recognition of something I'd always known but never consciously understood. Levi, the priestly tribe, the intercessors, those called to stand between heaven and earth on behalf of others. "Joined in harmony," if my childhood Hebrew lessons served me correctly.

I found myself grinning at him, actually grinning, despite the emotional carnage of moments before. "It's nice to finally meet you properly, Levi. I want to thank you for everything you've done for me. I understand you've been assigned to me from the very beginning."

Levi considered my words with the gravity of someone choosing them carefully. "Please don't thank me. Thank the Lord. It is He who has watched over you and shown you favor." His pause felt weighted with meaning. "He has heard you and knows you've thanked Him. Continue to tell Him, but don't forget to show Him your appreciation for your blessings, your gratitude for His word and His works in your life."

Another pause, deeper this time.

"But as for me, my greatest joy is the work given to me. My responsibility includes interceding on your behalf."

The words detonated in my chest like controlled explosions, each one bringing down another wall I'd built around my heart. God heard my prayers. After months of screaming into what felt like cosmic silence, believing I'd been abandoned to the wolves in expensive suits who had stolen my property and my faith in justice, He had heard me.

And more than that, He, God, had provided Levi. An intercessor. Someone whose very existence was dedicated to standing in the gap for me when I was too broken to stand for myself.

The tears came without warning, ugly and raw and completely beyond my control. I tried to stop them, tried to summon some dignity in front of these people who barely knew me, but that only made them worse. Years of suppressed grief and rage and despair poured out of me in waves that shook my entire body.

I cried for the life I'd almost thrown away. I cried for the sister whose illness had taught me that sometimes love isn't enough. I cried for the parents who had done their best with impossible circumstances. I cried for the judges who had looked me in the eye and chosen money over justice. I cried for every night I'd lain awake planning how to end the pain permanently.

And through it all, Levi stood beside our table like a sentinel, his presence somehow making it safe to fall apart completely.

"The power of his prayers is unequaled," Prisha said with gentle teasing in her voice, but her eyes were serious as she watched me crumble and rebuild simultaneously.

When I could finally breathe again, Levi began to speak.

"I left you in the arena so I could pray before the Lord on your behalf. I was concerned for your well-being. I believed you had lost hope and were unable to find your footing in this life."

His words were a key turning in a lock I didn't know existed. Someone had seen my desperation. Someone had cared enough to intercede when I couldn't even pray for myself anymore.

"I am what you might call a ferocious intercessor," Levi continued, and something in his tone made me smile through my tears. "I had a fourteen-point prayer plan for you."

Fourteen points. The specificity of it, the methodical care he'd taken with my broken life, undid me all over again.

"First," he said, his voice taking on the cadence of someone reciting something sacred, "I prayed that you would understand you still have a lot of life to live, and the end of your story has yet to be written."

The sob that escaped me was half grief, half recognition. Because he was right, I had been living like my story was over, like the courtroom defeats and financial devastation were the final chapters rather than difficult plot twists in something larger.

"Second, I prayed the Lord would bless you with a vision for your life. I hoped your vision for yourself would align with the Lord's vision for you. I noted your life has been one of service to others, and I prayed it would continue."

Service to others. When had I lost sight of that? When had the legal battles and property disputes consumed so much of my energy that I'd forgotten why I'd become a lawyer in the first place?

"Third, I prayed for wisdom and discernment in your decisions, choices that could benefit not only your life but the lives of others. Your experience, knowledge, and judgment will be the foundation for future growth through expanded wisdom."

Each prayer point landed like a stone thrown into still water, sending ripples through my understanding of myself and my circumstances. Levi continued, his voice steady and sure:

"Fourth, I prayed you would grow intellectually, psychologically, and spiritually. Intellectual growth affects knowledge, psychological growth impacts emotional well-being, and spiritual growth reflects your relationship with God's word and with God Himself."

"Fifth, I prayed for strength and fortitude to withstand opposition, criticism, and disapproval from others. You have sought others' approval to your detriment. It's time to stand on your own opinions and beliefs with God's guidance."

The accuracy of his assessment was surgical in its precision. How many times had I compromised my principles to avoid conflict? How many opportunities had I missed because I was too afraid of what others might think?

"Sixth, I prayed you wouldn't let past experiences adversely affect your future. You have a propensity to hang onto the past, refusing to let go. Those experiences get relived, preventing growth. Learn and let go."

Learn and let go. The words echoed in the chambers of my heart where I'd been hoarding grievances like treasure, polishing them with repeated attention until they gleamed with resentment.

"Seventh, I prayed you would accept and acknowledge who you are and who you're becoming. You must accept your failures and successes equally. You cannot remain in permanent grief or continue punishing yourself for past mistakes. Continued guilt taints future growth."

"Eighth, I prayed for patience with yourself and others. Perfection isn't the goal. No one is perfect. You will make mistakes but continue trying to be the best person you can be. When you fall short, don't criticize yourself or hold onto guilt. Be patient and try again."

"Ninth, I prayed for understanding of yourself and others. Specifically, to love your neighbors as yourself. People are difficult, with different attitudes and beliefs that make it hard to like them. This is considered one of the greatest commandments because it's one of the hardest to obey."

"Tenth, I prayed for your success. I asked God to touch your life so you could make a difference in others' lives. Through your success, others will succeed."

"Eleventh, I prayed you would be loved and have the capacity to love another. Love powers the desire to live, to move forward, to be the best person possible. Love changes all things."

"Twelfth, I prayed for experiences that would provoke laughter and amusement, they have positive impacts on attitude."

"Thirteenth, I prayed you would experience pure joy, the feeling of great pleasure and happiness. Disappointment, sadness, and difficulties already exist in abundance."

"And fourteenth," Levi's voice softened, "I prayed you would be in position to intercede for someone else. One of the greatest gifts to humanity is being able to help another. To help someone else, you must first have plenty for yourself."

When he finished, the silence that followed was different from the one that had started our conversation. This was the silence of something sacred having taken place, of prayers spoken in heavenly realms being acknowledged and received on earth.

I looked around the table at these people who had become my unexpected companions in this strange place. Ishita, who had been raped, betrayed by her family and found the strength to help others. Ling, who was born in a brothel, became a child prostitute and was saved, when others were not. Ho Sung, who had seen war's worst and chose peace. Simba, who had fought injustice without losing his humanity. Oliver, who had descended to hell and clawed his way back to redemption.

And now me, Andrea, who had almost thrown away the gift they had all fought so desperately to preserve.

The irony was sharp enough to cut: I, who had been given so much, loving parents, a stable childhood, educational opportunities, professional success. had been the one ready to surrender. While they, who had faced unimaginable hardships, had clung to life with fierce determination.

But perhaps that was the point. Perhaps I needed to hear their stories to understand the preciousness of what I'd been taking for granted. Perhaps they needed to hear mine to understand that suffering comes in many forms, and even the most privileged lives can harbor deep wounds.

"Thank you," I whispered to Levi, then louder: "Thank you all."

Because I was beginning to understand that this gathering wasn't accidental. These stories weren't random. This was orchestration on a scale I was only beginning to comprehend, a divine intervention disguised as chance encounters, designed to save a life that had nearly been lost to despair.

My story wasn't over. The end had yet to be written.

And for the first time in months, I was curious to see how my life would unfold.

30

— • —

THE LOVE MARCH

The Guides rose as one. We understood without words, it was time to return to the arena. But this would be different from our morning gathering. This would be the Love March.

"The Love March doesn't happen often," Prisha explained as we prepared to leave, her voice carrying reverence that made my spine tingle. "It has a sacred purpose, to wash away any remnants of darkness. When Satan comes before the Council of God, which is rare, the Love March cleanses his stench from the very air we breathe."

I paused at our table, taking one final look at the dining hall that had become the scene of such profound sharing. The sheer scope of it still took my breath away, room after endless room stretching into infinity, like standing between mirrors that reflected not just images but souls, stories, infinite variations of human experience multiplied beyond counting.

Thousands upon thousands of people moved through these halls, yet there was no pushing, no crowding, no impatience. Everyone moved with the fluid peace of those who had all eternity and knew it. As we walked toward the portal that would transport us back to the arena, I felt the weight of what we were about to witness settling over me.

The transition through the portal was still startling, one moment we were in the dining hall's warm intimacy, the next we were stepping into our arena seats, the grandeur hitting me like a physical force. I took my seat and immediately began cataloging details with my mind's eye, desperate to capture every nuance of what was about to unfold.

The air itself had changed. Where this morning it had been crisp and clear, now it was perfumed with frankincense and lemon, a combination that made me think of ancient temples and summer gardens. Candles appeared as if lit by invisible hands, their flames dancing without wind, casting light that seemed to come from within rather than without.

Then the music began!

At first, it was barely perceptible, the whisper of strings, the breath of wind instruments so soft I wondered if I was imagining it. But gradually, as my ears attuned themselves to the celestial acoustics, the orchestra emerged from below the arena floor, rising as they played, each musician bathed in light and dressed in white so pure they seemed to glow from within.

They arranged themselves in a perfect circle, suspended in midair as if gravity were merely a suggestion they'd chosen to ignore. In the center, on a small platform that rotated slowly, stood the conductor, a figure whose every gesture seemed to pull from the very fabric of creation itself, its music, the music to calm minds while taking flight.

As the orchestra's volume swelled, the choir emerged.

I had heard choirs before, church choirs, gospel choirs, even the renowned choirs of great cathedrals. But this... this was something beyond human experience. They surrounded the orchestra in concentric circles, their robes flowing gold and blue like captured sunrise and ocean, and when they began to sing, I understood why angels were said to make music in heaven.

Each voice was distinct, crystal clear, yet they blended into something greater than the sum of their parts. Sopranos that could shatter crystal with their purity, altos rich as honey, tenors that soared like eagles, baritones deep as mountain roots, and basses that seemed to emerge from the foundation stones of eternity itself.

And they sang Psalm 100:

"Make a joyful shout to the LORD,

all you lands!

Serve the LORD with gladness;

Come before His presence with singing.

Know that the LORD,

He is God;

It is He who has made us,

and not we ourselves;

We are His people and the sheep of His pasture.

Enter into His gates with thanksgiving,

And into His courts with praise.

Be thankful to Him and bless His name.

For the LORD is good;

His mercy is everlasting,

And His truth endures to all generations."

When they returned to the chorus, "Make a joyful shout to the Lord, all you lands!" the entire arena erupted. Every voice, from every culture, every language, every generation represented in this vast assembly, shouted as one. The sound was so powerful it seemed to shake the very pillars of heaven, and I felt it in my bones, in my soul, in places I didn't know sound could reach.

This went on for what felt like hours, each repetition building on the last, until the air itself seemed to vibrate with joy.

Then the music evolved.

Electric guitars materialized alongside synthesizers, their modern sounds weaving impossibly perfectly with the ancient orchestra. What should have been discord became harmony, what should have been chaos became a rock concert that would have made stadium shows look like whispered prayers. The fusion was so unexpected, so magnificent, that I found myself yelling, " Yes, Yes, Yes!" and singing along with with pure delight.

But even as I marveled at this musical miracle, the guitars faded, replaced by something primal and powerful, African drums that seemed to carry the heartbeat of the earth itself.

A Malinke drummer from West Africa appeared, his hands moving over the djembe with skill passed down through generations, tender yet commanding. The sound was both ancient and immediate, connecting every person in the arena to something deeper than culture, deeper than time. Soon a Yoruba drummer joined him, the Bata drums adding complexity and depth that made my chest tighten with emotion I couldn't name.

The entire arena began moving as one, not choreographed, but natural, organic, as if the rhythm had awakened something in our very DNA. We swayed side to side, our voices joining the chant: "Make a joyful shout to the Lord, all you lands!"

Then came the dancers.

African dancers appeared as if materializing from the music itself, encircling the choir and orchestra in flowing movements that told stories older than written language. Their costumes blazed with colors, red like sunset, yellow like summer sun, orange like flame, green like new life. Animal skins draped over their shoulders, leather belts crafted from natural materials, headdresses that caught the light and threw it back transformed.

They performed what looked like Indlamu, the war dance of the Zulu, but here it became something else, something that spoke not of conflict but of victory, of triumph over darkness, of the power of human spirit unified in purpose. They lifted their legs high, their hands moving with precision that was both disciplined and free, their bodies becoming instruments of worship that transcended denomination or doctrine.

As the drums gradually quieted, the dancers dissolved back into light, replaced by ballet dancers whose blue costumes seemed to capture pieces of sky. Where the African dancers had been earth and fire, these were air and water, moving with such grace to the choir's humming and the orchestra's strings that I felt my breath catch in my throat.

Arabesques that defied physics, assemblés that seemed to lift them beyond the reach of gravity, attitudes that spoke of joy, so pure it could only be expressed through movement. Each position, each leap, each turn was worship made visible, prayer given form.

The music shifted again, and a soloist emerged whose voice made my heart stop. Singing "Bridge Over Troubled Water" with such power, such soul, such perfect understanding of every note that I could have sworn it was Aretha Franklin herself, if Aretha had been able to sing with the voice of heaven itself.

"When you're weary, feeling small, when tears are in your eyes, I will dry them all..."

The words washed over the arena like a benediction, and I saw people weeping, not from sadness, but from recognition, from the overwhelming sense of being known, being loved, being cared for by something infinitely greater than ourselves.

A country artist followed, singing "Three Wooden Crosses" with a voice that carried all the wisdom of every small town, every rural church, every person who had ever found God in simple things and humble places. The song bridged every gap between sophisticated and simple, urban and rural, educated and intuitive.

But it was the trio that followed that shattered every remaining wall around my heart.

A countertenor, an alto, and a baritone, voices that should not have been able to blend but did, perfectly, impossibly, began singing "Way Maker." The song my mother had loved, the song that had carried her through her darkest days, the song that had played at my father's funeral when I thought God had forgotten us entirely.

"You are here, moving in our midst I worship You, I worship You.

You are here, working in this place I worship You, I worship You."

The arena caught fire, not with flames, but with something more powerful. Every person was on their feet, singing, clapping, crying, rejoicing, praising with abandon I had never seen before. Barriers dissolved, between cultures, between denominations, between the wounds we had carried and the healing we had never dared hope for.

"You are the Way maker, miracle worker, promise keeper Light in the darkness My God, that is who You are"

As the song swelled, the very architecture of heaven began to respond. The pillars that supported the arena started their slow, majestic journey toward the stars and sun, as if the music itself was lifting all of creation higher. The cherubim and seraphim took their positions around the arena's perimeter, beings so beautiful and terrible that looking at them directly made my eyes water, yet I couldn't look away.

The spirits that had been dancing through the air all day multiplied, became visible streams of light and color that wove between the singers and dancers and musicians like visible joy made manifest.

The twenty-four thrones that surrounded the great central throne rose into their appointed places, carrying their occupants; the elders, the representatives of all human history who had been found worthy to judge and rule, up toward their eternal positions. The orchestra and choir rose with them, their music becoming the soundtrack to the greatest elevation of souls in the history of creation.

And there, on the right side of the great white throne, a throne so massive and brilliant that looking at it was like trying to stare into the sun. I noticed a seat that hadn't been there this morning. Smaller than the Great White Throne but clearly significant, positioned in the place of honor, waiting for an occupant whose identity sent electricity through my spiritual senses.

The anticipation in the arena was palpable now, thick as honey, powerful as storm wind. Everyone remained standing, voices lifted in continuous praise:

"Way Maker, Miracle Worker, Promise Keeper, Light in the Darkness. My God, that is who You are!"

And then, the March began!

Every guide, every guardian angel, every spiritual being assigned to human care formed ranks with military precision that somehow felt like a dance. They filled every level of the arena, below the thrones, above them, surrounding the entire structure in formations that stretched as far as I could see.

The horn section and drums established a tempo that I felt in my chest, in my heartbeat, in the very rhythm of my existence. At first, they remained in place, lifting their right foot and then their left in perfect synchronization, side to side, building the cadence that would carry them forward.

Then they began to march, "Left, Right, Left . . ." and their voices rose in a call that spoke of victories, of battles won, of purpose fulfilled:

Let 'em blow,

Let 'em blow,

Let the four winds blow!

From the East to the West,

Alpha company is the best,

Dress it right and cover down,

Forty inches all around!

From the east to the west,

Alpha company is the best! . . .

But as they marched, something miraculous happened. Their physical forms began to dissolve, revealing their true nature, beings of pure spirit, beings of light and purpose and love so concentrated it was visible. Through their formations, threads of rainbow light began to weave, connecting each marcher to every other, creating a tapestry of such beauty that words became inadequate.

The arena filled with more than music, more than light, more than the presence of countless spiritual beings. It filled with love itself, love so pure, so powerful, so all-encompassing that it washed away every trace of doubt, every shadow of fear, every residue of the darkness that had dared to challenge the throne of grace.

This was why the Love March existed. This was how heaven cleansed itself when evil presumed to approach the throne of judgment. Not with force, not with anger, but with love so complete that darkness simply could not exist in its presence.

I felt tears streaming down my face, but they were tears of joy, of recognition, of coming home to a love I had been seeking my entire life without knowing it. Around me, thousands upon thousands of voices joined the eternal song, and I understood that this was just the beginning.

Something greater was coming. Someone greater was coming!

The empty seat beside the throne would not remain empty much longer.

And when it was filled, the real celebration would begin.

31

THE LOVE PRINCIPLE

A s I glance down, a wave of awe washes over me. Everyone and everything has returned to their sacred positions, as if drawn by an invisible, magnetism. The four living creatures, those magnificent beings with eyes like burning stars covering every inch of their forms, resume their eternal dance around the great white throne. How had I missed their six wings before? I must have been transfixed by those all-seeing eyes that seemed to pierce through time itself. The cherubim and seraphim stand in perfect formation, their presence both terrible and beautiful. The Seven Spirits rest upon their thrones, radiating power that makes the air itself hum with electricity.

The rainbow arcing over the massive white throne steals my breath away, not just colors, but living light that seems to sing. Gemstones, the size of mountains, reflect this celestial radiance, while gold purer than anything earthly gleams like captured sunlight. The entire arena pulses with glory so intense it should blind me, yet, somehow, I can see everything with crystalline clarity.

Then silence falls. Not the absence of sound, but the presence of something infinitely greater about to speak.

Jesus the Christ rises, and His voice, oh, that voice, fills every corner of creation with warmth that reaches into the deepest parts of my soul:

"This is the love principle. Love our Father with all of your mind, heart and soul and love your neighbors as yourself... Brothers and Sisters, let us not love in word or talk alone, but in our deeds and in truth."

The arena doesn't just erupt, it explodes with voices that shake the foundations of eternity itself: "LOVE! LOVE! LOVE! IN DEEDS AND IN TRUTH!" The sound rolls like thunder across dimensions, and I feel it reverberating in my bones.

Jesus the Christ continues, His words cutting through pretense like a sword of light:

"If I speak with human eloquence and angelic ecstasy but don't love, I'm nothing but the creaking of a rusty gate."

"NOTHING BUT A CREAKING OF A RUSTY GATE!" The multitude roars back, and I can almost hear the screech of metal on metal, the hollow emptiness of words without love.

"If I speak God's Word with power, revealing all his mysteries and making everything plain as day, and if I have faith that says to a mountain, 'Jump,' and it jumps, but I don't love, I'm nothing."

The arena convulses with energy: "JUMP! JUMP! JUMP!" I feel the ground beneath me tremble as if mountains themselves are leaping at His command.

"If I give everything I own to the poor and even go to the stake to be burned as a martyr, but I don't love, I've gotten nowhere. So, no matter what I say, what I believe, and what I do, I'm bankrupt without love."

"BANKRUPT WITHOUT LOVE!" The cry pierces my heart. I think of all the times I've acted without love, and shame and redemption wash over me in equal measure.

Jesus the Christ pauses, and in that moment, the entire universe seems to hold its breath. When He speaks again, His voice carries such tenderness that tears stream down my face:

"Love never gives up. Love cares more for others than for self. Love doesn't want what it doesn't have. Love doesn't strut, Doesn't have a swelled head, Doesn't force itself on others, Isn't always 'me first,' Doesn't fly off the handle, Doesn't keep score of the sins of others, Doesn't revel when others grovel, Takes pleasure in the flowering of truth, Puts up with anything, Trusts God always, Always looks for the best, Never looks back, But keeps going to the end."

Each line hits like a revelation. I see my failures, my successes, my desperate need for this kind of love. Around me, I hear soft weeping, not of sorrow, but of recognition and longing.

Jesus the Christ lifts His voice higher, and it carries the weight of eternity:

"Love never dies. Inspired speech will be over some day; praying in tongues will end; under-standing will reach its limit. We know only a portion of the truth, and what we say about God is always incomplete. But when the Complete arrives, our incompletes will be canceled."

"LOVE NEVER DIES!" The declaration shakes the stars themselves. I feel immortality coursing through my veins, not of body, but of spirit touched by unending love.

Jesus the Christ grows more intimate now, His voice like a father speaking to beloved children:

"When I was an infant at my mother's breast, I gurgled and cooed like any infant. When I grew up, I left those infant ways for good. We do not yet see things clearly. We are squinting in a fog, peering through a mist. But it will not be long before the weather clears, and the sun shines bright! We will see it all then, see it all as clearly as God sees us, knowing him directly just as he knows us! But for right now, until that completeness, we have three things to do to lead us toward that consummation: Trust steadily in God, hope unswervingly, love extravagantly. And the best of the three is love."

The arena becomes a thunderstorm of praise: "TRUST STEADILY IN GOD, HOPE UNSWERVINGLY, LOVE EXTRAVAGANTLY! TRUST, HOPE AND LOVE!" The words become a battle cry, a declaration of war against despair and hatred.

Jesus the Christ spreads His arms wide, and I can see the scars, beautiful, terrible re-minders of the price of love:

"Brothers and Sisters, we have poured our love into you, loving you freely, openly and without hesitation. From the time of creation, today and tomorrow. Know this, love is from God, and whoever loves has been born of God and knows God."

The response comes like waves crashing against eternal shores: "We love you... We love you... We love you..." Between each declaration, African drums beat with the rhythm of the human heart, and lightning splits the sky while thunder rolls from the arena to the farthest stars. "We love you... We love you... We love you..."

Then I see it! The arena begins to shimmer with gold light so pure it makes earthly gold look like mud. Near the great white throne, a form takes shape, tall, wide, unmistakably the outline of a man, yet infinitely more than any man could ever be. The rainbow expands, becoming a dome of living color that encompasses all the thrones. The four living creatures step back reverently, never taking their countless eyes off the throne. The cherubim rise from their positions like pillars of fire, while seraphim and other angelic beings create a symphony of flight overhead.

Our guardian angels, these beings who have walked with us through every moment of our earthly lives, drop to their knees in worship so pure it takes my breath away. I look right, left, everyone, from the humblest invited guest to the mightiest saint, has fallen to their knees. I, too, am on my knees and gratitude pours from my lips like water from a broken dam.

The shimmering gold presence moves, and Jesus the Christ speaks with authority that could command galaxies:

"I am the bread of life. He who comes to Me shall never hunger, and he who believes in Me shall never thirst. For your nourishment will be provided without fail. The word, my Father's word, is the feast that gives eternally. It is as sweet as honey. Melts in your mouth. While served on a silver platter."

The golden radiance flows around the platform like liquid light, and I taste honey on my tongue, the sweetness of promises fulfilled.

"I am the light of the world. He who follows Me shall not walk in darkness but have the light of life. You made your choice. Life through lightness, yet death through darkness lurks around the corner. Brothers and Sisters, the light will guide your feet to the love of our Father. Keep in mind, the Light of the world is the eye of the spirit conscious of a night of darkness, which has passed into the brightness of the Sun of Righteousness... Be the ray of light that sees the light of day, keeping the fuse lit!"

I feel that light burning within me, chasing away shadows I didn't even know existed.

"I am the door. If anyone enters by Me, he will be saved, and will go in and out and find pasture. Brothers and Sisters, there was only one way in and one way out and that was through the door of life. Our Father has created a sanctuary, a retreat, that provides a refuge. He has produced the necessary nutrition to allow you to become knowledgeable and wise, while providing the field so you can develop your strength and stamina. Remember, little children, I am the key to this heavenly door."

I see the door! Not wood or metal, but Jesus, himself, standing with arms outstretched in eternal invitation.

"I am the good shepherd. The good shepherd gives his life for the sheep. He loves his flock, caring for each and every one. He guides his flock, finding sustenance. He knows each lamb in his flock. And he keeps his flock safe. Just as the Father knows me and I know the Father."

The tenderness in His voice when He says "each lamb" makes me weep. I am that lamb. We all are.

"I am the resurrection and the life. He who believes in Me, though he may die, he shall live. For I died for the sins of Man according to the prophecies of the Scriptures. I was raised after the third day, appearing before men. Since death came through a man, the resurrection of the dead comes also through a man. Brothers and Sisters, the body will perish, but when raised, it will live, not in the natural body, but in the spiritual body. I declare to you that flesh and blood cannot inherit the kingdom of God. The death of the body is due to sin, but thanks to my Father who gave us the victory. STAND FIRM, brothers and sisters, let nothing move you. Always give yourselves fully because your labor in our Father is not in vain."

I feel death's sting being pulled from my heart, replaced by the certainty of forever.

"I am the way, the truth, and the life. No one comes to the Father except through Me. Through obedience and sacrifice, salvation of man is given. Our Father has appointed me, the Door, the Shepherd, the Light, to offer the gift of salvation. After all, I was the living sacrifice, dying for the sins of man, so he could be redeemed. I am the truth as promised through the prophecies of the Old Testament, transforming the law. I am the true way to eternal life, providing the only way of access to the Father."

The weight of absolute truth settles on my shoulders, not crushing, but strengthening.

"I am the vine; you are the branches. He who abides in Me, and I in him, bears much fruit; for without Me you can do nothing. Brothers and Sisters, the branch cannot grow without the vine that nourishes and sustains it. The branches need to be cultivated and supported in order to grow. If the branch does not bear good fruit, it will be cut down and thrown into the fire. Remember, you did not choose me, but I chose you and appointed you that you should go and bear fruit and that your fruit should abide. I am the true vine, and my Father is the vinedresser."

I feel the connection, the life flowing between vine and branch, between Jesus and my very soul.

Jesus the Christ stands taller now, His voice carrying across eternity itself:

"I am the light of the world, guiding your path. I am the door, the only door to my Father's house. I am the Good Shepherd, willing to die for you. I am the resurrection and the life. I died for you and was resurrected. I am the way, truth and the life. And I am the vine from which your branches grow. I love you!"

The silence that follows is not empty, it's full of the weight of divine love settling into every heart. Then praise erupts like a volcano of joy, voices joining in harmonies that make earthly music sound like noise. But I remember those moments during the seven "I AM" declarations when you could have heard a pin drop across the vastness of eternity, every soul hanging on every word, recognizing the voice of their Creator, their Savior, their eternal Love.

And at that moment, I understand, this isn't just a chapter in a book. This is the reason every story was ever written, every song ever sung, every heart ever yearned for something more. This is love incarnate, speaking truth that will echo through eternity, reminding us that we are chosen, beloved, and never, ever alone.

32

—•—

Be Ready and Keep Your Guards Up

L et me try to capture what I'm witnessing, though human words feel pitifully inadequate. Have you ever been to a concert with a superstar performer, Beyoncé commanding a stadium, Taylor Swift making 80,000 people sing as one voice, Blake Shelton turning an arena into a honky-tonk heaven? Picture that moment when the entire coliseum erupts to their feet simultaneously, a sea of humanity united in pure, electric joy. People hollering until their voices crack. Some singing along with tears streaming down their faces. Others, so overwhelmed with emotion they can barely stand. Cell phone flashlights creating a galaxy of earthbound stars.

Now multiply that energy, that raw emotional power, by a thousand. No, by infinity itself.

You have to understand! I'm not in some earthly concert hall with concrete walls and metal beams. I've been calling this place an "arena" because my finite vocabulary fails me, but imagine if you can: a vast, impossible space that seems to breathe with its own life. Circular tiers of seats rise like golden mountains, balcony upon balcony spiraling upward until they disappear into living light. There is no floor, just the earth spinning far below us in the cosmic dance. We exist suspended in the very heavens, with stars blazing like diamonds around us and the sun itself serving as our backdrop, as if God took the universe and turned it inside out to create the ultimate amphitheater.

But it's not the spectacular setting that steals my breath, it's the presence. The spiritual significance washing over me in waves defies every attempt at description. Try to imagine yourself transported back in time, sitting on that hillside in northern Israel, on the Korazim Plateau. Jesus Christ Himself stands before you, ready to deliver the Sermon on the Mount. His twelve disciples sit nearby, their faces glowing with wonder. Followers and seekers crowd around, hanging on every word that falls from His lips.

But here's what makes it unbearable in its beauty, you know. You know with absolute certainty that this man before you is the Son of the Living God, walking among humanity in flesh and blood. You know He will soon hang on a Roman cross, taking the weight of every sin ever committed. You know that in three days, He will shatter death itself and rise victorious. You know that salvation, real, eternal, unshakeable salvation, flows from His sacrifice. You know He is the fulfillment of every prophecy whispered by ancient voices, every promise carved in sacred stone.

You're looking directly at your Savior. Your Redeemer. Your eternal Hope.

How would that feel? Would your heart explode with gratitude? Would praise pour from your lips like water from a broken dam? Would you fall to your knees in worship so pure it hurts?

That's what's happening here in this celestial arena! Gratitude and thankfulness magnified beyond human comprehension, multiplied by the infinite love of God Himself. Across this vast space, voices join in a symphony of thanksgiving that makes angels weep with joy.

The shimmering gold radiance intensifies, growing brighter with each passing moment. Jesus the Christ stands majestically before the great white throne, no longer just speaking to us but radiating glory that transforms the very air around Him. The Seven Spirits on their thrones begin to shimmer in harmony, creating a light show that would put every earthly celebration to shame.

Jesus the Christ begins again, and His voice carries both infinite tenderness and steel-hard authority:

"My Brothers and Sisters, you are in our Father's house. This house has many rooms. It is your home, your residence. You, who are welcomed in the house of the Lord, you must remain vigilant and prepared. And you, who are not yet welcomed, but are invited guests, should not only be prepared but expect an attack upon you and your family. Be of sober spirit and be on alert. For our adversary is cunning and shrewd."

A chill runs down my spine at those words. Even in paradise, even surrounded by such glory, the battle is real. Jesus pauses, and in that silence, I feel the weight of cosmic warfare pressing against my soul.

He continues, His voice dropping to a tone that makes the very stars lean in to listen:

"Satan was before the Council today. He is our enemy. Once he lived among us, here in our Father's house. He, who was created, thought that he was better than the Creator, causing great turmoil. He and a third of the angels at that time were thrown out of heaven. Attempting to separate man from God, he deceived Adam and Eve in the Garden of Eden, causing them to sin. As a consequence, he was told that a woman would give birth. Her offspring would crush his head. Since then, he has chased women, seeking to destroy their offspring. He used Herod, King of Judea, to order the execution of all male children two years old and under in the vicinity of Bethlehem. And Pharaoh, who decreed that all baby boys of the Israelites be thrown in the Nile river for fear they might become too powerful. These were not random nor coincidental events."

My blood runs cold as the pieces fall into place. The massacre of innocents, the systematic attempts to destroy God's chosen people, all orchestrated by a fallen angel consumed with jealous rage. I think of every mother who wept, every father who raged, every child who died, and righteous anger burns in my chest.

Jesus the Christ doesn't flinch from the darkness. His voice grows stronger, more determined:

"Satan has been trying to destroy the man that is predestined to crush him. He has attempted to usurp the Lord God's authority and steal, kill and destroy humanity which was created in our image. He has roamed the earth like a ravenous wolf, seeking out people or acts that are opposite to that of the 'eyes of the Lord.' He is disdainful and disinterested as to the goodness of human beings. In fact, it is his desire that man would be contemptuous of God, our Father. And his goal is to prevent an intimate loving relationship between God and man. He has purposely sought to interfere with the Creator and his creation. His main function is to keep man in the dark, keeping him confused and keeping him distracted so he would be no benefit to the Lord, God. He will fashion himself as the angel of light. But he is the Deceiver as well as the Tempter, blinding the minds of those who do not believe, making it impossible for them to understand the Good News. Know this, he does not compare to the greatness of our Father. Never has and never will. He is his subordinate, at best. He may be the center of all evil in the universe and controls most of what takes place on earth, but our Father is the protector, the defender and the guardian from his darkness."

I feel the truth of those words settling into my bones. Every temptation I've ever faced, every doubt that's whispered in my ear, every moment I've felt separated from God, suddenly I see the puppet master behind the curtain. But more importantly, I see the Victor standing before me, the One who has already won the war.

Jesus the Christ shifts, His posture becoming that of a master teacher about to reveal a profound truth:

"Brothers and Sisters, do you remember 'The Parable of the Weeds'? The kingdom of heaven is like a man who sowed good seed in his field. But while everyone was sleeping, his enemy came and sowed weeds among the wheat, and went away. When the wheat sprouted and formed heads, then the weeds also appeared. The owner's servants came to him and said, 'Sir, didn't you sow good seed in your field? Where then did the weeds come from?' 'An enemy did this,' he replied. The servants asked him, 'Do you want us to go and pull them up?' 'No,' he answered, 'because while you are pulling the weeds, you may uproot the wheat with them. Let both grow together until the harvest. At that time, I will tell the harvesters: First collect the weeds and tie them in bundles to be burned; then gather the wheat and bring it into my barn.'"

The arena falls silent. Even the cherubim stop their eternal song. We all know what's coming, the final reckoning that every soul will face.

Jesus the Christ lets that weight settle before continuing, His voice now carrying the authority of ultimate judgment:

"What does that tell you? There will be a final harvesting, judgment, for all. The kings of the earth and their armies will be seized. The beast and the false prophet who worked signs that were meant to deceive and those that worshiped his image will be captured. The beast and the false prophet will be thrown into the lake burning with brimstone. While the rest will be killed by the sword and the birds will eat their flesh. But Satan, he will be bound with a great chain and cast into the bottomless pit by the angel from heaven using the key to seal him for a thousand years."

I can almost see it! The final battle, the cosmic showdown between good and evil. My heart pounds with anticipation and holy fear. Justice is coming. The scales will be balanced. Every wrong will be made right.

But then Jesus the Christ lifts His voice, and suddenly the arena fills with hope so bright it's almost blinding:

"There will be a voice from heaven saying, 'Be a witness to the greatness of the Lord. Our Father will be with all of his children and they will dwell together. He will wipe away the tears from their eyes, there will be no sorrow, no crying and no more death. The former things

will have passed away, leaving the oneness of the intimate relationship between the father and his children."

The arena explodes. Not just sound, reality itself seems to crack open with praise. Lightning fractures the sky in patterns of pure joy. Thunder rolls in harmonies that make earthly music sound like static. Rumblings of every kind cascade through dimensions I didn't know existed.

But it's what happens inside me that changes everything. Warmth floods my being, not just physical warmth, but the warmth of being completely, utterly, perfectly loved. Gentleness wraps around my heart like a mother's embrace. Kindness flows through my veins like liquid gold. Truth settles in my mind with the weight of absolute certainty. Love, pure, perfect, unstoppable love, envelopes every cell of my existence.

I have never felt anything like this. Never imagined it was possible to feel this complete, this whole, this home. Thankfulness doesn't begin to cover it. Gratitude feels like too small a word. Joy seems inadequate. This is something beyond human emotion, this is what my soul was created for, what every heartbeat has been leading toward.

I look over at Levi, and I see the same wonder, the same overwhelming joy, reflected in his eyes. Without thinking, I reach out and hug him tight, feeling like if I don't hold onto something solid, I might dissolve into pure light.

And then I feel it, a sensation like gravity releasing its hold, like the laws of physics taking a coffee break. The arena, the throne, Jesus, Levi, everything begins to shift and blur.

I'm falling!

But even as I fall, even as this magnificent vision begins to fade, I carry with me the certainty that burns brighter than any star: the battle is real, the enemy is defeated, and Love, perfect, eternal, unshakeable Love, has already won.

33

KICKED OUT OF HEAVEN!

The warmth hits me first, not the celestial radiance I'd grown accustomed to, but something smaller, more earthbound. Wet kisses peppered across my cheek, accompanied by the gentle weight of paws pressed against my chest. Princess. My sweet Princess, her chocolate-brown eyes staring into mine with an intensity that suggests she's been trying to wake me for some time.

"Hey, girl," I whisper, my voice hoarse and unfamiliar even to my own ears. She responds by licking my face with renewed enthusiasm, her tail creating a rhythmic drumbeat against the leather armrest of my recliner. When I try to turn away, she follows, determined to cover every inch of my face with her particular brand of canine affection.

I hold her close, feeling the silky texture of her fur beneath my fingers, the steady rise and fall of her breathing, the frantic beating of her heart. She's real. Tangible. Present. Everything heaven had felt like and everything it now isn't.

Opening my eyes fully, I take in my surroundings with the disorientation of someone waking from the most vivid dream imaginable, except I know it wasn't a dream. My living room stretches before me, exactly as it had been before Levi's visit. The throw pillows are arranged just so on the couch. The coffee table holds yesterday's mail and my reading glasses. The afternoon light filters through familiar curtains, casting shadows I could map with my eyes closed.

I gently lift Princess and set her on the floor, then force myself to stand on unsteady legs. Room by room, I move through my house like a detective searching for evidence of the impossible. The kitchen, spotless, undisturbed. My bedroom, the bed made exactly as I'd left it. The guest room where Levi had... but no, everything is pristine, untouched, as if no angelic visitor had ever graced my home.

I peer through windows, hoping to catch a glimpse of something, anything, that might bridge the gap between there and here. But outside, life moves with its usual mundane rhythm. A neighbor walks their dog. A delivery truck rumbles past. Children's laughter drifts from a backyard somewhere.

It's official. I'm home. I'm in my living room. And I'm having the most profound case of spiritual whiplash imaginable.

The emotions hit me like a tidal wave, gratitude for Princess's warm presence tangled with an ache so deep it feels like grief. I was in heaven. I stood in the presence of Jesus Christ, himself. I heard the Love Principle from His own lips. I witnessed cosmic warfare and eternal truth. And now I'm back to sorting mail and wondering if I remembered to pay the electric bill.

But even as that thought forms, I slam the door on it with fierce determination. No. I will not allow doubt to creep in like morning mist, subtle and suffocating. I know doubt's signature, recognize its whispered questions because I've heard them before, not just in my own mind, but echoing through history itself.

"Did God really tell you not to eat of the tree in the middle of the garden?"

"Did He really mean that you were going to die, or did He mean that you would be like Him?"

The serpent's questions to Eve, designed to erode certainty and plant seeds of rebellion. I've felt doubt's corrosive power in my own life, doubting my choices, my worth, my purpose, my truth. I know the cost of doubt, how it can transform blessing into burden, faith into fear, hope into despair.

What I experienced was real. More real than this chair I'm sitting in, more solid than the walls surrounding me, more true than anything I've ever known. I will not let the enemy steal this from me.

But knowing something intellectually and feeling it emotionally are two different countries entirely, and right now, I'm caught at the border between them.

"I was kicked out of heaven," I say aloud, and Princess tilts her head as if considering the theological implications. The words feel strange on my tongue, tinged with humor and heartbreak in equal measure.

I didn't want to leave. God knows I didn't want to leave. I understood my status as an "invited guest," but understanding and accepting are distant cousins. There were so many questions burning in my mind, so many mysteries I'd barely begun to unravel. The feeling of perfect love that had enveloped me like a warm blanket on the coldest night, I want to wrap myself in that again. My guide, Levi, with his gentle wisdom and protective presence, I miss him with the intensity usually reserved for family members.

The dining hall with its impossible manna that tasted like hope and forgiveness combined. My tablemates who had shared fragments of their stories with such vulnerability. Ling with her quiet strength, Ho Sung's infectious laugh, Oliver's thoughtful questions, Simba's warrior spirit, and Ishita's radiant joy. I had thought they would become friends, not just beautiful, fleeting encounters.

The Love March that set my soul ablaze. The Love Principle that rewrote everything I thought I knew about love itself. The arena, that magnificent, impossible space where earth and heaven met in cosmic celebration. The sounds that no earthly orchestra could replicate, lightning that sang, thunder that comforted, rumblings that spoke of God's pleasure in His children.

And most of all, most of all, the presence of the Trinity. God the Father, whose love felt like coming home after a lifetime of wandering. Jesus Christ, whose voice could command galaxies and comfort broken hearts with equal ease. The Holy Spirit, moving through everything like divine breath giving life to lifeless places.

But there's another ache, smaller but somehow more personal. I didn't see them, the people who had walked through my life and stepped into eternity ahead of me. My father, whose funeral just months ago had left a father-shaped hole in my world. My sister and brother, taken too soon, whose laughter I still expect to hear around corners. Cynthia's mom Cat, Catherine, who had been like a second mother to me. Zela, my mother's "ride or die" friend, who could make anyone feel welcomed and loved.

Where were they? Are they in a different part of heaven? Are they busy with their own eternal purposes? Or is there something about timing, about readiness, about the mysterious ways God orchestrates divine encounters?

And what about my pets, my beloved companions who had shared my life with such loyalty and unconditional love? Lady, whose sudden death had sent me into mourning so deep I questioned everything about loss and eternity. Tiger, with his dignified purr.

Noodles, who never met a stranger. My current Princess, sleeping peacefully at my feet now. Bapsey and Ali, each with their own precious personalities.

I remember the desperate conversations I'd had after Lady died, cornering anyone who would listen with my burning question: "Do dogs go to heaven?" The responses were maddeningly divided. Some people, usually with gentle smiles, would assure me that yes, there's a heaven for pets. Others, often with theological certainty, would declare that animals have no souls and therefore no eternal destiny.

To those people, I would always ask, "Why would God give us loyal, loving, protective companions to share our earthly journey if there was no place for them in our eternal one?" The question was never academic for me, it was deeply personal. I honestly didn't know if I would want to go to a place without the animals who had taught me so much about unconditional love.

I never received an answer that satisfied my heart.

But as I sit here now, stroking Princess's soft fur, those questions shift into something larger, more significant. The weight of what I actually witnessed begins to settle into my consciousness like sediment in still water.

The Adversary, Satan himself, had sought immediate judgment for mankind. Not in some distant future when God's timing was perfect, but now. His argument had been devastatingly logical on the surface: humanity's complete failure to keep even one of God's commandments, particularly the greatest one that Jesus Himself had emphasized. Love God with all your heart, mind, and soul, and love your neighbor as yourself.

How many times, I wonder, has humanity stood on the precipice of final judgment while going about our daily lives, completely unaware of the cosmic legal proceedings taking place in heavenly courts? How many times has the enemy made his case for our destruction while we worried about traffic jams and grocery lists?

The Adversary had methodically listed humanity's failures, our inhumanity to each other, our selfishness, our pride, our violence, our greed. For a terrifying moment, his arguments had seemed irrefutable. I had felt the weight of every sin, every failure, every moment I had chosen myself over God or others.

Until the fifth voice spoke up, was it one of the Seven Spirits? The memory shimmers just out of reach, but I remember the power in those words, the reminder that Satan himself was the author of humanity's corruption. He was the one who had been "going to and fro on the earth," as the book of Job describes, influencing and deceiving humanity so we couldn't know truth or walk in light.

The breathtaking audacity of it still stuns me. Satan, the father of lies, accusing humanity of the very sins he had spent millennia orchestrating. It would be like an arsonist blaming the building for burning.

His words, I realize now, echo in the rhetoric of so many earthly leaders, the same patterns of manipulation, the same divisive strategies. The Adversary had acknowledged that family was one of God's greatest gifts to humanity. After creating Adam, God saw that it wasn't good for man to be alone, so He created Eve for companionship and partnership. Then He commanded them to multiply, establishing the first safety net, a place of identity, belonging, and mutual care.

Yet from the very beginning, the family has been under attack. First, the serpent's deception drove a wedge between Adam, Eve, and their Creator. Then Cain murdered Abel, shattering the first family with fratricide. The pattern was established: attack the family, and you attack the foundation of human society.

Now, like then, the Adversary continues his assault. Nearly a quarter of American children under eighteen live with only one parent. Housing costs have spiraled beyond the reach of working families in what's supposed to be one of the world's richest nations. Healthcare, basic human care when we're sick and vulnerable, is treated like a luxury item, debated and rationed while those in power enjoy the finest medical care money can buy.

I think about the United States President who contracted COVID-19 and received experimental treatments because he was a "celebrity," while on that same day, over 200,000 Americans were diagnosed and 3,000 died without access to those same treatments. Families received a one-time payment of $1,200 per adult and $600 per child while businesses were infused with nearly three trillion dollars, sending the stock market soaring to record highs even as families faced eviction and hunger.

Are these the natural decisions of fallible humans, or are they the carefully orchestrated influences of the Adversary? When we allow thousands to die daily from a disease that could be slowed by something as simple as wearing a mask, whose wisdom are we following? When we create systems where "celebrities" receive life-saving treatments denied to ordinary people. Whose values are we implementing?

The audacity of Satan's courtroom performance still takes my breath away. Here was a being who had contributed to every human failure, influenced every selfish decision, whispered doubt into every moment of potential faith, and he had the unmitigated gall to demand punishment for the very corruption he had authored. It was like a drug dealer demanding the death penalty for addiction, a con artist calling for justice against fraud.

Who was he to stand before God and argue for humanity's judgment? He wasn't our creator, God was. He wasn't our redeemer, Jesus was. He wasn't our sanctifier; the Holy Spirit was. He was nothing more than a fallen creature whose pride had corrupted his purpose and whose jealousy had twisted his love into hatred.

I remember studying Isaiah 14, that chilling catalog of Lucifer's hubris before his fall from grace:

"I will ascend into heaven, I will exalt my throne above the stars of God; I will also sit on the mount of the congregation on the farthest sides of the north; I will ascend above the heights of the clouds, I will be like the Most High."

Five "I will" statements that reveal the heart of rebellion, the creature attempting to dethrone the Creator, the servant trying to become master, the finite challenging the infinite. It truly is delusions of grandeur on a cosmic scale.

Recognizing the dangerous territory my thoughts are treading, I deliberately shift focus. Dwelling on the enemy's strategies is like staring into darkness, eventually, it begins to stare back.

Instead, I wonder about my role in all of this. Why was I chosen as an "invited guest"? With my collection of losses and failures, my ordinary life and unremarkable accomplishments, what could I possibly have to offer? The question isn't born from false humility but from genuine bewilderment.

I close my eyes and try to remember Levi's fourteen-point prayer on my behalf, each petition a building block for something I couldn't yet see:

Understanding, that I might see with spiritual eyes.

Vision, that I might perceive God's perspective.

Wisdom, that I might make choices aligned with heaven's values.

Growth, that I might not remain static in my faith.

Strength, that I might endure whatever lies ahead.

Freedom from the past, that old wounds wouldn't limit new possibilities.

Acceptance, that I might embrace God's will even when it differs from my own.

Patience, that I might trust God's timing over my urgency.

Obedience, that I might follow even when the path seems unclear.

Success, defined not by worldly standards but by heavenly ones.

Love, that I might reflect the heart I witnessed in the arena.

Humor, that I might find joy even in difficulty.

Joy, that deep, unshakeable peace that transcends circumstances.

And intercession, that I might stand in the gap for others as Levi had for me.

Sitting here with Princess in my arms, I begin to cry. Not tears of sadness, but tears of overwhelming need. I need prayer. I need strength. I need guidance. I need to hold onto what I experienced without being crushed by the weight of it.

I try to visualize the Love March, to recapture that moment when thousands of voices joined in perfect harmony. I try to remember every word of the Love Principle, every inflection in Jesus's voice as He spoke the seven "I AM" statements. I try to feel again that perfect love that had enveloped me like divine atmosphere.

And I take to heart His warning to be prepared and remain ready.

I know I was an "invited guest," temporary visitor to eternal realities. But I can't shake the feeling that I was sent back, not dismissed. There's an expectation lingering in the air around me, a sense of assignment yet to be revealed. What's the likelihood that I would be invited to something so special, so life-altering, without some expectation of purpose or mission?

It's possible, of course, that the experience was pure gift grace poured out simply because God wanted to bless me. But every instinct tells me there's more. I feel a calling on my life, as real as the chair I'm sitting in, as certain as Princess's weight in my lap. I just don't know what it is yet.

But I'm ready to find out.

The late afternoon light is beginning to fade, casting longer shadows across my familiar living room. Soon it will be evening, then night, then morning again. The world will continue spinning on its axis, people will continue living their lives, and I will continue looking like the same person I was yesterday.

But I'm not the same. I've seen behind the curtain of reality. I've witnessed the cosmic battle between good and evil. I've heard Love define itself in its own voice. I've been in the presence of perfect holiness and unlimited grace.

I've been to heaven and back.

And now I have to figure out what to do with that impossible, beautiful, terrifying gift.

Princess stirs in my lap, opens one eye to check on me, then settles back into her nap with a contented sigh. Even she seems to understand that something has fundamentally changed, that the woman holding her is the same person but somehow more than she was before.

I stroke her soft fur and whisper a prayer that's part thanksgiving, part desperation, and completely honest: "God, I don't know what comes next. But I'm ready. Use me however You see fit. And please, please, don't let me forget what I've seen."

Outside, a neighbor's wind chime catches the evening breeze, creating a melody that sounds almost like... no, not like the music of heaven. Nothing earthly could replicate that.

But it's beautiful in its own way.

And for now, that's enough.

34

THE ZOOM CALL

D ays had passed since my return from heaven, each one blending into the next like watercolors bleeding together on wet paper. The question followed me everywhere, a persistent whisper that turned mundane moments into opportunities for existential wrestling. What was I called to do by God? Was there truly a divine assignment waiting for me, or was I simply a witness to glory beyond comprehension, expected to carry the memory like a secret treasure? And if I was meant to testify, to whom would I speak? Who would believe such an impossible story?

The questions circled my mind like vultures, patient and relentless.

I'd been spending more time with Mom lately, drawn to her quiet strength and practical wisdom. Today, like many others, she needed someone present while she showered, not because she was weak, but because fear had taken up residence in her bones since her fall. The bathroom tiles, slick with steam and possibility, had become enemies in her mind.

"I just need to know someone's here," she'd said with the vulnerability that comes when we acknowledge our limitations. "Just in case."

While the sound of running water created a gentle percussion from behind the bathroom door, I moved through her small apartment with the efficiency born of routine. Stripping her bed, I replaced worn sheets with crisp, clean ones that smelled of lavender fabric softener. The vacuum hummed across her carpet, erasing the evidence of Princess's latest adventure, scattered kibble and mysterious crumbs that seemed to multiply overnight.

In the kitchen, I arranged her groceries with the careful precision of someone who understood that order brought comfort. Distilled water for her morning routine. Pre-washed spinach salads that would ensure she ate something green. Everything found its designated place in cabinets and refrigerator, maintaining the organization that helped her feel in control of her shrinking world.

The pill organizers sat on her counter like colorful sentries, green for morning medications, purple for evening. I filled each compartment methodically, counting out pills that kept her heart beating steadily, her blood pressure stable, her joints functioning. Sunday through Saturday, each day portioned out in tiny pharmaceutical promises.

When she emerged from the shower, pink-cheeked and wrapped in her favorite terry cloth robe, I helped smooth lotion across her back, that impossible-to-reach territory that reminded us both of the indignities of aging. Then came her ritual spray of Estée Lauder perfume, the same scent she'd worn for forty years, because some things were worth preserving exactly as they'd always been.

"Now where did I put those shoes?" Mom muttered, padding around in her slippers.

I already knew the answer. Princess, my thirteen-pound accomplice, had struck again. We found the evidence under Mom's bed; two chewed, soggy shoes that bore the telltale marks of tiny teeth. Princess had developed this particular obsession, treating Mom's footwear like the world's most challenging puzzle toy.

"She thinks it's a game," Mom said with a mixture of exasperation and affection. "That little rascal waits until I'm distracted, then sneaks them away one at a time."

"Maybe it's time to try those new shoes I ordered for you," I suggested, though we both knew Mom's attachment to her old, comfortable pairs ran deeper than practicality.

"They probably just smell interesting to her," Mom replied diplomatically. "Like rawhide chews."

After we located Princess's latest victim and I kissed Mom goodbye, promising to call later, I settled into my car for the drive home. The late afternoon sun slanted through my windshield, and I found myself thinking about purpose again, about calling, about the weight of extraordinary experience pressing against ordinary life.

That's when my phone rang.

The sound startled me from my reverie, and when I glanced at the screen, my heart skipped. A Zoom call from an unfamiliar number. My finger hovered over the decline button; strange calls were usually telemarketers or worse. But something deeper than logic urged me to answer.

"Hello?" I said tentatively.

And then faces began appearing on my screen like miracles materializing in digital space.

Ishita first, her warm brown eyes lighting up with recognition and joy. Then Ling, her serene expression breaking into a smile that could have powered cities. Simba appeared next, his presence commanding even through pixelated connection. Ho Sung's face materialized with a grin that seemed to reach through the screen. Finally, Oliver's familiar features completed our impossible reunion.

My heart hammered against my ribs. I pulled into the nearest parking lot so quickly I nearly hit the curb, my hands shaking as I fumbled for my iPad to see them better.

"I knew it was real!" The words burst from my lips before I could stop them, accompanied by a smile so wide it hurt my cheeks. "How are you all? How have you been since..." I couldn't finish the sentence. Since heaven. Since we sat together at that impossible table, sharing manna and stories and the beginning of friendship.

Each face on my screen transformed with the same progression, surprise melting into joy, wonder replacing doubt.

"I almost convinced myself I dreamed the whole thing," Ling admitted, her voice carrying the relief of someone who'd been carrying a beautiful burden alone. "How did you get my number? I've had it blocked for weeks because of spam calls."

Simba's laugh rumbled through my speakers. "I've been in the mountains with practically no cell service. Your timing is absolutely perfect!"

"I just finished an eleven-hour flight," Ishita said, exhaustion and excitement warring in her expression. "I was literally about to step into the shower when this call came through."

Ho Sung shook his head in amazement. "I just walked out of the most boring budget meeting of my life. This is definitely divine intervention."

Oliver and I spoke simultaneously: "Who made this call?"

Silence.

Each face on the screen reflected the same confusion, the same dawning realization.

"I didn't call anyone," Ling said slowly.

"Neither did I," Simba confirmed.

"My phone just started ringing," Ishita added.

"Same here," Ho Sung nodded.

Oliver's brow furrowed. "But that's impossible. None of us know each other's full names, let alone phone numbers."

The technological impossibility of our connection settled over us like a holy mystery. Someone or something had orchestrated this reunion with the kind of precision that made miracles look like coincidences.

"Well," Oliver said finally, his voice carrying the weight of someone choosing to embrace the impossible, "if we're all here, maybe we should talk about what we experienced. What we witnessed."

The floodgates opened.

"I didn't want to leave," I admitted, the words carrying months of longing. "I keep feeling like there's a purpose behind the visit, a calling of some kind. But I can't figure out what it is."

Ishita leaned closer to her camera, her expression growing serious. "I've been re-searching something that's been bothering me since we returned. The Adversary, Satan. I don't think people on earth take him seriously enough."

Her words sent a chill through me. "What do you mean?"

"I've been looking into public opinion, surveys, cultural attitudes. The vast majority of people either don't believe he exists at all, or they think of him as some cartoon character in red pajamas with a pitchfork." Her voice grew urgent. "Can you imagine having an enemy who's actively working against you, but you don't even believe he's real? How much damage can someone cause when there's no opposition, no defense against his strategies?"

The truth of her observation hit me like cold water. We'd witnessed cosmic warfare, seen the Adversary make his case for humanity's destruction with the skill of a master prosecutor. But here on earth, most people treated spiritual warfare like fantasy.

Ling jumped in, her usually calm demeanor showing cracks of concern. "Think about COVID-19 in the United States. Nearly 400,000 people have died. If the disease had been acknowledged seriously from the beginning, if proper action had been taken immediately, would the loss of life have been so devastating?"

Ho Sung's voice dropped to barely above a whisper. "Are you suggesting COVID-19 is a tool used by the Adversary?"

"It could be," Simba replied grimly. "Weren't we told that the Adversary is cunning and shrewd? Division, fear, death, the breakdown of community and trust, those are exactly his strategies."

The conversation was heading into territory that made my skin crawl, but I needed to ask the question that had been haunting me. "Why do you think God selected us as 'invited guests'? What does He expect from us?"

The pause that followed felt pregnant with possibility and responsibility.

Ho Sung spoke first, his words carrying the weight of someone who'd wrestled with the same question. "God's actions are always purposeful, even when the purpose isn't immediately obvious. Isaiah 55:8-9 reminds us: 'For my thoughts are not your thoughts, neither are your ways my ways, declares the Lord. As the heavens are higher than the earth, so are my ways higher than your ways and my thoughts than your thoughts.' We need to pray for wisdom and understanding."

His words settled over us like a benediction, creating space for deeper reflection.

Simba cleared his throat. "Peter wrote something in his first letter that's been echoing in my mind: 'God has given each of us a gift from his great variety of spiritual gifts. Use them well to serve one another. Do you have the gift of speaking? Then speak as though God himself were speaking through you. Do you have the gift of helping others? Do it with all the strength and energy that God supplies. Then everything you do will bring glory to God through Jesus Christ.'"

Gifts. The word hung in the digital space between us like a key waiting for the right lock.

"Gifts that we can use to help others," I murmured, my mind beginning to race with possibilities.

Ling's face brightened. "Remember the Love Principle? We heard Jesus speak the greatest commandment, love God with all our heart, mind, and soul, and love our neighbor as ourselves. Then came the seven 'I AM' statements. I am the Good Shepherd. I am the Door. I am the Vine. I am the Way, the Truth, and the Life. Maybe we're supposed to demonstrate these principles."

"How?" Ishita asked, leaning forward. "What would that look like practically?"

Ling paused, choosing her words carefully. "Maybe 'demonstrate' isn't the right word. Imitate? Reflect? Live them out in ways that make the invisible Kingdom visible?"

Oliver's expression grew thoughtful. "The Adversary's argument was about man's inhumanity to man. What if we're called to take actions that reverse some of the damage humans have inflicted on each other?"

"Explain that," I urged, sensing we were approaching something crucial.

"God denied the Adversary's request for immediate judgment," Oliver continued, his voice gaining momentum. "But the consequences of human actions are creating judgment-like conditions anyway. Remember the first trumpet in Revelation? It announced that one-third of trees and grass would be burned. This year alone, we've witnessed wildfires unlike anything in recorded history. What if there are actions we can take to slow the forest fires, to heal the damage?"

Simba's eyes lit up with understanding. "Climate change, global warming, environmental destruction, these could be the natural consequences of human choices that mirror divine judgment. But if we have gifts, if we're called to action, maybe we can interrupt those consequences."

"Exactly!" Ishita exclaimed. "Each of us has unique gifts that could benefit humanity. My passion is clean water access, preventing people from getting sick, and keeping them from drinking contaminated water. What did Revelation call the bitter water? Wormwood? What if I'm called to address that specific issue?"

The connections were forming like lightning between clouds. "And my interest might be social justice," I said, my voice growing stronger with conviction. "Issues around racism, poverty, inequality, the very 'inhumanity to man' that the Adversary used in his accusations."

Ideas began flying across our connection like sparks from a fire. Environmental restoration. Healthcare access. Education equality. Economic justice. Community building. Each passion, each burden, each area of expertise represented a potential front in the cosmic battle between good and evil.

"But how do we know what God specifically wants us to do?" I asked, the weight of infinite possibilities both thrilling and overwhelming.

Ling's voice brought us back to center. "Remember Levi's fourteen-point prayer over you? He should be our example. He's in heaven, and he stands before God interceding for us. We should be praying constantly, seeking God's direction and purpose."

The profound simplicity of her statement settled over us like peace. Before action came communion. Before strategy came surrender.

"We should exchange contact information," Ho Sung suggested practically. "Real numbers this time, assuming this supernatural conference call doesn't become a regular thing."

Laughter rippled through our connection, nervous, hopeful, tinged with the recognition that we were stepping into something far bigger than ourselves.

"Let's commit to speaking again within the next few days," Oliver proposed. "We'll each spend time in prayer, seeking God's specific direction for our individual callings."

"And for our collective purpose," Simba added. "If we were brought together, there might be something we're meant to do as a group."

One by one, we shared our actual phone numbers and email addresses, the practical details that would anchor our supernatural connection in earthly reality. The conversation that began with confusion was ending with clarity of purpose, if not yet clarity of specific action.

"Until soon," Ishita said, her smile radiant even through the pixelated connection.

"Until soon," we echoed, each face disappearing from my screen like doors closing on a house I wasn't ready to leave.

As I sat alone in the parking lot, the silence felt different, not empty, but pregnant with possibility. I pulled out of the lot slowly, my mind spinning with ideas, dreams, fears, and hopes all tangled together like Christmas lights that needed patient untangling.

The implications were staggering. If we'd been chosen for a purpose, if our heavenly experience was preparation for earthly action, then everything was about to change. My quiet, ordinary life was about to become something extraordinary, something that mattered on a cosmic scale.

But even as excitement built in my chest, a familiar whisper began in the back of my mind. Doubt. Cold, persistent, wearing the mask of realism.

Who do you think you are? What makes you believe you can make any real difference? You're just ordinary. You have no special training, no advanced degrees, no platform, no influence. How could God possibly use someone like you?

I recognized the voice immediately, not my own thoughts, but the enemy's strategy. The same doubt that had whispered to Eve in the garden, the same questioning that sought to undermine every divine calling throughout history.

"No," I said aloud, my voice firm in the enclosed space of my car. "I will not let fear defeat me before I even begin."

As I drove through the gathering dusk, I began to pray with an urgency that surprised me. "God, please defeat my fear. You said if I have faith like a mustard seed, I could move mountains. I don't need to move mountains, Lord, I just need to move forward. Show me what You want me to do. Give me courage to do it. And please, please, don't let me waste this gift You've given me."

The streetlights began flickering on as darkness settled over the city, but inside my car, something else was settling too, a quiet determination that felt like the beginning of everything.

I had been to heaven and back. I had witnessed the cosmic battle between good and evil. I had heard Love define itself in its own voice. And now, impossibly, beautifully, terrifyingly, it seemed I was being called to join the fight.

The question was no longer whether I had a calling.

The question was whether I had the courage to answer it.

35

---•---

WAIT FOR GOD

The Zoom call replayed in my mind like a song I couldn't stop humming. Every face, every word, every moment of supernatural connection had etched itself into my memory with the permanence of carved stone. "Who made the call?" The question followed me through the day like a gentle ghost, not haunting but comforting, a reminder that Someone beyond our understanding was orchestrating events with divine precision.

Seeing each of my tablemates had been like finding pieces of myself I didn't know were missing. If any whisper of doubt had still lingered in the corners of my heart, and truthfully, there hadn't been, that call would have incinerated it completely. It was confirmation wrapped in pixels and delivered through fiber optic cables, proof that the impossible could become as real as morning coffee and evening news.

But who else could I share this with? Who else would understand?

The answer had crystallized during Bible study when our teacher asked, "Why did Mary, the mother of Jesus Christ, visit her cousin Elizabeth after the angel announced she would give birth to the Messiah?"

My hand shot up before I could think. "Because she needed someone who could share in the experience of a divine encounter. Someone who could confirm the nature of what had happened to her without questioning its legitimacy."

Elizabeth, pregnant with John the Baptist after decades of barrenness, would understand miraculous conception. She would believe because she, too, had experienced the impossible made manifest in her own body.

That's what I felt about my tablemates, they were my Elizabeths, the only people on earth who could hear my story and respond with recognition instead of referrals to mental health professionals.

Because let's be honest about what would happen if I tried to share this with anyone else.

Picture it: Your lifelong friend, someone you've known since childhood, someone whose sanity you've never questioned, sits you down for what they call an "important conversation." They tell you they felt the presence of a man in a small examination room while waiting for a doctor, though you were there too and saw nothing. Oh, and by the way, they were there seeking drugs, this was the second doctor, the first having already refused. They were literally doctor-shopping for controlled substances, medications that alter thought processes and perception.

Then that same friend tells you an angel appeared and transported them to heaven. In heaven, they witnessed God the Father on His throne, saw Jesus Christ in His glory, watched Satan himself make legal arguments for humanity's destruction. They claim to have dined with saints from across history, eaten the same manna that sustained the Israelites for forty years in the wilderness, attended a cosmic concert where angels marched in perfect formation. They describe thrones and beasts and creatures covered in eyes, culminating with Jesus Christ delivering prophecies and warnings directly to them.

What would you say to that friend? Would you nod thoughtfully and ask for more details? Or would you gently inquire about the medication they'd finally obtained and how long its hallucinogenic effects typically lasted?

Exactly.

You wouldn't believe them. Not for a second. And you'd probably start googling local psychiatrists while they were still talking.

So the Zoom call wasn't just confirmation, it was salvation from the isolation that comes with carrying impossible truth alone. It satisfied a desperate hunger I hadn't fully acknowledged: the need to share what had happened, to speak it aloud and have someone respond with understanding instead of concern for my mental health.

But our conversation had revealed something else, a golden thread woven through each of our stories: we all sensed a calling on our lives. None of us could articulate exactly what that calling entailed, but we felt it like a low-frequency hum in our souls, persistent and undeniable.

I'd been wrestling with this question for days now, turning it over like a puzzle piece I couldn't quite fit into place. What were my gifts? What could I possibly offer that would matter in the cosmic battle between good and evil?

Ideas had begun sprouting like wildflowers after rain. A business, maybe, or a nonprofit focused on housing needs, helping people find safe, affordable places to call home. Perhaps writing, a book about my experiences, a blog that bridged earthly struggles with heavenly truths. Maybe counseling, using whatever wisdom I'd gained to help others navigate their own spiritual journeys.

The possibilities excited and terrified me in equal measure. Was it possible to use spiritual gifts in work that was actually enjoyable? Hadn't Levi prayed specifically for my humor, joy, and success? Maybe divine calling didn't have to feel like martyrdom. Maybe it could feel like coming alive.

Something fundamental was shifting inside me, like tectonic plates rearranging them-selves to create new continents of possibility. The feelings of failure that had clung to me like smoke for so long were beginning to dissipate. The doubts and anxiety that had plagued my thoughts were being replaced by something I'd almost forgotten how to feel: adventure. The sense that my life could matter, that my story could have chapters I hadn't yet imagined, that hope wasn't just wishful thinking but rational expectation based on divine intervention.

I'd begun researching opportunities that could help others while allowing me to make a living, something I could be proud of and that would receive God's blessing. What I really meant was that I'd started praying differently, for understanding, wisdom, vision, and growth. Levi's fourteen-point prayer had become my template, teaching me what to ask of God instead of just asking God to fix what I thought was broken.

Two Bible verses had become my anchors, words I repeated like mantras when doubt tried to creep back in.

The first was Isaiah 40:31: "But they who wait for the LORD shall renew their strength; they shall mount up with wings like eagles; they shall run and not be weary; they shall walk and not faint."

This verse had become my permission slip to be patient with the process. Waiting on the Lord wasn't passive resignation, it was active anticipation. God had called me for a purpose that would be revealed in His timing, not mine. And while I waited, something miraculous would happen: my strength would be renewed.

I thought about the years I'd spent running on empty, working endless hours that blurred into endless days. Evenings, weekends, vacations. I'd worked through all of it. My assistant used to get so frustrated she'd physically try to take my phone away. "Turn it off!" she'd plead, but I couldn't. I was driven by something I couldn't name, fueled by a restlessness that no amount of achievement could satisfy.

But this verse promised something different. Energy that would last. The ability to soar without burning out, to run without growing weary, to walk without fainting. The language was figurative, but the promise felt literal, I would be able to do what God called me to do with supernatural endurance because I wouldn't be doing it alone.

The second verse had found me during a particularly vulnerable moment: Psalm 27:13-14: "I believe that I shall look upon the goodness of the LORD in the land of the living! Wait for the LORD; be strong and let your heart take courage; wait for the LORD!"

I'd discovered this passage after watching a YouTube video by a popular rabbi discussing the afterlife. I'm a Christian, but I've always believed wisdom can come from unexpected sources, especially when it comes to understanding Old Testament concepts.

Someone had asked the rabbi, "Is there life after death?"

His response had initially sounded like theological double-talk: "How can the living die, or the dead live? The living lives and the dead dies."

I'd been ready to click to another video when something made me pause and really listen. His argument was beautifully simple: God breathed life into man, and that breath, the soul, was eternal. But God formed man from dust, and dust was dead matter. When the body dies, it returns to dust, but the soul continues to live.

This insight had unlocked Psalm 27:13-14 in a way I'd never considered before. The phrase "land of the living" wasn't just about earthly existence, it encompassed both the literal land where we currently live and the eternal realm where souls continue to exist after physical death.

When I was in heaven, every being I encountered was vibrantly, eternally alive. Those who believe in Jesus Christ, accepting Him as Savior, don't just receive eternal life, they are eternal life. But those who choose darkness, who reject the Light of the world, don't just die, they choose non-existence, separation from the Source of all life.

Before my heavenly experience, I would have read this verse superficially. Now, everything carried deeper meaning, as if my spiritual eyes had been fitted with new lenses that could perceive dimensions previously invisible.

The verse also spoke about courage: "Be strong and let your heart take courage." This wasn't just cheerleader encouragement, it was a command based on spiritual reality. Living takes courage. Having faith in a faithless world requires the kind of strength that only comes from supernatural sources. Sometimes, being strong is simply having the courage to do what's right, to stand up for truth when lies are more popular, to choose light when darkness offers easier paths.

Courage to wait on the Lord.

That's where I found myself now, in the sacred space between calling and clarity, between invitation and instruction. I was waiting on the Lord to show me direction, and for the first time in my adult life, the waiting didn't feel like punishment.

It felt like preparation.

God had shown me heaven not as an ending, but as a beginning. He'd given me a glimpse of the cosmic battle between good and evil not to overwhelm me, but to recruit me. He'd connected me with fellow travelers not to form a social club, but to build a team.

Now came the hardest part: trusting His timing over my impatience, His wisdom over my plans, His methods over my expectations.

I was learning to wait with wings like eagles, not the desperate waiting of someone hoping for rescue, but the confident waiting of someone who knows rescue has already come and is now preparing for flight.

The adventure was just beginning.

36

○

DOCTOR VISIT

The alarm pierced through my sleep like a sword through silk, dragging me from dreams I couldn't quite remember but somehow didn't want to leave. Princess had claimed most of my pillow during the night, her small body curled into a perfect circle with her rear end positioned directly in front of my face, her favorite sleeping arrangement and my least favorite wake-up call.

"Really, Princess?" I mumbled, gently nudging her toward the foot of the bed. She opened one eye, gave me a look that clearly communicated her displeasure at being disturbed, then hopped down with the dramatic flair that only small dogs can muster.

I turned off the alarm and sank back into the mattress, staring at the ceiling as reality settled around me like morning fog. Today was the day that I was supposed to return to the Doctor's office. I should have cancelled yesterday. Twenty-four hours' notice, that was the rule. Cancel now and face a twenty-five-dollar penalty for my indecision.

But indecision wasn't really the right word, was it? I had changed. Fundamentally, completely, irrevocably changed since my last visit to that office. The woman who had sat in that examination room weeks ago, desperate for Xanax to quiet the screaming anxiety in her head, felt like a stranger now. A stranger I pitied and barely recognized.

I still carried some anxiety, I wasn't completely transformed, not yet. The human condition doesn't evaporate overnight, even after divine intervention. But the crushing weight that used to sit on my chest like a concrete block? That was gone. The panic that used to claw at my throat when I thought about the future? Replaced by something I was still learning to trust: faith.

I was trying to lean on God's guidance and His word, though I had to admit I still needed to mature and grow in understanding. Some days felt like spiritual boot camp, learning to walk in faith when my old instincts screamed for control.

But waiting for God to reveal His calling carried its own brand of apprehension. What if He asked me to do something I couldn't do correctly? What if I was unwilling to do what He asked? The consequences of failing God felt infinitely more terrifying than failing myself.

And God had made some... unusual requests of His people throughout history.

Take the Prophet Ezekiel. God told him to stage an elaborate performance art piece to portray Judah's coming captivity. By day, Ezekiel was to pack his belongings and relocate in full view of the Israelites. By night, he was to dig through the wall of his home, carrying his possessions while covering his face, again, in front of an audience. When people asked why he was doing this bizarre pantomime, he was to explain that this was their future: captivity in Babylon if they didn't change their rebellious ways.

Or Jeremiah, commanded to wear a linen sash that could never be washed, then bury it under a rock near the Euphrates River. After it had rotted underground, God told him to dig it up and wear the ruined, stinking thing as an object lesson about the ruined pride of Judah and Jerusalem.

Then there was Isaiah, ordered to walk naked and barefoot for three years as a sign that Egypt and Ethiopia would be conquered by the Assyrians. Three years! The scripture says he would represent how the captives would be led away "young and old, naked and barefoot, with their buttocks uncovered," bringing great shame.

And poor Hosea, commanded to marry a prostitute who would be unfaithful to him, their dysfunctional relationship serving as a living metaphor for Israel's unfaithfulness to God. Even their children's names were prophetic messages: Jezreel ("God will sow"), Lo-Ruhamah ("no mercy"), and Lo-Ammi ("you are not my people").

I know how this sounds! I'm not completely crazy, and I'm certainly no prophet! But these stories had always struck me as both profound and absurd. They made me wonder: would God ask me to do something equally outrageous? Would I be willing to walk around naked for three years? If I tried, would I be committed to the nearest psychiatric facility before I made it to the end of my driveway?

Or would I chicken out and claim I was just trying to lose weight for vanity reasons?

I know I'm being ridiculous, but you have to maintain a sense of humor when contemplating divine assignments. Levi had prayed for my humor, after all.

But what if God asked me to communicate His message and people refused to listen? What if I was unable to speak with sufficient eloquence for the word of God? What if my calling required skills I didn't possess or courage I couldn't summon?

What am I called to do? The question followed me like my own shadow.

I went through my morning routine with deliberate care, as if normal activities could anchor me to sanity. Princess got her walk around the block, her breakfast served in her favorite bowl, and a goodbye kiss that she tolerated with regal patience.

As I drove to the doctor's office, my mind wandered to my tablemates from heaven. I'd been curious about each of them but hadn't wanted to violate their privacy by digging into their earthly lives. Today, though, I decided I would look them up online when I got home. If we were meant to work together in some divine capacity, maybe I should know more about their backgrounds, their skills, their earthly roles.

The medical building looked exactly the same as it had weeks ago, but I felt like I was seeing it through different eyes. The parking lot, the automatic doors, the sterile smell of disinfectant mixed with industrial carpet, all of it familiar yet foreign, like returning to a childhood home after decades away.

"Good morning," I said to the receptionist, offering my insurance card. "I have an appointment."

"Of course, Ms. Evans. Please have a seat. Someone will be with you shortly."

The waiting room was populated with the usual collection of people avoiding eye contact; elderly couples holding hands, mothers with fidgeting children, individuals staring at their phones with the desperate focus of people trying to avoid thinking about why they were there.

When my name was called, I followed the nurse down a hallway that seemed both longer and shorter than I remembered. She stopped at the same examination room where I'd first felt Levi's presence, where my spiritual journey had truly begun.

"Just have a seat," she said cheerfully. "I'll take your vitals, and then the doctor will be right in."

I positioned myself on the same stool where I'd sat in terrified confusion weeks ago, half-expecting to feel that supernatural presence again. I found myself hoping Levi would appear, this time, I wouldn't be afraid. This time, I would welcome him with gratitude instead of panic.

But the room felt ordinary, empty of anything beyond medical equipment and the faint scent of sanitizer.

"Good morning, Ms. Evans. How are you doing today?" The nurse bustled in with practiced efficiency, wrapping the blood pressure cuff around my arm.

Temperature: 97.4. Blood pressure: 129/82. Oxygen: 98%. Weight: ... well, let's just say the scale and I were no longer on speaking terms.

"The doctor will be in shortly," she said, making notes on her tablet before disappearing again.

I sat alone with my thoughts and the steady hum of fluorescent lights, wondering if divine appointments ever happened in places that smelled like antiseptic.

"Ms. Evans? Good to meet you."

The voice belonged to a tall, striking African American woman who carried herself with the confident bearing of someone accustomed to being the smartest person in most rooms. She was heavier than me, impeccably dressed, and radiating an all-business energy that suggested she didn't suffer fools gladly.

Something about her face seemed familiar, though I was certain we'd never met. Maybe she just reminded me of someone, that strange recognition you sometimes feel when meeting a kindred spirit.

"I'm Dr. Williams," she continued, settling onto her rolling stool with the efficiency of someone who'd done this thousands of times. "I see from your previous visit that you were seeking a prescription for Xanax. Can you tell me why?"

The directness of her question caught me off guard, though I suppose I should have expected it. This was, after all, why I'd originally come.

"That's true," I said carefully. "I was dealing with severe anxiety and was hoping Xanax might help. But honestly, I no longer need it. I've... found other ways to manage my anxiety."

Her eyebrows rose slightly. "What's changed in your life that's reduced your anxiety levels?"

I gave her the safest answer I could think of: "I haven't been working lately. I've been staying home, getting plenty of rest, keeping out of harm's way. My anxiety just isn't as severe as it was."

Dr. Williams leaned back slightly, her expression shifting from professional interest to something that looked suspiciously like . . . suspicion.

"I spoke with your previous primary care physician," she said, her tone cooling several degrees. "He told me you were quite determined to be prescribed Xanax. He was concerned you might be developing a dependency and wanted to prevent addiction. Yet here you are, claiming you no longer need it after waiting in my office just a couple of weeks ago." She paused, studying my face with the intensity of a detective examining evidence. "Are you getting it somewhere else, Ms. Evans?"

The question hit me like a slap. I felt my back straighten, my jaw clench, my entire demeanor shift from patient to plaintiff.

"I'm not sure you heard me clearly," I said, my voice taking on the crisp, professional tone I'd perfected during years of difficult conversations. "I said I'm no longer interested in being prescribed Xanax. The only reason I'm here today is because I forgot to cancel yesterday and didn't want to pay the penalty for same-day cancellation." I paused, letting that sink in. "I need a new primary care physician due to insurance changes. I also need referrals to a gastroenterologist and an orthopedist. Did I come to the right place for primary care, or should I look elsewhere?"

"Ms. Evans," she said, her tone softening slightly but her suspicion remaining intact, "I heard what you said. I just don't understand the sudden change of heart. Many people who claim they no longer need controlled substances are obtaining them elsewhere. I want to make sure you're not doing anything that could harm you down the road."

Something inside me snapped, not into anger, but into absolute clarity.

"Are you accusing me of being a drug addict, Doctor?" My voice was steel wrapped in silk. The transformation was instantaneous and complete, I went from anxious patient to formidable advocate for myself. "If you need to know why I no longer desire Xanax, it's not because I'm getting it elsewhere. It's because God interceded in my life. I went to Heaven."

I didn't care what she thought. I didn't care how it sounded. I stood up, grabbed my purse, phone, and keys, and headed for the door.

"Wait!" Her voice stopped me mid-stride. "You died and went to Heaven?"

I turned back, seeing the expression I'd expected, a mixture of concern, disbelief, and the particular look medical professionals get when they think they're dealing with someone who's lost touch with reality.

"No, I didn't die," I said with the patience one uses when explaining something obvious to a child. "If I had died, would I still be dead?" I softened my tone slightly. "I guess I should say I'm going through a transformation with God's help. I'm trying to lean on Him instead of my own understanding."

Still standing at the door, I decided to redirect the conversation to safer ground. "I have new health insurance. My previous primary care physician didn't participate in my new plan. I called the insurance company for recommendations, and your name was one of several who accepted new patients. I know I need referrals for specialists, so I thought it best to establish care as soon as possible."

The atmosphere in the room had shifted completely. We were studying each other like chess players trying to anticipate the next move. She was trying to figure out if I could be trusted with controlled substances. I was trying to figure out if she could be trusted with the truth.

"I really want to know your story," she said finally, her voice carrying a vulnerability that hadn't been there before. "I want to understand what you meant when you said you went to Heaven, and it transformed you."

I weighed my options. This could go very badly, very quickly. "Doctor, aren't we limited to fifteen minutes per visit based on insurance guidelines?"

"I'll only charge for the first fifteen minutes," she said without hesitation. "I don't have another patient for a while, and I genuinely want to hear what happened to you."

Something in her tone made me reconsider. Maybe it was the way her professional mask had slipped, revealing something raw and desperate underneath.

"Okay," I said, moving back into the room but remaining standing. "The last time I was here, in this exact room, I felt a presence. I couldn't explain it, but I knew someone was with me. It terrified me. I fled your office, trying to escape whatever it was."

"Who was with you?" she asked quietly.

"My angel, Levi. When I got home, he was waiting for me. He said God had sent him on a mission. I was an invited guest to Heaven." The words felt surreal even as I spoke them. "He took me to what he called the hall of halls, like a massive arena. I witnessed Satan, the Adversary seeking judgment against humanity. I experienced the Love March and heard the Love Principles directly from Jesus Christ. I met other people like me, with their own guardian angels."

I watched her face as I spoke, seeing the familiar struggle between skepticism and something that looked almost like... hope?

"There aren't words to express the full glory of what I experienced," I continued. "It was magnificent beyond description. It reminded me that everything begins and ends with God. Since my visit to Heaven, my anxiety has decreased dramatically. I realized my anxiety was rooted in feelings of failure and defeat, but I was reminded that I'm not defeated. Only God could truly defeat me, and He's chosen to build me up instead."

I paused, studying her reaction. "I don't know why God chose me and the others as invited guests, but He did. I know there's a calling on my life, though I'm not sure what it is yet."

Dr. Williams sat in absolute silence for what felt like an eternity. Then, slowly, tears began to form in her eyes.

"I was there," she whispered. "I was in Heaven, too."

The words hung in the air between us like a bridge across an impossible distance. Then we were both crying, and somehow, we were hugging, and the professional boundaries that should have kept us separated dissolved in the face of shared impossible truth.

Someone knocked on the door.

"I'm okay," she called through her tears. "I'll be out shortly."

I could hear footsteps outside, someone clearly concerned but respecting her privacy. The door remained closed.

"I told my husband what happened," she said, her voice breaking. "He said I was just daydreaming, but I knew I wasn't dreaming. Eli visited me, my angel. I was on my way to the grocery store, parked in front of Wegmans, just sitting there for a minute. I'm always surrounded by people, patients, staff, my Husband, etc. I never get quiet moments. So, I turned on some music and just... relaxed."

Her tears were flowing freely now. "Before I knew it, I was having the deepest conversation with the gentlest person you could ever imagine. He asked me questions about myself, but he already knew me. He said God had sent for me. I was in that arena you described, saw the thrones, heard the voices, witnessed the four living creatures, the cherubim and seraphim. I heard the argument about humanity's failures. I experienced the Love March and the Love Principles."

She looked directly into my eyes. "I knew it was real. I had been touched by God. But my husband said what I described was impossible. He said no time had passed, I was only away from the office for thirty minutes. He said there's no evidence God exists, and if there was a God, would He allow such violence, poverty, and inequity in the world?"

Another gentle knock interrupted her.

"I began to doubt my own eyes," she continued urgently. "Not until now. Not until you and your story."

She stood and went to the door. Her husband, the office manager, was checking on her. He mentioned another patient waiting and a pharmaceutical sales rep at the front desk. As he spoke, his eyes found me over her shoulder, examining me with the particular suspicion reserved for people who keep doctors from maintaining their schedules.

"I haven't finished reviewing her medical history," Dr. Williams said firmly. "When I'm done, I'll be out." She closed the door and returned to her seat.

"Before Eli, I was in a really dark place," she said, her voice barely above a whisper. "I was suffering from severe depression. Every day I came to work scared. Would someone bring COVID-19 to my office? Would I be the one who got just a headache and cough, or would I die on a ventilator without friends or family by my side?"

The vulnerability in her voice was crushing. "People think being a doctor means you're perfect, making money, no problems. They don't consider that doctors get sick and die just like everyone else. We don't have all the answers. How many of the people who died from COVID were doctors, nurses, technicians?" She looked at me with eyes that had seen too much loss. "I didn't want to die. At least, I didn't want to die then."

I listened, barely breathing.

"I was confused after my heavenly experience. I knew what I'd experienced was real, but I couldn't convince my husband. He called my doctor. He requested a sleeping aid and antidepressants. For me! He scrutinizes me like I'm falling apart in front of him, but I'm not falling apart. Not anymore."

Her voice grew stronger, tinged with frustration. "The pressure is constant. He wants to be with me every minute of the day. I think he's planning to have me committed to the psychiatric ward at the local hospital." She paused, pain flickering across her features. "I love my husband, but I'm beginning to wonder if he's under the influence of the Devil. He's caused me to doubt something so real, so transformative."

The depth of her confession left me speechless. Without knowing it, I had been sent to this appointment not for medical care, but for confirmation. Like Elizabeth greeting Mary, recognizing the miracle each carried, we had found each other in the most unlikely place.

Two women who had touched Heaven were sitting in an examination room, confirming each other's impossible truth.

And I realized this was exactly what God had meant when He called us to wait on Him. He hadn't been asking us to sit passively. He'd been preparing divine appointments, orchestrating encounters that would strengthen us for whatever came next.

The calling I had been waiting for wasn't coming.

It was already here.

37

FOOT IN THE MOUTH DISEASE

As I walked past the office manager, the weight of the unspoken tension pressed against my shoulders like a physical force. His eyes tracked my movement with the intensity of a predator studying prey, and I could practically hear the questions grinding through his mind like gears in desperate need of oil.

Who was this woman to his wife?

The thought radiated from him with such force that I felt it in my bones. He watched me emerge from the examination room, observed my passage by the receptionist's desk, followed my exit through the front door with the kind of scrutiny usually reserved for suspected criminals. I wasn't just another patient to him, I was an anomaly, a variable in an equation he couldn't solve.

The poor man looked like someone trying to catch smoke with his bare hands.

He'd heard his wife crying in that exam room. Witnessed her emerge looking simultaneously shattered and illuminated. Seen us embrace like old friends reuniting after years apart, though we were supposed to be strangers meeting for the second time. The receptionist had been watching him watch her, which meant he couldn't linger at the door as every instinct demanded. He couldn't get answers to the questions burning holes in his peace of mind.

And he didn't trust that he could get a straight answer from his wife anymore.

She'd been acting strange. She claimed she'd been to heaven, experienced impossible things she couldn't fully explain. But it had taken only thirty minutes for her to leave the office, drive a mile to Wegmans, go in and out of the grocery store, and return. Thirty minutes. In his rational, scientific mind, she'd lost her sanity in the span of a coffee break.

His world was changing right before his eyes, shifting in ways that were subtle yet seismic, completely outside his control. He loved his wife, that much was certain. And she loved him. But since that day, the day she claimed to have visited heaven, her love had... changed. Not diminished, but transformed into something he didn't recognize, couldn't predict, couldn't control.

I could almost hear his internal monologue as I reached my car: Could I have handled the situation differently? Could I have told her I believed her? Could I have sat down and asked her to tell me everything about her visit to heaven? What was God like? Did you see Jesus Christ? Could I have pretended to be something I'm not?

Maybe I was too quick to call her doctor. Maybe I...

She's dried up on me. My wife has dried up.

My phone rang just as I reached for my car door handle.

"Ms. Evans." The voice was muffled, thick with emotion I couldn't immediately identify. "Who are you to my wife?"

I froze, keys dangling from my fingers. Slowly, I turned toward the medical building I'd just left. At a side window, several blinds had been pushed up, creating a small viewing portal. He was there, the office manager, Dr. Williams' husband, staring at me with the desperate intensity of someone watching their life unravel in real time.

"I'm sorry," I said carefully, "can you tell me who's calling, please?"

We studied each other across the parking lot like chess opponents trying to read each other's next move. I knew who he was. More importantly, I knew what he wanted from me, and what he feared I might represent.

The blinds snapped shut. Footsteps retreated from the window.

"Ms. Evans, you were just in the examination room with my wife, your... doctor." The pause before that last word carried the weight of accusation, suspicion, and barely contained panic.

I continued to my vehicle, processing the conversation I somehow knew was coming. "Mr. Harris, I'm your wife's patient. You met me several weeks ago when I couldn't stay for my appointment, so I rescheduled for today. She gave me two referrals, one for gastroenterology, one for orthopedics."

This wasn't the answer to his real question, but it was a response to what he'd actually asked. While he gathered courage to voice his true concerns, I found myself contemplating the deeper tragedy unfolding. Here were two people who needed each other desperately, yet he was unknowingly working to extinguish the very fire that had been placed within her, the divine spark that would enable her to fulfill her Kingdom purpose.

The biblical parallel hit me like lightning: When Jesus told His disciples what would happen to Him, Peter had assured Him of his protection, declaring that Jesus's predictions would never come to pass. Jesus's response had been swift and devastating: "Get behind me, Satan! You are a stumbling block to me; you do not have in mind the concerns of God, but merely human concerns."

Peter, in his human love and protection, had been used as an instrument of spiritual opposition.

Just like this husband was being used now.

Through my phone, I could hear Mr. Harris weeping, ragged, broken sounds that spoke of a man watching his world crumble. He cried, broke, stopped, then started again. I heard rustling, the distinctive sound of tissue being pulled from a box, a nose being blown.

I remained in my car, still parked in the same space in front of their building, somehow unable to leave.

"Why are you lying to me?" His voice cracked like thin ice under pressure. "I know you're lying. Are you... are you lovers?"

The question hung in the air like a toxic cloud. Why was I still on this phone? I should have disconnected the moment he called. Should have driven away without looking back. But something, divine appointment, human compassion, or simple curiosity, kept me anchored to this increasingly disturbing conversation.

"No, we are not lovers," I said as gently as I could manage. "This is my second time speaking with her and the first time actually meeting her. Why would you accuse me of being her lover? What's really wrong, Mr. Harris?"

His answer came wrapped in pure anguish: "I don't want to lose my wife. I can see her changing, getting further and further away from me every day. Then you walk in, smiling, glistening, and she sits down with you like you're the answer to prayers and I didn't even know she was praying. She cries and talks to you like you're her confessor. She should be talking to me. My shoulders can handle her tears. Why you? Why not me?"

The raw pain in his voice made my chest ache. "I don't know why," I answered honestly. "Have you tried sitting down and really talking with her?"

"The last time we talked, really talked, I told her she was crazy." The admission fell from his lips like broken glass. "I said I was going to send her to the hospital for a mental evaluation. I... I really didn't mean it. Well, I think I didn't mean it. But I did call her doctor. She said something so unexpected, so unlike her, that I wanted to put an end to the conversation. Really, it scared me."

"What scared you?"

"She said she went to heaven." The words came out like a confession of defeat. "She told me about all these things she witnessed, these impossible experiences. But she'd only been away from the office for thirty minutes. How could all of those things have happened? It didn't make sense. But now I wonder..."

He stopped, the silence stretching between us like a bridge neither of us was sure we should cross.

"What do you wonder?" I pressed gently.

"I wonder if things would be different between us if I had just believed her. If I had just listened, really listened, instead of trying to fix her or diagnose her or save her from herself." His voice broke again. "I wish I hadn't acted the way I did."

"Have you apologized to her? Have you told her you just didn't understand?" I found myself probing deeper, guided by an instinct I didn't fully understand. "Why did her claim about heaven bother you so much?"

His answer came in a rush, like water breaking through a dam: "First, she'd been terribly afraid of catching COVID-19. We're both big people, both people of color. The bullseye was on our backs from day one. She'd been having thoughts about dying, making statements and innuendos about death. I didn't want to live my life afraid all the time, and I didn't want her to either."

He paused, gathering momentum for the deeper confession: "Second, we're scientists. We believe in what we can prove, measure, replicate in controlled conditions. God is mere speculation, wishful thinking for people who can't handle reality."

The final blow came with devastating honesty: "Third, she hadn't been to church since she moved away from her parents' home almost twenty years ago. Never mentioned the Bible, Jesus Christ, or God in any meaningful way. When my parents insisted we attend church with them one Christmas, she refused point-blank. My father told me not to marry her because we weren't equally yoked. I married her anyway, but now..." He trailed off, then finished with desperate confusion: "Is she going to become some bible-thumping doctor? What does she know about God or Jesus Christ?"

"What should she know about God or Jesus Christ?" I countered.

"I'm sorry, what do you mean?"

"You asked what she knows about God or Jesus Christ. I want to know from you, what should she know?"

Silence stretched between us like a chasm.

"Mr. Harris, your wife told you she went to heaven. She shared her experiences with you. How do those experiences take away from your relationship with her?"

More silence. My phone showed we were still connected. I could hear rustling, breathing, the sound of a man wrestling with concepts that threatened to upend everything he thought he knew about reality.

Something compelled me to press further, though I wasn't sure where the words were coming from: "Jesus told His followers that He was the way, the truth, and the life, that no one comes to the Father except through Him. Do you think your wife has discovered Jesus Christ? Has He changed her life? Has her visit to heaven transformed her?"

I stopped talking, surprised by my own boldness. Why was I asking about their relationship? About Jesus Christ? He'd opened a door, and somehow I'd walked through it without conscious decision.

I glanced toward the building, toward the window where the blinds had been raised. He wasn't visible now. It felt almost like talking to myself, but I knew he was there, listening, wrestling.

Nothing. No response. Just the weight of silence and unasked questions.

"Mr. Harris, have you seen a change in your wife?" I pushed gently.

Finally, reluctantly: "Yes. There's been a change. She's stronger, more confident. She hasn't been afraid of dying, in fact, there's been a peace, a calmness that's come over her. I almost thought she was at peace because she was planning her own... exit."

The word hung between us like a blade. "Why did you think she was planning her own exit? We're talking about suicide, right?"

He considered the question carefully. "She went from being terribly depressed to never mentioning her fears and worries. But before this change, she'd talked to me about a patient who had committed suicide. She said she understood why that patient had taken that action." His voice grew quieter, more vulnerable. "When she changed so dramatically, I thought she might have solved her problems by developing a plan. She knew I was tired of hearing her complain, so she stopped having normal conversations with me about her fears. That made me watch her more closely, but I was afraid to talk to her. I didn't understand her."

The admission came with a weight that threatened to crush us both: "She talked about being in heaven, but she hadn't picked up a Bible or joined a church. Something had profoundly changed her, but she refused to share the truth with me."

"What happens if she has told you the truth, but you refused to hear it?" I asked gently. "Would it be so bad if she really went to heaven? Certainly that's better than suicide or having an affair, right?"

"Have you heard yourself?" His frustration and anger were building like pressure in a boiler. "Heaven? How can I compete with heaven? You're asking me to believe that she died and went to heaven, then was sent back to me, happy, joyful, and calm."

"No, I never said she died."

"You're wasting my time," he spat, his voice thick with disbelief and rage. "You really are an asshole!"

The line went dead.

I sat in my car, staring at my phone, feeling like I'd just witnessed a marriage imploding in real time. The man's pain was real, legitimate, heartbreaking. His wife had been transformed by an experience he couldn't accept, couldn't understand, couldn't compete with. From his perspective, he'd lost her to something that didn't exist.

But from my perspective, from his wife's perspective, she'd been found by the only thing, the only person, that could have saved her.

And I'd just stuck my foot so far in my mouth that I'd probably made everything worse.

Sometimes being a messenger of hope felt an awful lot like being a messenger of destruction.

The question was: which one was I really?

38

— ◆ —

PURPOSE

As I pulled out of the parking lot, the weight of two conversations pressed against my chest like competing storms. The doctor's tears of recognition and relief. Her husband's rage and desperate fear. Both conversations swirled in my mind, creating an emotional whirlwind I couldn't quite navigate.

I remembered the last time someone had called me an "asshole." Ironically, that insult had been a blessing in disguise, it had stopped me from doing something truly foolish. But this time felt different. This time, the accusation bothered me in ways I couldn't fully articulate.

Because part of him knew the truth about his wife.

He knew she was sharing something personal, intimate, transformative. Deep down, he knew she hadn't lost her mind, yet he acted as if she had. It struck me that he understood the power of God but was terrified to acknowledge it, terrified to let her acknowledge it. The implications were too threatening to his carefully constructed world.

Something he'd said nagged at me. When his parents had wanted them to attend church one Christmas, he hadn't said he wouldn't go, he'd said she wouldn't. A man raised by church-going parents, familiar with faith's language and expectations. Did he have a relationship with God that he was now denying? Had something interfered with his faith? Had he once believed but lost that belief somewhere along the way?

He'd seemed suspicious of me, yet he'd opened up completely. Cried. Admitted his fears. Was it his wife he was afraid of losing, or his lifestyle with his wife? Was he protecting something deeper than just their marriage? Was he terrified that if she changed, her love for him would change too?

His demeanor had shifted during our call. Even though he'd hung up in anger, I sensed that my questions had provoked something within him, planted seeds in soil he'd thought was barren.

But the conversation with Dr. Williams filled me with something I could only call joy. I'd known I was called to fulfill a purpose, though I hadn't understood what. Today, I'd glimpsed it. The appointment hadn't been an accident, it had been divine confirmation. Not so much for me as for her. She'd needed to know her experiences were real, not dreams or delusions. She was being told her story was false, nonexistent. But for God's work to take place, doubt had to be eliminated.

I'd been sent as her Elizabeth, the one who could confirm the impossible.

After such an intense day, I craved the simple comfort of my bed and mindless television. I kicked off my shoes, grabbed a pillow, and pulled a blanket over me. Princess navigated her doggie stairs to claim her spot beside me. I clicked on the news.

The anchor was discussing the Capitol riot that had shaken the nation two days earlier. People were still reeling from the unprecedented assault on democracy, the shocking images of the President's involvement in undermining the very government he'd sworn to protect. The implications were staggering, contrary to everything America claimed to represent.

I turned off the television. The chaos of earthly politics felt small compared to the cosmic battles I'd witnessed.

Before I knew it, I was dreaming.

Or was I?

_____

I found myself standing inside massive gates that defied human comprehension. They towered above me, crafted from gold so pure it seemed to sing with its own light. Intricate designs were inlaid throughout, people, animals, entire histories carved with divine artistry. Cherubim perched on the gates like living sentries, their wings creating gentle shadows that danced with celestial rhythm.

Beyond the gates, clouds stretched into infinity. Far below, I could see Earth spinning in its cosmic dance. Above, stars blazed with the intensity of diamonds against black velvet, and the sun burned with perfect fire.

When I turned around, beauty and light radiated from every surface, every corner, every molecule of air. This wasn't just the absence of darkness, this was pure light, the kind that existed before darkness was even a concept.

The road beneath my feet was paved with gold, but not the cold metal of earthly treasure. This gold was warm, alive, pulsing with divine energy. On either side, mansions rose like monuments to eternal architecture, brick, granite, and stone adorned with gemstones that caught and reflected light in ways that made rainbows look monochrome.

As I began to walk, sounds of joy filled the air. People talking and laughing, their voices carrying notes of happiness so pure it made my heart ache with longing. And then, the sound that made me stop in my tracks, a dog barking. Not one dog, but several, their barks creating a symphony of canine celebration.

Movement caught my peripheral vision. I was surrounded by beings, not quite people, but spirits in translucent form. They shimmered with glittering colors, defined by their radiant shapes and sizes rather than facial features. As they passed through me, I felt waves of warmth, love, and kindness so intense, it took my breath away.

"Sweetie!"

The voice calling my childhood nickname made my heart leap. I began walking faster toward the sound emanating from one of the magnificent mansions. As I moved, glittering colors bounced around my legs, a familiar sensation that triggered memories I couldn't quite place.

The colors jumped on me, around me, through me, radiating excitement so pure it was infectious. When I stopped to look closer, recognition hit me like lightning.

My dogs. All of them.

Lady, Tiger, Bapsey, and Ali, my beloved Boxers, bouncing and running into each other with the boundless energy of eternal youth. In their midst, Noodles and my first Princess fought to reach me, their joy so tangible I could taste it.

I tried to touch them, but my hands passed through their spirit forms. Yet I could feel them in my soul, could see enough to recognize each precious personality. I dropped to my knees, trying to greet each one individually, wanting to memorize every second of this impossible reunion.

I'd loved each of them with the fierce devotion usually reserved for children. They had been my children, my furry family who'd taught me about unconditional love, loyalty, and the pain of inevitable loss.

"I told you I would take care of your babies while you took care of mine."

The voice made me look up. My sister stood before me, radiant and beautiful, slender in a way she'd never been in life, joy radiating from every pore. She embraced me for what felt like eternity, and as she did, Elton John's "Bennie and the Jets" filled the air, her favorite song, the one she'd hummed while doing dishes, the soundtrack to a thousand memories.

As we spoke, something miraculous happened. She transformed from spirit form to human appearance, and the dogs followed suit, becoming the tangible companions I remembered. I touched her face, hugged each pet, desperate to memorize every detail.

"I have a surprise for you," she said, linking her arm through mine.

The entourage followed as she led me to the mansion's patio, where a figure sat that made my heart explode with joy.

"Daddy!"

I ran to him like a child, and he enveloped me in arms that still smelled of Old Spice after-shave. He looked like a younger version of himself, wearing his familiar Sherwin-Williams painter's clothes, as if he were about to head out for another job.

"My pride and joy," he whispered, the same words he'd spoken countless times in life.

Several Boxers tried to claim my lap simultaneously, creating the kind of chaos that used to drive me crazy but now made me laugh until tears streamed down my face. This was what I'd always hoped for, confirmation that God wouldn't provide such loving companions on earth only to abandon them in eternity.

For precious moments, we reminisced about life, hopes, dreams, joys, and disappoint-ments. They told me about watching over the family, how they could check on us but couldn't influence outcomes. My sister knew intimate details about her living children, offering guidance and warnings with maternal precision.

She told me to stop harassing the youngest child. She laughed when she overheard me jokingly tell him I was going to live in his basement and smoke marijuana all day, funded by my monthly social security check. She also laughed at his response. Ironically, this came from the child I once thought might become a weed head but who instead grew into a responsible adult.

She spoke contemplatively about her middle child, warning me that although he's quieter and more sensitive than the others, I must make sure to keep him close. She wanted me to tell him that she loves his music, not just one favorite song, but all the tracks on his first and second albums. She wants him to keep pursuing it. She also mentioned liking his girlfriend, cautioning me that she's sensitive too, so I should be careful with my words around her. What moved her most was that he was the only one who remembered her on the twentieth anniversary of her death. Finally, she noted his knowledge of God's word, which made her wonder about the calling on his life.

When she discussed her oldest child, she said, half-jokingly but with underlying truth, that he really wasn't hers but mine, her gift to me. Her concern for him was evident. She wants me to tell him she loves him and that he must learn to release family conflicts. If he doesn't, she warned, Satan could use those conflicts to push him further from both his purpose and his family. She also observed that he's unhappy and feels trapped. She didn't elaborate on these insights, and he's never expressed such feelings to me directly, but I trust that she can see what remains hidden from my view.

But then my father's expression grew serious, and the atmosphere shifted.

"You don't have much time," he said, his painter's clothes somehow making him look more official, not less. "So I need to tell you why you're here."

I waited, sensing the weight of what was coming.

"You can probably sense that something's about to happen. You likely have a sense of impending doom. A war is brewing on earth." His words fell like stones into still water, creating ripples that would change everything.

"At first glance, it will look like war between nations, China, Russia, Brazil, several Middle Eastern and African countries against America, Europe, Canada, Australia. But the war isn't between nations. It's between light and darkness, good and evil, truth and lies."

The cosmic scope of his revelation made my knees weak.

"The same dark forces working on one side are infiltrating the other. Millions will die in this conflict. You've been called to warn the masses of what's coming." His voice carried the authority of someone speaking divine truth. "You were present when the Adversary sought judgment of humanity. He comes periodically, but this time was different. Remember when he was cast from heaven? A third of the angels followed him. Now he seeks judgment so he can build his army, but the Lord knows his true motivation."

My father's eyes blazed with prophetic fire. "Remember when the Elders asked whether humanity was suffering consequences that resembled the four trumpets? This time will be different. This time, it will be the seven seals."

The words hit me like physical blows: "A rider will come out to conquer. People will slay one another. Starvation will take hold while alcohol and drugs remain plentiful. Pestilence and famine will spread across the earth. The Lord will gather His army. Everyone will run and hide when they witness the day of wrath. And then the seven trumpets will begin to blow."

The magnitude of what he was describing, the end times themselves, made it hard to breathe.

"You must figure out how to call attention to what's about to happen. The more people who turn to the Lord, the more will be saved. But death will be knocking at countless doors, and everyone will suffer."

My sister placed her hand on my shoulder, her touch both comforting and weighted with urgency. "Remember, you know what is written. This will be a difficult time for you, but God will be with you as always. Daddy and I, and all your babies, will be waiting for everyone."

Her voice grew tender: "Stay close to the word of God. And did you know? Levi made the request before God to allow you to come back to us."

I awoke with a gasp.

Princess was still sleeping in the exact same position. I sat up, looking around my familiar bedroom, trying to reconcile the impossible vividness of what I'd experienced. Had it been a dream? A vision? Another divine appointment?

As I swung my legs over the side of the bed, something on my nightstand stopped me cold.

A picture that hadn't been there when I'd fallen asleep.

My father and the Boxers. An old photograph I kept stored in a box in my closet, one I hadn't looked at in years. Yet there it sat, perfectly positioned where I couldn't miss it, physical proof of a spiritual encounter that defied every law of reality I'd once believed.

My hands trembled as I picked up the picture. My father's smile. Lady's tongue hanging out. Tiger's dignified expression. All of them together, all of them waiting.

All of them real.

I knew what I had to do. Tomorrow, I would call my tablemates. Tomorrow, the real work would begin.

Because this wasn't the end of my story.

This was my beginning.

The call had come. The purpose was clear. The war between light and darkness was about to begin, and I had been one of many, chosen as a messenger, not for comfort, but of urgent warning.

God help me.

God help us all.

THE END, NO THE BEGINNING!

About the Author

Arlene A. Smith-Scott brings a wealth of knowledge and experience to the table, making her an authority in bankruptcy practice, business development, and legal consulting. Her impressive tenure includes packaging compelling grant proposals and business plans, developing transformative course content, and authoring several influential books.

As Managing Attorney at Strategic Law Group, LLC, Arlene oversaw more than 200 legal cases, specializing in client relationship management and legal retention. Her work involved drafting contracts, researching intricate legal matters, writing appellate briefs, and litigating civil and criminal cases. In her capacity as a certified Civil Mediator, she promoted effective communication, empathy, and balanced problem-solving to help parties reach lasting resolutions.

Previously, as CEO of Strategic Alliance Funding, Inc., Arlene brokered both residential and commercial mortgage loans, originating, processing, and closing them with precision. She performed in-depth credit assessments, created dynamic

Arlene's extensive experience in grant writing, legal consulting, and business development, combined with her ability to leverage video production tools, and emerging technologies like AI, makes her an invaluable asset to clients, students, and readers alike.

STAY CONNECTED

DocWriteReview understands that your time and money are valuable! We want to offer insightful, encouraging, and informative books, videos, music, and other media, that will make a difference in your life at an affordable price.

Enroll in periodic giveaways, discount programs, event information, and new releases by providing your email. Look for us on Facebook, Twitter, and Instagram.

WEBSITE: www.DocWriteReview.com

EMAIL: Info@DocWriteReview.com